WONDER

CHRISTINA C JONES

AUTHOR'S NOTE

This project has truly been a labor of love. It's a departure from my "usual" novel, containing many elements that made more than a little nervous about bringing this project to life.

If you're interested, this video has my pre-release thoughts about this project, and I think provides some context that enhances the experience.

Am I scaring you, LOL?

It's packaged a little differently that usual, but just like all my work, there's a love story at heart - one I feel amazing about.

I hope you enjoy it!

ONE

"I need you to handle Ruby for me today."

I nearly choked on my coffee. Half of my daily four-ounce ration spilled down my throat in a sudden, wasteful gulp. Usually, I spent my ten-minute break savoring it in careful sips, suppressing the desire to lick the tiny ceramic mug at the end, so as not to waste a single drop.

I glared at Harriet, who groaned and then moved over to the coffee machine, plugging in her employee code to dispense her serving of brew. With a huff, she poured half into my mug, replenishing it.

"There. Now, seriously Aly, please?"

Harriet wasn't one to ask for favors – that whole "*I owe you one*" thing could be dangerous nowadays, even for something as innocuous as this. You never knew what you'd be asked to do, or what trouble you might get into for doing someone a solid.

I knew Harriet well enough to understand that if she was asking, it had to be serious. But still...

"Ruby? As in, your absolute hardest to please client? I don't think so."

"Nessa is sick." Harriet glanced around, making sure we were alone in the break room before she stepped closer, lowering her voice. "I have a hookup. Someone who can get antibiotics for me. But I have to go *now*. I can't miss this opportunity."

She was telling the truth. Even if it wasn't clear in her big gray eyes, I knew how it worked around here. The doctor was expensive, *if* you could get an appointment, and it meant missing work, missing school, for who knew how long. Then, you'd be prescribed medicine you may or may not afford – and even if you *could* afford it, meds were in high demand. If you were lucky enough to purchase what you needed, there was still the *un*lucky chance of getting knocked upside the head and robbed leaving the pharmacy.

Sickness was dangerous, in more ways than one.

But Nessa was still so small.

Only seven years old, born *just* before pregnancy became a luxury only the rich could afford, and the *Division Three Sterilization Program* posters went up all over the city.

Well, not *this* part of the city.

The other parts.

Harriet would do anything for her little girl, even risk a shady deal for black market antibiotics. Honestly, I wanted to help her, but...

"If I mess it up—"

"You *won't*," Harriet insisted. "Aly, you're the only person I trust to ask this. But you *know* what will happen if I don't get somebody to cover for me."

I did.

And getting fired would be the blow that banished Harriet's family from the relative comfort and safety of where we lived to another area.

"You can have my coffee for two weeks," Harriet offered.

Tempting.

"And I'll clean your station for you, for the same two weeks. No complaints. I swear."

A smirk danced at the corners of my mouth until I gave in for a full-blown smile. "Fine, Harriet. I'll do it. You don't have to clean my station, but I *will* take your coffee. And if I get fired..."

"You *won't*." She propped a hand on one hip. "You will absolutely kill it and get a big enough tip to buy a dress and dance in the Apex – like other girls your age."

She said that like "my age" wasn't twenty-five, like I didn't have more pressing matters than dresses and dancing, even though I didn't have a family like her. I knew she meant well though.

"*Or*, I can put more money on Gran's account," I reminded her. "It won't be much, but every little bit helps."

Every little bit meant a little less debt, meant a little closer to the impossibility of not owing anyone anything. A dream, but one that had my singular focus.

Harriet put a hand to her mouth. "Oh Aly, I'm sorry. I didn't consider that," she admitted, pulling me into a hug. Her vanilla-scented sheets of thick brown hair tickled my skin as she squeezed, then stepped back. "But it makes my point even more. You're doing this for your Gran. I'm doing this for Nessa. And neither of us will fail."

The distinct click of boots against the cold tile floor made us step further apart, and I snatched up my mug, swallowing my tepid coffee in one swallow. My break was over.

Lori's beaky nose appeared around the corner to the break room before she did, wearing her usual half-scowl. Her thin blonde hair was, as always, slicked back into a perfect knot, exaggerating her already birdlike features – that nose, those beady, crafty eyes.

"Alyson will take Ruby for me this afternoon," Harriet spoke, before Lori complained, which she'd undoubtedly come to do. "I have a personal matter to attend to."

Lori's nose rose in the air. "We should handle Personal matters on *personal* time."

"Yes. And typically, I would, but—"

"I do not care." Lori raised a hand for silence, cutting her off.

"Alyson, you understand how important Ruby Hartford's patronage is to us, correct?"

I nodded. "I do."

Those beady eyes gave me a slow once-over, but she didn't comment on my appearance, which was an approval.

"Good. Don't fuck it up."

Lori turned on her high-heeled boots and stalked away as Harriet and I exchanged a look.

"On *that* note, I have to get out of here before I miss this meetup," she said. "Ruby will be here in twenty minutes. *Don't* make her wait."

"Duh," I countered, disposing of my mug in the stack with the others. "Now go, don't be late. I have work to do."

Once Harriet left, I went the opposite direction, toward the floor. I needed time to set up the private booth where I'd service Ruby, but I took a moment to check my appearance in the mirror first, to make sure it was just so.

Black shoes, black pants, black logo top, hot pink lip, no jewelry. That was our "uniform" here, and deviation would earn you a demerit at best, and at worst, fired on the spot. We could do whatever we wanted with our hair – it was encouraged, the more intricate/interesting the better.

I always had braids.

Now, I pulled them all over one shoulder, taking comfort in their familiar swing against my hip as I moved to my station. It was fortifying – a concrete feeling to connect to in a moment that was feeling more and more surreal.

My hands were going in Ruby Hartford's hair today.

I was great at my job – you had to be, in a place like this. Working at a salon in *The Apex* meant a wage where you could do more than keeping yourself alive – another high commodity. As much as the world had changed, the obsession with beauty had not.

But that was no complaint.

Though I'd hated growing up in a salon, spending long days at my mother's feet on the weekends, inhaling the odors of chemical straighteners and acetone, I was grateful now. I was grateful then too, but as an adult I had a better understanding of *why* she taught me formulations with painstaking precision, made sure I had an eagle eye for split ends, perfect braiding techniques – *everything* I could need to know, to wear the title of *stylist*.

She knew it could keep me alive after she was gone.

I'd watched Harriet's prep work for Ruby enough times to know what I needed to gather, but I still smiled when I saw the note she'd left.

"Sure of yourself, are you?" I muttered to myself as I grabbed a basket from my station to head to the repository. There, I handed the masked attendant a list of what I needed, and was careful to double-check before I signed the slip to leave with the basket. Back at my station, I took my time to arrange everything the way I liked it, and then with one minute to spare before my appointment, I was done.

Ruby Hartford walked in thirty seconds later.

Security guards flanked her, which wasn't uncommon for the ultra-wealthy residents of *The Apex*. Violent crime was virtually nonexistent here, but being able to afford your own security was a status symbol. Not that Ruby needed men in black uniforms and heavy boots for us to understand how wealthy she was.

She *oozed* it.

Like me, Ruby was dressed in all black. *Un*like me, her blacks were all lush, luxury fabrics – skintight black leggings, and a cropped tank, topped with a cashmere kimono she shrugged off, tossing toward one of the security guards in a fluid motion that *had* to be rehearsed, with how seamlessly he collected it before it hit the floor.

Ruby walked – well, more like *glided* – up, stopping to give me a once-over similar to the one Lori had given earlier. There was no disapproval in her gaze though, just a mild interest that made my cheeks go hot before her eyes, emerald orbs framed by long, delicate lashes came back to my face. Up close, her caramel skin was just as flawless as it seemed from a distance, sprinkled over with dark brown freckles.

"You're beautiful," she said, in a way that didn't exactly feel like a compliment. "Why are you here, instead of working as a *Diamond*?"

I swallowed, hard, then couldn't do anything other than shrug. "I... this is what my mother taught me to do," I answered.

Somehow, that amused her. "Right.. The passing of knowledge. It wouldn't do for a hairdresser to have taught you to be a whore, would it?"

My eyes went wide. "I suppose not."

"Of course you do. You're the one serving as Harriet's replacement today." She wasn't asking a question – she was telling me, and took the empty seat in my salon chair to deepen the point. "Don't fuck it up."

Yeah.

I'd already heard that one.

"Fucking up" wasn't typically a part of my day, and I had every intention of keeping up that streak. Ruby Hartford had nearly three feet of natural coils, that she expected colored, blow-dried, and styled to perfection, and I did that.

Carefully.

I was the picture of professionalism, bringing her dark roots to match the cinnamon tone of the rest of her hair, then drying and styling it into her signature beachy waves. While I worked, she conducted a few business calls I paid no attention to – I wasn't curious about anything except hair when I had a client in front of me. The only thing that registered interest was a heart-shaped birthmark behind her ear, and I quickly pushed even that from my mind as I curled and combed and laid every strand in the perfect place.

When I finished, Ruby surveyed her appearance in the mirror, accepting the comb I handed her to part through various sections to check the color. When she finished, she sat back, sounding slightly disappointed when she complimented me on a job well done.

My face must have registered confusion because her lips quirked into a smile. "I haven't ruined anyone's life yet today," she explained. "I was hoping you'd give me a reason, but this is flawless. I may come back to you next time, instead of Harriet."

"No," I stammered. "You're Harriet's client, I couldn't—"

"Be telling *me* no?" Ruby spoke over me, still wearing that smirk that made an insidious feeling creep up my back. "You're right. You couldn't be doing that."

She made a gesture for me to remove the styling cape so I did, keeping my lips pressed closed. I wanted to say something ugly, wanted to chew her out, but I couldn't risk my job – my livelihood – on having the last word with a client.

So I swallowed it.

Once she was back on her feet, towering over me in her heels, she gave me her attention again. "I'd like you to think about what I said earlier," she told me, as she held out her arms for one of the guards to put that kimono back on her. "Girl like you could make good money – much more than the scraps here. Isn't that right Alonso?" she asked one guard. He remained stone-faced, his presence only made *more* imposing by the tattoo on his face – a trio of spades, at the corner of his eye.

When he didn't answer, Ruby laughed, then snapped her fingers. It happened so fast I couldn't tell where it came from, but suddenly there was a thick fold of money between her fingers.

She peeled off much more than her service cost and handed it to me, walking off before I could realize the error. I tried to catch her, but the guard who'd taken the position closest to her gave me a look so petrifying that I shut my mouth, stuffing the money in my pocket and considering it a blessing.

They were few and far between around here.

TWO

It started with heat waves.

At least, that was what my father's grandparents said. My mother's said the ice was first, biting and slick under the wheels of cars belonging to people for whom "freezing rain" was a foreign concept. It didn't matter though, because none of them were here now, and no matter where it started, it had evolved.

Devolved.

The heat got so bad it was dangerous to be outside, and when it was the right time of the year, the weight of the ice brought down power lines and cracked windows. The beaches were empty, because of the smell – if the sea life didn't wash up already cooked from the water, it died on scorching sand. Frost killed the palm trees.

And in between that, there was rain.

Torrential downpours dumping unholy amounts of water, flooding the streets and washing away the soil and soaking so deep into the earth it disrupted concrete building foundations. The lightning was indiscriminate, destroying homes and blowing past precautionary insulation to cause power surges and blackouts that fried everything from air traffic control systems to home microwaves.

And the thunder?

So loud you'd feel it for days. So loud that the government sent out mobile units to provide ear protection – the same insulated ear muffs you'd get at a gun range.

So loud that fault lines moved.

The ones that hadn't moved in years and years, the ones our books said were "dormant".

The earth was tired of us destroying her and had struck first.

A "patriot" wasn't supposed to think this way, let alone say it out loud, but she'd won. All our science and technology and politics had meant nothing once she decided she wanted us off, that we'd done too much and gone too far.

Three-quarters of the world's population, *gone*.

It wasn't what ended up in the sleek books they gave us at school now, a hundred years later. As the earth remapped itself, so had history, both guided by the hand of those who'd been cunning and self-serving and *evil* enough to negotiate power from an extinction level event.

Not that I was into all that.

I didn't care who was in power because they were all the same. They didn't bother with the sham elections anymore – why, when there were barely "states" anymore? There were "divisions" now – ten, separated by guarded walls I'd never been to and didn't care to see.

I wanted to keep my head down and stay alive.

That was exactly what I did as I approached the gates that separated the *Apex* from the *Mids* – what we called the section of our city that lay between the spotless, lush environment of the *Apex*, where the wealthy lived, and the lawless *Burrows*.

Even in the *Mids*, the further you got from the *Apex*, the more likely you were to get robbed, assaulted, killed, or worse. Especially a woman traveling alone as the sun disappeared from the sky. The APF – *America's Police Force* – were prowling around, sure. Allegedly to help keep us safe, but I knew better. Knew the uniform meant nothing if the person wearing it was a criminal too.

Honestly, it was hard to know *who* to trust these days.

That was why I was careful to tuck my thumb over the house number and street name when I showed the guard my ID to get through the gate that would lead me home. A few years ago, one of them had flirted with me – had gotten angry when I declined his advances. A day or so later, he was waiting across the street from my home.

Luckily, my father had preached diligence enough that I spotted him before he saw me. I snuck around through the back, and watched him through a crack in the blinds as he waited, and waited, and then left. They found his body the next day.

The streets were dangerous for *everybody* at night.

Once I got through the gate, I breathed out a sigh. Even with its flaws, the *Mids* were home – the only one I'd ever known. In some ways, it was relieving to be back on this side of the gate where I belonged, away from the glossy facade of the *Apex*. Mostly though, my slow, deep sigh was resigned.

The world had ended, rebooted itself, and this was what we got.

It was ungrateful of me to view the palm trees and balmy weather with such disdain, but I chalked it up to cabin fever. Anybody would be sick of the same thing every day, would want something more than what they've always known, right? *Division Two* got lots of rain and ice, sometimes *snow* – a phenomenon I'd only ever seen in pictures.

Here?

Sometimes it rained.

Often, that rain smelled like death, and the *Apex* would all but shut down, because their delicate noses couldn't handle the stench. I loved those days. I got to sip my coffee ration slower, watching the toxic rain streak down the windows. Other times though, the rain came with storms.

I didn't love those.

Those were terrifying messes of destructive lightning and sonorous thunder and sheets of rain that made you wonder if yet another reckoning was coming. Before she passed, I remembered my father's mother fussing that back when she was my age, they didn't have to worry about being wiped out by a thunderstorm, that they were common occurrences that rarely had the potential to remap the earth.

I always bit my tongue instead of reminding her they *should* have worried.

They should have worried a lot.

But now, here we were.

Unpredictably destructive weather, drastically different climates, all packed onto what was left after the world decided to try to take us out, just trying to live.

I moved, before one of the guards noticed I'd been standing there too long and decided I was suspicious. I had errands before I got home, and dinner to make once I arrived, and had already spent too much time daydreaming.

My first stop was the specialty dry cleaner I couldn't afford to not be able to afford. The salon's strict dress code even included the shade – no faded, off-black. Inky pure black, always, or you'd be sent home without your wages, which wasn't an option for most of us. So I paid what I had to for another week of work clothes, to keep the job that kept me alive.

With that bundle draped over my arm, I headed for the market. My heart clenched at the sight of the armed guards that flanked the doors, demanding ID from anyone who wanted to enter. I pulled my same address-hiding trick here, and they waved me inside with barely a glance. I dumped my clothes over the side of a cart and started down the aisles, grabbing only the absolute necessities. It hurt every day to wheel my meager collection past the coffee display, the aroma goading me, wrapping around me to remind me that nice things would never be a part of my life. Not as long as—

"*Keep it moving!*" an armed guard barked in my ear, shoving me forward in the line. I used my grip on the basket to steady myself, knowing better than to say anything back or look his way.

I kept it moving, like I'd been told.

Weighed down with bags, I moved much slower leaving the market than I did on the way there. I glanced up at the sky, willing the sun to relax a little, not to run so fast to get behind the horizon, to turn everything dangerous and dark. I was ready to drop everything and run if necessary.

It wasn't today.

This time when I sighed, it was out of relief to be on the right side of my locked front door, in the relative safety of home. Maybe I was being paranoid, but so far, that paranoia had kept me alive, and I saw no reason to change it.

I stopped by the kitchen first, allowing the low, familiar hum of the old, beat-up refrigerator to soothe me. I remembered the whole family eating light to afford the extra cost the week my father brought it home, but I'd never seen my mother smile so much. Now that they were gone, it had a dual utility – cold storage, and a warm memory.

Once I'd put away the groceries, I moved to my room – the main bedroom, which had been my parents'. I hung my work clothes in the closet, then went to check the panel that monitored our electricity usage – yet another thing that was rationed. A rare smile lit my face when I saw that my house was well under-budget for the month, which meant I could indulge myself with a hot shower that lasted longer than three minutes.

"*Maybe a whole ten...*" I mused to myself as I sat down on the end of the bed to take off my shoes and give my aching feet some relief. "*Or I should wait until the end of the week...*"

It wasn't until I was putting my shoes in the closet that I realized something was *off*. I'd been so absorbed in my own thoughts that the overwhelming emptiness of the house hadn't struck me.

It did now.

Barefoot, I padded across the worn carpet and flung my door open, heading down the hall. I didn't stop moving until I reached another door, where I listened first. When I heard nothing, I knocked. When the knock went unanswered, my heart dropped.

Where the hell is Nadiah?

I opened the door just to check, but I already knew she wasn't there. Panic gripped my chest as I looked around for a note, a clue, *anything*, but found nothing. I swallowed hard, choking down the disappointment of what I knew I had to do next.

There goes that long shower.

In fact, there went a lot of day-to-day comforts our meager ration of electricity afforded. I went back to the panel in my room, dreading the necessary but not putting it off.

I had to make a call.

When the new government took over, they'd confiscated any electronic that had a memory or storage. They called it anti-terrorism, and had torn up homes and ended lives, over cell phones and laptops. Eventually, citizens were given access again, but at a cost. Only the hyper-rich could afford the devices sold at *Apex* stores, and anyone caught making, selling, or owning a counterfeit was subject to prosecution.

Persecution.

And they made sure we knew.

Instead of subjecting myself to those possibilities, I was content with the call function on the panel – monitored and recorded, and they ate up electricity like a vacuum. I rarely used the ability, largely because I didn't know many people to call. But now, with the sun long-gone from the sky, and Nadiah nowhere to be found, it was necessary.

So I made the call.

It took Gran a bit to answer because of the time. I knew I'd woken her up, and felt bad about it, but I'd feel worse if I didn't do everything I could to figure out where the hell my sister was.

"What happened?" she asked, as soon as her face appeared on the screen. Momentarily, Nadiah left my mind as I processed Gran's gaunt likeness. Before the illness, she'd been vibrant – full cheeks and full of life. Her face was hollow now, and her floral robe hung loose over bony shoulders. Just two days ago I'd made the trek to see her in person, and had fought to stay upbeat, to not let her see the impending doom I felt. Even more of the light was gone from her eyes now.

"Are they giving you your treatments?" I asked, ignoring her question. Most of my peers at the salon lived somewhat worry-free lives, in the *Upper Mids,* the neighborhoods nearest the *Apex.* They didn't worry about electricity, or food, or much crime. Unfortunately, that wasn't my life.

My grandmother had already needed round-the-clock care, when my parents were still alive. Between their two incomes, they could afford it, even though it was tight.

They weren't here anymore.

It was just me now, taking care of two other women – one elderly and sick, the other a near-genius who *needed* to be in school. Just yesterday, she'd gotten a letter about a potential scholarship to finish her post-secondary schooling up in the *Apex,* which was huge. We couldn't ignore that.

So Gran went to the "retirement" community, which I hated, but was cheaper than the private care she'd had before. It wasn't ideal, but we managed, and I could afford a luxury here and there for her – nice bed linens, tea in the mornings.

But then she got sicker.

Which meant no luxuries for any of us.

"They're giving me the treatments," Gran coughed. "I'm just an old woman. Saving the mascara for special occasions," she rasped, trying to make me smile.

I didn't.

I couldn't.

"If they're not, I need you to tell me. I'm *paying* for—"

"I keep telling you, you should stop," Gran interrupted, shaking her head. "Let me die with some dignity before I lose anybody else."

Swallowing hard, I averted my gaze from the screen. This wasn't her first time making this request – one I was too selfish to honor.

I didn't want to lose anyone else either.

"You're talking crazy," I told her, in a soothing tone. "You're not dying. Don't talk like that."

"I'll talk how I want to," was her brittle response. "Now what do you want? You didn't interrupt my sleep with an expensive call for nothing. What happened?"

I scoffed over her changing the subject, but she was right. "Did Nadiah make it to see you today, after school?"

Gran's half-empty smile gaped across the screen. "Yes, I saw my pretty grandbaby today. She was excited. Had found something in a book about some ruins."

I frowned. "Ruins?"

"Yeah, the destroyed city, the bridge, all that. She was going to go poke around."

"Today? She said she was going today?"

"She didn't say. Just that she was excited about it."

"Okay," I sighed. "When did she leave?"

Gran thought about it for a moment, then answered, "Must've been about four o'clock. Why? Did something happen?"

I contemplated not telling her, but knew she'd just chew me out about it when she found out. "She's not here. She's not home. And there's no note or anything. I'm worried."

"She's not home at this time of night, and you called me instead of the police?" Incredulity laced her tone, but *my* tone was the same when I replied.

"What exactly were the police going to do?"

Maybe in the *Apex* or *Upper Mids*, the APF would mount up to find a missing young woman, in hopes of returning her to her family. Everywhere else, reporting something like this to the police could be just as easily putting a target on her back – a blaring beacon that there was an attractive young woman out somewhere in this city, alone.

I had *no* intention of doing such a thing.

A tiny chime sounded, letting me know the call had surpassed five minutes – I could only afford seven before I started digging into credit, and debt was absolutely non-negotiable for me. I rushed my grandmother off the phone, urging her to get some sleep, and promising that I would keep her updated on Nadiah.

I couldn't bring myself to look at how much the call had cost once it was over.

Instead, I went to my closet, digging out the heavy boots I wore when it rained. They'd belonged to my mother, and didn't look nice by any stretch of the imagination. But they were sturdy and reliable, and the protection I needed if I was going into ruins to find my sister.

I put them on, along with a jacket I stashed full of granola bars and two canteens of filtered water. I thought for a moment, then stuffed an inside pocket with alcohol pads and gauze, just in case. And then I stood in the living room, lost.

I had *no* idea where my sister had gone.

No idea where to even start.

That realization made me sink to the floor as emotion bubbled up from somewhere deep. Nadiah had always been curious, always digging into facts and possibilities, always so intrigued by how we'd gotten here. About our history.

Whenever she could, she went as far as she allowed, exploring vacant houses and bringing back little treasures for whoever wanted them – me, Gran, her friends. But that was the key – she *always* came back. When I got home from work, from running my errands, Nadiah would be in her room, poring over some magazine or book she'd found.

I tried my best to choke back impending sobs over the possibility of not seeing Nadiah's face again – of her not walking through the door with a big smile and a handful of ink pens she'd scavenged for my collection.

I didn't know what to do next, and that was a very specific sort of horror.

Before I could give in to it, someone knocked at the back door.

A frantic, desperate knocking that pulled me to my feet and into a full sprint to get there, flinging the door open without checking through the window first, hoping that it would be my sister on the other side of the threshold.

It was not.

THREE

"Bunny?" I said, then pulled Nadiah's friend into the house, glancing around the yard before I locked the door again. "What are you doing here? It's late!"

"I know," she said, looking at me with glassy eyes. The sweet, almost cartoonish face that had earned her nickname was pulled into a frown, her voice anxious as she tugged at the hem of her white sweater. "But Nadiah, she's—"

"You know where she is?!"

Her front teeth – just slightly too large for her face, another contributing factor to the nickname she'd embraced – came down over her bottom lip, digging in. "Uh, yes and no."

"What the hell does that mean?!" I hissed, grabbing her by the shoulders. "Where is my sister?!"

"Oakland, I think. At least that's where I last saw her."

I frowned. "*Oakland?* It doesn't even exist anymore. And what do you mean *that's where you last saw her?*"

"Well, it was the area that *was* Oakland. Before the earthquake smashed everything in."

I shook my head, still confused. "You're not making any sense girl. Make it make sense, *now*."

"Out in the ruins."

"The ruins that are all covered in poisonous plants and teeming with dangerous wildlife? *Those* ruins?" I asked, eyes wide.

Bunny grinned. "That's what they tell us, but that's not it. There's nothing out there. It's quiet, and you can see the stars. It's beautiful."

"And that's where Nadiah is? Why didn't she come back with you?"

That grin melted off her face. "Well, we kinda went too far. The ruins connect to the *Burrows* without having to go through the gate. And neither of us had ever seen them before, so we..."

My heart rocketed past my stomach, landing somewhere near my feet. "You went to the *Burrows*? Are you... you've *gotta be kidding me!*" I gritted those last words through my teeth, trying my best to temper my anger. Nadiah and Bunny were both young, nineteen. They were kids, and kids did stupid things, but this was...

"I'm so sorry, Aly," Bunny whimpered, fidgeting now with the hot pink watch on her wrist – a gift that had undoubtedly come from my sister. Now though, I wondered if her explorations had been as safe as she'd always assured me. "We wanted to see for ourselves, but then some guy started yelling at us, and we ran, to hide. But then Nadiah fell, and—"

"She fell?! Is she okay?!" I asked, though I could already guess the answer. If she was okay, she'd be here.

With her head hung low, Bunny admitted, "There's something wrong with her ankle. There was no way she could make it back on it. I got back here as soon as I could, and that's it. That's the whole story."

I cupped a hand over my mouth, clamping it tight to keep myself from screaming. After a deep breath, I asked, "So where is she? Is she somewhere out in the open, is she safe?"

"She's in a house. An abandoned house out there that we got into. She's hidden. No one knows she's there, no one saw us go in or out."

My eyes narrowed. "You sure?"

"I'm *sure*," she insisted. "And I can lead you there. With two of us, we can get her back."

"If we don't get arrested, for being in a restricted area," I countered, shaking my head. It was a risk I was willing to take to get my sister back, but I had to be realistic. This was dangerous.

"If you follow me, we'll be there in no time. Nobody will see us."

I scoffed. "With you in that bright white sweater? Shouldn't you change into something dark, so you don't get caught?"

"I *always* wear white," she said. "And *I've* never gotten caught."

"*Except today*," I wanted to counter, before I caught the implication of her words.

She wasn't the reason they'd gotten caught.

"We have to go," Bunny spoke up, already moving toward the door. "Nadiah was in a lot of pain, and I've already been gone almost two hours."

My eyes bugged wide. "She's two hours away?!"

"Just about. I stopped by my house, to get her something for the pain before I came to you." She looked at her watch again, then back up at me, bouncing anxiously on the balls of her feet. "We gotta go."

Knowing she was right, I glanced around the house one last time, trying to decide if there was anything I'd forgotten. And then, I followed Bunny out my back door.

The earthquake got one paragraph in our history book.

Our teachers didn't want to get in trouble for going outside the text, so they didn't, but our parents and grand-parents, and so on, filled the gaps where they could. Once upon a time, the San Francisco Bay had been the largest estuary on the coast, but after a 9.2 magnitude earthquake that spread hundreds of miles had remixed that area, all traces of it were gone. Whatever the earthquake didn't destroy was taken by fire, which the subsequent tsunami quelled.

The paragraph was in a chapter full of short descriptions of how all the former major cities got destroyed. There was too much horror to give any of it the full color it deserved, at least in a basic classroom textbook. They wouldn't have had space for all the government indoctrination then.

Those pages contained few pictures, and the *Bay Area Disaster* wasn't one. After sneaking through the *Mids* with Bunny as my guide, I thought my mind had already been blown. But once she'd led me through a partially destroyed underground tunnel that let out in what she and Nadiah referred to as the *Ruins,* I understood that no, I hadn't seen anything yet.

I'd heard from my grandfather that *"That big ass bridge just folded up like a pocket knife and fell over"*. Maybe the "pocket knife" thing was why I'd underestimated the size of the San Francisco Bay Bridge, likening it to the simple bridges that dotted the *Apex*, connecting one part of the city to the other.

No.

This was *massive.*

A mess of concrete and steel and cables and *cars.* This was yet another place where mother nature had taken over again, with grass and plants and moss and vines snaking over and through everywhere it could reach. There was no mistaking the quiet beauty of the area – the sounds of civilization only present in the background, no human presence for miles.

But still.

All I could think about as we picked our way over the ruined bridge – the route that Bunny insisted was the clearest, and safest – all I could think about was the never-reported toll of the lives lost on the heavily populated passage. How many bodies were still here, unreachable. How many must have died slowly, trapped in their cars.

And though I knew it was silly, maybe if any of them were *undead*.

We were living post-apocalypse, after all.

Once we were past the overgrown bridge, I pushed the ridiculousness from my mind and focused on getting to Nadiah. Bunny's footsteps were fast, and confident, while I tested and double-checked every time I placed my weight anywhere that wasn't the ground. She disappeared and reappeared, glancing back with an impatient frown as we picked our way through a hilly area populated with colorful, half-fallen houses. Suddenly, she stopped – so sudden I nearly ran into the back of her.

I eased my way up onto the hill beside her, my chest clenching when I saw the fear in her eyes.

"Bunny, what is it?" I asked, trying to bring her back into our present, less-than-desirable situation. "Do you not remember which house?"

She blinked, shaking her head. "No, it's not that. It's the house right there."

I looked where she was pointing, down the hill, to a house tucked into the trees. The back door was open.

"Is that how you marked it?" I asked, turning to face her. "Your signal to yourself, that this was the house?"

Bunny looked at me, shook her head.

"No."

I swallowed, hard, but didn't outwardly react.

Because I already knew that.

I picked my way down the hill as quickly as I could without hurting myself – it wouldn't do for *both* of us to be injured. On the patio, I froze. What would I do if I walked in here and got attacked, or found someone attacking Nadiah?

Glancing around, my eyes fell upon a patio set that had seen better days. Bending, I wrenched off one of the rusting metal legs, brandishing it like a bat as I stepped into the house. On the way here, Bunny had run down where Nadiah was in the house, so there was no need for either of us to speak.

Bunny had the flashlight, trailing it in front of us as we crept along, moving straight to where Nadiah was supposed to be. Part of me already knew she wouldn't be there, but opening the closet to find the floor empty still pulled a scream of rage from deep in my belly.

"Are you *sure* this is the house?" I growled at Bunny, who shrunk away from me as she nodded.

"Yes, I'm positive. She was supposed to wait here and not leave. I don't know why she would leave!"

"She didn't *leave*, someone took her!" I snapped, tugging a handful of braids in frustration. "We have to figure out where. And who? And we have to get her back. Okay?"

Bunny nodded. "Yeah. Yeah, of course, Aly. But *how*?"

I didn't have any ideas.

Just like back at my house, I had no clue what to do next. The helplessness made me sick to my stomach. With my hands propped at my hips, I paced, hoping that the movement would get some blood flow to my brain, which would lead to... *something*.

I cringed when my boot landed on something crunchy.

"*Ugh*," I muttered, imagining all kinds of horrible possibilities to have crushed underfoot. I pulled out my flashlight, pointing it at the floor as I lifted my foot, one eye open, the other closed, as if that would limit the grossness of whatever I was about to see.

It was a cheeseball.

Of *all* the things to have survived the destruction and subsequent rebuilding of the world, the crunchy balls of... whatever the hell they made those things of, covered in disgusting powdered "cheese", these things were Nadiah's favorite. She *still* came after me with "cheese" coated fingers like when we were small children, threatening to spread it on my face.

Somehow, I felt like it was talking to me.

On pure hunch, I trailed the flashlight along the floor, going back the way we'd come in. Sure enough, there was another one – not in the direct path of the door where it was obvious, but close enough it felt like something I shouldn't let go of.

So I didn't.

Ignoring Bunny's question of what I was doing, I kept going, chair leg in one hand, the flashlight in the other. When I spotted yet another cheese ball on the path leading around to the front of the house, I had to catch myself from yelling in triumph. Their little adventure may have been reckless and dangerous, but if nothing else, Nadiah could think outside of the box- a quality I admired in my little sister.

She was trying to save herself.

"Aly, I think we should just stay here," Bunny insisted, grabbing my arm before I could follow the trail for another cheeseball. "Or you stay here in case she comes back. I know this area, and I can go look for her and report back."

My face curled up. "So you can end up missing too? No, I don't think so. We go together."

"Maybe she got thirsty, went for water." She glanced at her watch. "We got back fast, faster than what I told her. She's probably going to come through that door any second."

I sighed as I met Bunny's gaze. "I know you want to believe everything is just going to be okay, but we both know she didn't leave to go get water. We know she didn't leave willingly at all. It doesn't make sense. So we will follow this trail, I'm maybe going to hit somebody with this chair leg, and we *will* get Nadiah back? Okay?"

Bunny glanced around, then gave me the barest hint of a nod. "Okay."

Not that it was up to her, anyway.

If she wanted to turn back, get home to her parents, I wouldn't blame her. This was scary, and as confident as I hoped I sounded, I was terrified. But going home without my little sister wasn't an option.

I gave her an encouraging smile, then turned to find the next item on Nadiah's improvised rescue trail. It didn't take long to come out of the ruins, into the lawless area of the *Burrows*.

Only, it didn't look like I expected.

From the way they preached about it, I expected trash lining the streets beside piles of dead bodies, abandoned cars blocking the roads, fires everywhere. Instead, it looked like the *Mids* – a normal city block, the usual graffiti, a standard amount of litter on the roads.

The main difference was the people – there was a curfew in the *Mids,* and God help you if you were out past that time. Here though, there were people out – in groups, laughing and smoking, loners with gleaming guns on their hips, one or two staggering along inebriated.

Bunny and I kept to the shadows, picking our way along the trail Nadiah had left. A deep sense of dread washed over me, yet again, as the trail moved down an alley which I hesitated to step into, not knowing what I'd find.

"Well, *well,* what do we have *here,*" I heard, in a gravelly tone that made my skin crawl. Before I could make myself move, a first, then a second man stepped from the dark, both wearing menacing grins.

"Bunny. *Run,*" I commanded, and to my relief, she took off without questioning it. Wildly, I swung that metal chair leg, forcing their attention to me instead of her, hopefully giving her enough of a head start.

That made them angry.

I swung more as they approached, as hard as I could, as fast as I could, knowing there was no way I could take them both on. I still wasn't going down without a fight though. My weapon connected with flesh with a satisfying, sickening crack, sending one man howling.

I didn't see the other one, but I felt the blow to the back of my head.

I went down.

The chair leg fell from my hands, and with the consciousness I had left, I curled myself into a ball, tucking my hands over my head in an attempt at protection. My eyes were squeezed too tightly to see anything, but I heard – and felt – every bit of abuse that got hurled my way. I pulled a happy thought to the forefront of my mind – a warm memory, focusing on holding onto it until I couldn't feel the blows anymore.

It took a second to realize that I *wasn't* that great at disassociating myself.

I wasn't being hit anymore.

Distantly, I could hear arguing, and then what sounded like fighting – the violent connection of skin on skin, the splatter of blood, the crack of bones breaking.

And then it was over.

And everything faded to black.

FOUR

I woke up.

The details of that weren't important, at least not initially. When I closed my eyes in that alley, it had been with a certain level of confidence it was permanent, and it happened so fast I'd had no time for the usual near-death experience emotions.

Or was that yet another relic of the past, relegated to the pages of books?

In a half-destroyed world, did *anybody* weep and moan over the things they'd never done or seen, the people they were leaving behind? When death and decay were so normalized that you might be the only one left in your *entire* family, out of all the grandkids and cousins and aunts, did fading into the veil even matter?

Apparently so.

Because there was undeniable gladness coursing through me as I sat up on what I realized was a bed. That gladness was replaced with ear-splitting pain, coursing through my head, pouring down my back and shoulders, and left arm.

I fell back onto the bed and the pain dissipated, some. The worst of it faded, but a dull ache remained, bringing what had happened in that alley into sharp focus.

Telling Bunny to run.

Trying to defend myself.

Hitting one of those men.

Getting hit.

Over, and over, and over.

Then fading to black.

Somewhere in there, someone else had come along, someone who'd stopped the assault against me. Whether that was benevolence, I didn't know, but I assumed that's why I wasn't rotting in that alley now. Somehow, I doubted those first two guys had a warm, comfortable bed in mind for me – especially after the way I was swinging that rusty chair leg.

It couldn't have inspired kindness.

Instead of trying to sit up again, I stayed on my back to survey my surroundings. They were simple – no furniture except the bed, a little table beside it to hold a lamp, a bare dresser, and a straight-backed chair across the room. The walls were blank, and the window was covered in a simple shade. Still – compared to that alley, I was in the lap of luxury here.

Now that I somewhat had my bearings, I turned my gaze on myself, to take inventory. My mother's boots were gone from my feet, but I still had my socks, jeans, long-sleeved tee and all underwear, which was relieving. Feeling around revealed my jacket beside me on the bed, the pockets still full of everything I'd stuffed in there before I left my house.

At least I wasn't robbed, with everything else...

That was a small comfort once I looked at my arm. Even in the soft lamplight, I could make out ugly purple bruising that had to be deep to show up against my red-brown skin. My back had been the larger target, so I assumed there were worse bruises there, and my head... that was still throbbing. With my right hand, I reached back to feel for any swelling. I jerked back, horrified at how wet it felt. Shakily, I pulled my hand in front of my face, expecting it to be coated in blood.

The moisture was clear.

"*It's water,*" I muttered to myself, after smelling my hand and detecting nothing. I sat up again – slowly this time – then turned toward my pillow to see the ice pack laying there. Ice *packs.* I'd been lying on them for a long time, because none of them were cold anymore.

I've been here too long.

Nadiah's face sprang to mind, and I imagined her waiting for me at the end of that alley, wondering why I hadn't come for her. Had she heard the altercation? Had hope sprang up in her, at the thought of being rescued, only for me to have failed?

Had those guys gotten to her?

Shit.

As fast as I could – which was slow – I pulled my jacket back on. Once I was sitting up, I could see my boots on the floor beside the bed, with my weapon laying beside them. I got them on, got them laced up, then drug myself up from the bed, into a standing position. Once I felt confident I could stay upright, I moved.

Through the door of the room I'd woken up in, into a hallway lined with other doors. I kept moving until I found a staircase at the end which opened into a huge foyer. There was a rhythmic thump, coming from somewhere in the distance, but I ignored it in favor of searching the area for human presence. When I saw none, I headed down the stairs.

The closer I got to the bottom, the louder that sound came, joined by others. Abruptly, I realized it was music – not the canned stuff that played in the salon, or the impromptu concerts that sprang up in public spaces with improvised instruments before they were disbursed.

Music, recorded in a studio, mixed and mastered, like my grand-mother talked about. It had been a casualty of all the electronics being confiscated, making it – like the heavily monitored cell phones and computers – a luxury for the rich.

But... I thought I was in the Burrows?

I shook my head, blinking a little as my feet hit the floor, and the music vibrated through me. Someone was speaking, but in a weird cadence that flowed along with the sound. I couldn't tell what she was saying – a combination of the sound being muffled, and the words just not making any sense – but somehow it felt *good*.

This wasn't the time for that though.

Where the front door should have been was closed off, so I went the other way. This time when I heard voices, they were louder – not part of the music, but a conversation happening on the other side of a cracked door. As quietly as I could, I crept up to it, relying on the music to help muffle my steps in the heavy boots.

"...Know goddamn well the 'Queen' is just looking for a reason to storm my shit, and you attack her Knights over some pussy?!"

"I don't have to do anything special to get pussy, Ches. You know that just as well as any other motherfucker around here."

*"You're right – my bad. **New** pussy."*

*"It ain't about that either way. They had no business over here doing **anything**, and damn sure not attacking anybody. You're just gonna let that rock?"*

*"I don't have a choice now, because your wild ass didn't wait for an answer before you went in swinging. I can't go to her complaining about her Knights on my territory if they're **dead**."*

"They're not dead."

"We both know they probably wish they were."

Too late, I realized the conversation was over. Before I could back away, try to hide, the door swung open. The action took me by surprise, throwing me so off balance I pitched backward and hit the floor with a hard *thump*.

Adding more bruises to my collection.

Pain pulled my face into a squint as a tall figured stepped over me, peering down. At first, I thought I was being looked on with a sinister smile, but as my vision cleared, I realized I was looking at a mask, pulled up over the woman's mouth and nose.

"Look at this shit," she snapped, tugging the mask down to speak to someone out of my view. "You see? You bring your *stray* into my place, and she's already sneaking around." Her nose curled as her gaze returned. "I should kick your ass, girl."

"Wait!" I exclaimed, pulling up on my good arm to scoot away. "I don't mean to be sneaky, I don't know where I am. And I'm looking for my little sister. I don't want any trouble."

A smile curled across her face now, just as sinister as the mask, and nearly as wide. "Oh honey, I *know* you don't want any trouble. Not up in here. You must be telling the truth about not knowing where you are. Or who *I* am."

Someone I had no business in front of.

That was for sure.

She was dressed in jade leather – pants that hung low on her hips, baring miles of golden skin between there and the halter top covering her breasts. Her lips, eyebrows, and hair – a short, sleek bob that curled around her ears – were all the same shade of seaweed green. Unconventional, sure, but striking when taken together with undeniably beautiful features.

She was terrifying.

"I'm sorry," I told her, scooting back a little more, out of the way of the pointed toe of her high-heeled boots. "I didn't mean any harm."

"Relax," a male voice sounded – the other half of the conversation I'd listened in on. "Ches is just in a bad mood, don't mind her."

"*Ches*" frowned, dragging her glare away from me to turn it on him. Once she wasn't looking at me anymore, I felt free to adjust my sightline, turning to see the man who dared speak so casually to such a frightful woman.

My gaze landed and stuck on deep brown skin, covered with the blue-black lines of permanent graffiti. It swathed both of his arms – powerful arms, with thick biceps – disappearing under the tight-fitting sleeves of a black tee shirt that stretched over his chest, then appearing again at his neck, stopping somewhere under his jaw. The glossy ends of two braids rested on his shoulders, their origins hidden under a black cap pulled backward on his head.

He had kind eyes, and that made me feel a little safer.

Just a little.

He approached me with his hand extended, helping me up from where I was splayed on the ground. I had to tip my head back to keep my eyes on his face – I couldn't keep my eyes off his face – even once I was back on my feet.

"Ches hasn't had any this week," he said, flashing a wicked smile full of white teeth, with silver fangs decorating the bottom row. "Her regular dick is off on a diplomatic mission, so she's on one."

"Maddox, you keep playing with me and I'm putting you in the cage," Ches hissed, stepping into his face as if he didn't have at least a foot of height and about seventy pounds of weight over her.

Over *me*.

"You won't," he countered, not blinking. "Unless you want 'em all out of commission for a few weeks."

I didn't know who "*they*" were, but he must've been right, because Ches let out of huff before she turned her attention back to me.

"Where are you from, little girl? And what the hell are you doing in the *Burrows*?"

"I'm looking for my sister. She's just a teenager. We're from the *Mids*."

One perfectly groomed green eyebrow lifted. "A teenager? She looks like you?"

"Yes!" I answered, hopefully. "You've seen her?"

Ches chuckled, shaking her head. "No. But an attractive teenage girl, around here? *Alone?* You might as well go on home, break the news to your parents."

"Our parents are dead," I shot back, with a venom level that was probably ill-advised. "But what do you mean, break what news?"

"What I mean is that it ain't safe around here for a young girl who doesn't belong to anybody. Hell…" Her eyes narrowed as she looked me over, stepping in a little more. "It might not be safe for *you* either."

Maddox stuck an arm between us. "You're scaring her."

"*Good*," Ches countered. "She ought to be. This is *my* shit." Her sharp gaze turned to Maddox, and she cupped his chin. Her long, jade lacquered nails were filed into points that pressed into his skin. "You're the only motherfucker around here who *isn't* scared of me, and I'd like to keep it that way."

Maddox smirked at her, moving her hand from his face before he looked at me, locking his piercing black eyes with mine. "Your sister. That's what you were doing in that alley?" he asked, and I nodded.

"She was exploring the ruins with a friend and got hurt. I believe someone got to her, but she left a trail for me. That's where it led, but then those guys popped out. I told Bunny to run, and then…"

His thick eyebrows went up. "Bunny? That's who came sprinting out of there?"

"Yeah, you saw her?" I asked, halfway afraid to sound optimistic.

He nodded. "That's what got my attention, made me go see what was going on. I don't know where she is though."

"I told her to go home," I explained, hoping like hell she'd been able to get there. I looked back to Ches, since it was obvious she held power not just here in the house, but in the Burrows themselves. "But *I* can't go home. Not without my sister."

Ches rolled her eyes. "You can keep the cute puppy act to yourself honey. I'm not sentimental. You understand… post-apocalypse, every woman for herself, all that?"

"*Goddamn*, Ches, can you cut the shit, please?" Maddox interjected. "Ya ass wasn't always *Franchesca Catlan,* Baddest Bitch of the *Burrows.* You forgot what you used to do? How you helped peo—"

"*That's enough,*" Ches hissed, with a sharp hand motion that Maddox must've understood as the end of her rope, because his mouth shut. Nostrils flared, she turned with a sneer. "I'm gonna do one thing for you, and then I want you out of my face, unless you've got something to offer."

She turned and walked away, and I looked to Maddox, confused, hoping he knew what was happening. He shrugged, then crossed his arms, waiting.

It only took a moment before she was back, rifling through a small silver pouch. She took out a green tube, shoving the rest of the pouch at Maddox to hold.

I flinched as she grabbed me by the chin, lifting it to expose my neck. "Hold still," she demanded, and I did, barely breathing as she unscrewed the tube to reveal metallic green lipstick she used to draw something on my neck. "This is my mark. It won't come off for a few days unless you purposely scrub it off. This will let you move around the *Burrows*."

She took her bag back from Maddox, who pointed to his own neck, where a green lipstick print – tattooed- was set apart from his other ink.

"Maddox will escort you," she said, wiping the perpetual smirk from his face, replacing it with a wrinkled brow and a frown.

"I will?" he asked, in a tone that implied this was a serious affront. "But what about—"

"I don't give a fuck," she informed him, waving off whatever excuse he had. "This is *your* mess, not mine. You're the one who brought her here."

"Yeah, cause I didn't want to leave a battered woman in an alley, not because I planned to play babysitter. I have things to *do*," he said, looking past both of us, with enough focus that I glanced back. I hadn't noticed until then, but the music was louder now, like a door had opened somewhere, and people were gathering in the foyer.

Maddox was looking in one specific direction though.

I followed his gaze to twins – literally – two gorgeous, mahogany-skinned women with bald heads. Curiosity drove me to look them over – strappy high heels, tiny shorts, and crop tops with words printed across in white letters.

Eat Me, with an arrow pointing down on one. *Suck Me,* with arrows on either side, pointing to hard nipples prominent through the thin fabric of the shirt.

Oh.

That's what he had to do.

"Dee and Dem will be here when you get back," Ches assured Maddox, rolling her eyes as the twins waved at him, and he waved back, cupping his groin through his jeans. "I thought you wanted to help her?"

"I wanted *you* to help her," he countered with a heavy sigh as he looked me over, probably comparing me to the twins, then turning back to Ches once he realized I wasn't as appetizing. "But, fine. She's gotta sleep off that concussion first though, before I take her anywhere."

Ches sucked her teeth. "You're just trying to get rid of her so you can get your dick serviced, but luckily for you, you're right." She glanced at me again, her lip curling in disgust. "She looks like hell. Feed her, put her to bed, and then take her to see Blue. If anybody knows anything about her sister..."

"Blue does. Got it," Maddox said, making a gun motion at her as he backed away. He grabbed me by the good wrist. "Come on."

He tugged at me, but I resisted, turning to Ches to meet her eyes. "Thank you."

She smirked. "You're welcome honey," she replied, grabbing the edge of her mask and pulling it back up over face. "Good luck," she told me, from behind that painted-on sinister grin. "You'll need it."

FIVE

"So you never told me what your name was."

Maddox made that statement from the confines of a half-circle booth, where instead of sitting opposite me, he'd chosen immediate proximity. His legs were spread wide – one *touching* mine – and he draped his arms along the back of the seat, enveloping me in ambient heat from his body.

"Aly. Alyson."

"Okay. Nice to meet you, Alyson."

I felt, rather than saw, his grin. All the tables had a single bulb hanging over them for illumination, but the bench seats sank into the shadows. Sitting back like he was, I could only barely see him, but still.

His presence was potent.

He'd ordered for me, when I'd sat there gaping stupidly at the menu upon being asked what I wanted. It was embarrassing, really – I couldn't tell you if the *Mids* had a place like this... a *restaurant*. I rarely deviated from my specific route, and if I did, there was no way I'd ever part with an amount so large for a meal that would only feed one person.

He ordered me a waffle, which I'd never had, and chicken, which I hadn't tasted in years and years. Once it was just me and Nadiah, with Gran sick in assisted living, the budget had been cut to the bone. Meat was a luxury I couldn't afford.

It didn't feel like something I could argue against though. This place – *Underground,* as they apparently called it – belonged to Ches. We were underneath the foyer where we'd been introduced, where I'd felt the music under my feet. After Ches had offered her ominous farewell, Maddox led me through a heavy steel door and down another set of stairs, through a mass of sweaty bodies writhing to pounding music, to the area where we were now.

I drew enough curious stares along the way to understand that I didn't fit. Desperately, I wanted to sit back, out of the light, but that would mean sinking into Maddox – a thought way more mortifying than the stares were.

I'd seen a man before – the *Mids* were full of them. Over the years, I'd dated a little, with varying levels of success.

Mostly very, *very* low.

And *none* of them made me feel as flustered as Maddox did.

"So you're from the *Mids*, huh?" he asked, right in my ear, nearly making me jump out of my skin.

I swallowed hard, steadying myself, not looking back when I nodded. "Yeah. Been there all my life."

"Damn. How do you manage out there with that curfew?"

"I don't notice it," I shrugged. "Nadiah and I are never out that late anyway, so it means nothing to us."

"*Never?*" he asked, with such skepticism I turned then, to meet his eyes in the low light.

"Never."

"Not even like... out with your man or anything, sneaking around?"

My face heated as I shook my head. "No, not even that."

"Ah, damn," he grinned, then laughed. "That's not surprising though, not really. Typical good girl from the *Mids*. You probably never even got your cherry popped."

"I'm not a *child*," I defended, suddenly feeling parched. I used my tongue to wet my dry lips, wishing I'd had the sense to put lip balm in one of my overstuffed pockets. "I've... you know?"

That enthralling smile spread wider. "Nah, I don't, cause you can't say it."

"But I've *done* it."

"If you say so."

Ugh.

I clenched my teeth together, practicing my *difficult client* protocol to calm myself. A count to five, with a closed mouth, and then a smile. Another count to five, and then a swallowing of the anger that would only get me in trouble if I let it out. Maddox wasn't a client, but that didn't mean I shouldn't practice a similar decorum. Working ensured my survival. Cooperating with Maddox would get me answers about my sister.

At this point, they were of equal importance.

The food helped quell my emotions. It was impossible to focus on my self-conscious irritation when the plate in front of me smelled like happiness. My mouth watered as they loaded the table with food and drinks and condiments, reminding me that Harriet's coffee at the salon was the last thing I'd consumed.

That coffee – and the salon, and that conversation – felt like something that had happened *days* ago, instead of hours.

Maddox tucked into his food without hesitation, probably expecting me to do the same. Instead, I stared at the golden, syrup-drowned waffle piled high with fried chicken like it was going to come alive and attack me. Like I was waiting to wake up from a dream.

But then Maddox took a piece right off my plate, biting into it. "It's good, Aly. You should eat."

So I did.

Using every detail of the table manners my mother and grandmother had taught me, I prepared myself and then took my first bite. I tried my best not to moan, but the rush of flavor in my mouth made that impossible.

Quickly, I forgot most of my manners.

Long-term hunger – a feeling I'd become accustomed to, to make sure Nadiah had plenty to eat – and great food created a situation where I tuned out my surroundings – there was nothing there except me and my plate, and I had every intention of cleaning it.

Until I realized Maddox was looking at me.

Thinly veiled amusement was apparent on his handsome face, and for about the hundredth time in the last few hours, embarrassment rushed through me.

"You've got a little..." he picked up a napkin, aiming for my chin before I snatched the cloth from his hand to do it myself.

It was syrup.

A line of syrup I had to scrub at to get off, like it had been there for a bit and had time to dry. When I put the napkin down, my fork went with it. I took a big gulp of water I halfway choked on, not expecting it to taste so *clean*.

And then I put my hands in my lap and sat still before I humiliated myself any further.

"What's wrong?" Maddox asked, and I shook my head.

"Nothing. Just waiting."

"So you're done? You're full?"

"I'm fine."

"I didn't ask if you were fine, I asked if you were *full*."

"I'm done eating."

His expression softened to understanding. "Because I was looking at you?"

"Because you were *laughing* at me."

"I wasn't laughing at you. I was looking at you, because you seemed happy – like you were enjoying yourself, which I hadn't seen before. Eat your food."

I shook my head. "I had enough. I don't want to make myself

sick." That was true. But I only had enough sense to think it because he'd embarrassed me out of stuffing my face.

Maddox stared for another few seconds, then shrugged, sliding my plate over to join the *plates* of food he was already working on. "May as well not let it go to waste."

I gave him a tight smile – approval he didn't need to polish off the rest of my food with his own. I finished my water, knowing I needed the hydration, then refilled the glass with the pitcher that had been left on the table.

The longer I sat, the worse I started to feel.

It wasn't about being ashamed anymore, but *physically*. My head was swimming, body aching, and my tongue felt too big for my mouth.

"Did you... did... you *drug* me?" I asked Maddox, trying to resist the urge to put my head down on the table. "Something... in the water?" Just getting that sentence out was exhausting.

Through bleary eyes, I watched him shake his head as he wiped his mouth. "Nah. You got drugged hours ago, when Doc checked you out. It's wearing off."

Oh.

Yes.

You got your ass kicked, remember?

"Come on," Maddox said, already on his feet, moving to the outside of the booth. He extended a hand, and I accepted it, allowing him to help me up. I barely had any strength in my legs, but his grip around my waist was steady. I blinked, and we were back in the foyer. I blinked again, and I was back in the room where I'd woken up, sitting on the edge of the bed while Maddox stripped my jacket off, and someone I couldn't make out flashed a light in my eyes.

The last thing I processed was Maddox telling me not to leave the room, that he'd come by for me in the morning.

And then I was out, again.

I had to pee.

Even though I'd been told not to leave the room, at some point physiological need overrode that instruction, leading me out of the bed and out of the room, sneaking as quietly as I could down the hall.

Luckily, a cracked door caught my attention before I could build up the courage to try any of the closed ones. I snuck toward it, relieved that my suspicion of it being the bathroom was correct. Slipping inside, I flipped the light switch, then locked the door behind me.

First, I relieved myself, taking care of the primary reason for sneaking out of bed. Then, I took advantage of the big vanity mirror, checking for visible bruising to match all the tenderness I still felt.

My face was fine, which was a relief.

My looks weren't usually of any concern – the men I encountered on my curated schedule were so underwhelming that I didn't care if they thought I was cute. It was – unfortunately – safer to not be worth a second glance. I wasn't, however, naïve enough to believe a pretty face and slim waist weren't contributing factors to me getting my job. Not that I had control over either one. I inherited my face, and the slim build was a result of a tight budget. But that was of no concern to anyone except me, and maybe Gran and Nadiah.

In the *Apex*, it was the facade that mattered.

And maybe not just there...

The way Maddox looked at the twins hadn't escaped my notice. Not that I could blame him – they weren't *pretty*. They were *beautiful*, strikingly so, and very comfortable with their bodies – healthy, filled-out bodies that didn't have the slightest concern for where their next meal might come from.

Hell, I'd been looking too.

In the mirror, I saw nothing special – that wasn't self-deprecation, just the truth. I pulled all my braids to one side, noting that while my face remained blemish-free, there was an ugly purple bruise at the back of my neck, disappearing under my shirt to spread onto my shoulder.

Gingerly, I grabbed the hem of my tee shirt, pulling it up as I twisted in the mirror. My back was mottled like a watercolor painting – red-brown skin, black and purple bruises.

Wherever she was, I hoped Nadiah wasn't checking for bruises in the mirror. Just the thought of that had me tugging my shirt down and tucking it in, ready to get moving. I wasn't sure what time it was, but the light coming through the windows in the hall told me the sun was coming up, which meant it was approaching 24 hours since I'd seen my sister.

I needed to be out there looking for her.

There were no extra toothbrushes, but I found the cabinet under the sink well-stocked with tiny bottles of mouthwash. I took one, figuring it was better than nothing – and better to ask forgiveness than permission – and cleaned my mouth as well as I could. Once I washed my face, depositing the towel I used in a marked basket, I left the bathroom to go back to the room I'd woken up in.

The door was locked.

I stepped back, trying not to panic as I counted again to make sure – I'd been in the third room from the corner. I knew I hadn't turned the lock behind me, so *what the hell?*

The only people I knew here were Ches and Maddox, and I wasn't confident in calling either of them a friendly face – not this early in the morning.

Especially after I'd been told to stay in the room, and Ches hadn't seemed thrilled about my presence.

The sound of footsteps on the stairs sent my heart rate into overdrive – I didn't know who was coming, or how much trouble I'd get into for being in this hallway. I tried the doorknob again, silently willing it, *begging* it to *pleasepleaseplease* open this time.

It didn't.

"This is why I told you not to leave your room."

Behind me, Maddox laughed. Somehow, the sound of his voice was both relieving and anxiety-spiking.

"I had to pee," I explained, hating how weak the excuse sounded, true or not. "I didn't know the door would lock behind me."

Wearing that same disarming grin from last night, Maddox leaned into the wall beside my door, hands tucked into his pockets. Today's tee shirt was the same jade as the lips tattooed on his neck, paired with a thick tungsten chain – I only knew what it was because it was the "it" metal in the *Apex* this year. All forms of gold were passé.

His cap was pulled forward today, creating a shadow over half his face. "You don't know how to hold it?" he asked, casual, as if he weren't, yet again, asking for information that was personal.

"I *tried*," I snapped, once more using anger to cover embarrassment.

"Try harder next time."

He pulled a ring of keys from his pocket, and opened the door, motioning for me to go in ahead of him. Without being asked, I moved straight to putting on my scuffed boots, trying not to compare them with the pristine boots Maddox wore.

Trying not to pay too much attention to him, period, which was a hard task.

He looked good.

He smelled good.

And my insecurity about going out with him in yesterday's clothes shot up, landing somewhere near the roof. *At least,* I thought to myself, *the expensive high-performance deodorant I use for work is doing its job. But things aren't going well for you, if your only selling point is "at least I don't stink."*

"I'm glad you're already awake. We'll hit Blue up while he's having breakfast – guaranteed good mood. How you feeling?"

My shoulders went up for a shrug that made me cringe, which I tried to play off by sucking my teeth. "Like I got my ass kicked, but I'll manage. I want to find my sister."

"Understandable, but there's no reason for you walk around any more uncomfortable than you have to. We'll grab something simple for you on the way out, after you change."

"Change?" I asked, my eyebrows going up. "This is all I have."

He nodded, then gave me a different smile this time – more *calculated* than the usual one. "Yeah, I've got that covered."

Those words were barely out of his mouth before there was a knock at the door. He opened it and stepped back, revealing the twins.

"*Good morning, Maddox,*" they chimed, in unison, both fawning over him as the door swung closed. After he'd enjoyed a few moments of their attention – lots of winking and groping and giggles and whispered comments – he came up for air.

"Aly – meet Deneira and Demaris – Dee and Dem. They're gonna get you together, then we'll head out. I'll see you in a few minutes," he said, disappearing through the door before I could protest.

It wasn't until then I realized they'd both been carrying large duffels they'd dropped to sweet talk Maddox, but they retrieved them now to head in my direction. Like last night, they wore tiny shorts and cropped tops, but there were no words this time – stripes for one, and polka dots for the other.

"Um... ladies, I don't mean any offense, but I don't know that your look is my style?"

Like mirror images, their flawlessly made-up faces pulled into scowls, and they looked to each other.

"Does she think we want to make her look like us?" Dem – *I think* – asked Dee, and Dee scowled a little deeper, then responded, "Look like us? She thinks that's what we want?"

Still frowning, they turned to look at me. "No offense sweetie, but you could *never*," Dee said, and Dem nodded. "*Never*, sweetie. No offense."

My mouth dropped open. "I'm sorry, I—"

Dee – *Or Dem?* – raised a hand, quieting me. "We're professionals, okay? We *know* what we're doing."

"Okay?" Dem nodded, stopping forward, clearly expecting me to nod too. "*We* know what we're doing. We're *professionals.*"

I couldn't argue.

"Okay," I agreed. "Fine. Just tell me what to do."

Both frowns disappeared, and they looked at each and smiled.

Dee pulled piles of clothes from her duffel, and Dem pulled makeup from hers.

"How do you know what size I need?" I asked Dee, straining to look as Dem patted something on my face.

"She has an eye for it," Dem answered for her, before Dee answered, "Yeah, I have an eye for it, you know?"

Dem grabbed my chin, making me face her, staring at me for a moment before she picked up a tube of something that was the same color as my skin. "You have a really pretty face, you know? Like, a perfect canvas."

"You do," Dee chimed in. "A perfect canvas. Just like, a really pretty face."

"Um, thank you?"

"You're welcome," they trilled, at the same time.

It went on like that, with them repeating after each other, "*We have to lay these baby hairs down – these baby hairs? We have to lay them down.*" until my makeup was done. Then, Dee dressed and undressed me several times, something I only tolerated because I was so grateful to see the underwear she'd brought for me to choose from, really nice stuff, with all the tags still on.

When they were finished with me, they stood me up, opening a closet door I hadn't noticed. On the other side was a full-length mirror, and they flanked me as I looked at myself.

"You're so totally pretty I went natural with your makeup, none of the men will think you have any on. They're so dumb," Dem laughed, as I admired her work. Sure enough, it was still my face, but perhaps what I could've looked like... pre-apocalypse.

On my other side, Dee laughed. "Yeah, the men are so dumb, they're gonna like, see how natural she went with your makeup – cause you're totally pretty – and think you don't have any on."

I returned her smile and nodded. "Yeah, Dem did a beautiful job."

"And I saw you had your little conservative girl thing going on, so you see I put you in some cute jeans, with the vintage boots you already had, and gave you a vintage top. It's like a century old, so don't lose it, okay? And you can put your same jacket on."

"Mmmhmmm," Dem added. "Your same jacket, and your same vintage boots, some cute jeans, and a vintage top, so you can keep your little conservative girl thing going on, you know? Dee saw that for you, she told me about it. Don't lose that top either, it's like a century old."

Looking down, I read the words across the shirt in the mirror. *Ivy Park* meant nothing to me, but I looked cute, and the only vintage things I owned were because they'd been handed down.

I wasn't complaining.

"Thank you, Dee. Thank you, Dem," I told them, and they smiled.

In the mirror, Dee winked at me. "Maddox is *totally* gonna want to fuck you now."

My eyes got big.

I was *not* expecting that.

"*Totally*," Dem agreed, laughing. "Now, he is *so* gonna want to fuck you."

"But, I–" I stammered, but they waved me off, moving to pack up their things.

"It's nothing to be nervous about, Maddox is totally a gentleman," Dem assured, as Dee nodded. "He's a *total* gentleman, don't be nervous."

They exchanged another grin, and Dee turned hers in my direction. "Unless you don't want him to be."

"Yeah," Dem agreed. "If you don't want him to be, he won't. But don't be nervous either way."

"Right, either way, don't be nervous!"

"I'm *not* doing that with him!" I said, my voice going sharp as I tried to stop this whole line of conversation.

With their duffels on opposite shoulders, they looked at each other, then looked at me.

"Why not?" they harmonized, in a tone that made it obvious they thought I was crazy. Before I could answer, a knock sounded at the door, and they forgot about encouraging me to *"fuck Maddox"* in favor of doing it to him themselves, with their eyes.

A deep, quiet sigh blew from my nostrils as I watched their exchange, full of lip biting and teasing, and Maddox giving them a perfect simultaneous smack on the ass as they moved on their way. He watched them walk down the hall, enjoying the view before he turned, wearing the friendliest of smiles.

"You look nice. You ready to go see Blue?"

SIX

I wasn't expecting the motorcycle.

I'd never been inside a vehicle smaller than a bus, and I found *that* nerve-wracking, so the idea that I was supposed to ride on the back of this fast-moving thing with no protection except the helmet Maddox handed me was daunting.

He must have sensed my hesitation, because he gave me another one of those grins as he pulled the helmet from my hands, tucking my braids behind my shoulders before he put it on me.

"Let's *go*," he said, with an impatient edge that suggested *I* was the holdup – like I'd somehow been responsible for the mini-makeover *he* found necessary. I'd have much rather had a shower and toothbrush to go with it all, but again, I was in no position to complain.

I climbed up on the bike behind him, at his instruction.

"Put your feet here," he told me, pointing. "And keep your arms around me, unless you want to fall off."

Two seconds later, he took off.

I kept my feet where he said, and kept my arms around him.

Tight.

In the bright light of day, the *Burrows* looked normal. From all the stories, from the reputation, I'd expected it to look like a hellscape of toppled buildings, animals roaming the streets, decaying bodies scattered around. I'd realized last night this wasn't the case, but now, as we came out of the area where *Underground* was, into an area that was more populated, I wondered if the *Burrows* was *better*.

Appearances were deceiving – this was wisdom I understood. But looking around this "lawless" place and seeing happy children playing together in a park, to see a fresh market with no armed guards flanking the entrance, to get a nod of acknowledgment from a stranger, instead of narrowed eyes and mistrust... it was hard not to wonder what the hell was going on.

In fact, once the motorcycle stopped, and Maddox helped me climb off, curiosity overruled my determination to not seem naïve.

"Hey," I said, stopping him before he could move along the sidewalk. "We're still in the *Burrows*, right?"

Confusion wrinkled his brow. "Uh, yeah. What makes you ask?"

"Well..." I held my hands out, gesturing around me. "For a name like the *Burrows*, this is sure as hell a lot of open air and sunshine and... life."

Maddox chuckled. "Ahh, you thought we were like, mole people or something, right?" he laughed again, nodding. "I see the *Mids* still doing a thorough job with their indoctrination protocol."

"I'm not *indoctrinated*," I snapped, offended. "I know the government isn't some benevolent entity with the good of man at heart."

"Maybe so, but you believe the other lies they feed you to keep you in line, and you follow all of their rules, don't step a toe outside of the boundaries."

I curled my nose. "How can you say that when I'm *here*?!"

"Only because of an extreme circumstance, to find your little sister," he countered. "Which is admirable. Impressive. I wouldn't think a good girl from the *Mids* had it in her."

"This *good girl* has a *lot* in her, actually. Not that you'd know, because you don't know *me*. I follow the rules because it keeps me alive, to take care of Nadiah, to take care of my grandmother. I'm doing what I *have* to do."

Maddox shrugged. "So that's your answer, huh? That's it? Just being alive – not happy, not thriving, just *living*, that's worth your rights and freedom?"

"Oh *hell*, don't tell me you're of those," I snapped, shaking my head. "Your *"freedom"* over everything?"

"Damn right. I'm supposed to be satisfied with just the air I breathe, while motherfuckers living lavish off the shit they murdered, raped, and stole for? *Fuck that.*"

"No *fuck you!*" I shot back, drawing a sideways look from a couple passing by. "Because people like *you* get the rest of us in trouble – dragged off for questioning for being your neighbor, accused of a crime from dropping off a package as a favor. Or blown to pieces, for being in the wrong place at the wrong time," I finished, my voice cracking as I turned away, only to have him grab my arm, turning me back to face him.

"What are you talking about?" he asked, catching me under the chin to make me look at him. "I'm not taking you to see *anybody* unless you tell me."

I huffed, blinking away tears. "My parents. Six years ago when I was Nadiah's age. They were passing through the gate between the *Apex* and the *Mids* to get home. They were just trying to get home. But terrorists decided that sending their message was more important than the innocent people who might come through, and they blew it up. There weren't even bodies for us to bury. But freedom, right?"

Maddox was quiet for a moment, then swiped a hand over his chin. "I didn't know your parents died like that. I'm sorry."

"Yeah, well now you do. Can we talk to this guy now? I need to see my sister."

"We will, but hold up a second," he said, not taking a step. "I get you aren't a big fan of... you call it terrorism, I call it resistance. I *get* it. You lost half your world. But understand that this—" he motioned around us "- the 'open air, and sunlight, and life', this shit came with a price I'm glad the people before me paid. It wasn't free, and it wasn't *pretty*."

"Why are you telling me this?" I asked, shaking my head. "Nothing you say will make it be okay."

"You're right, it won't. Because the shit *isn't* okay. But instead of being angry at the people fighting for something better, you can spare some loathing for the ones who made it that way."

He didn't wait for a response – not that I had one. He walked, and I followed, into a brick-front building where the smell of food hit me right in the pit of my empty stomach. The chicken and waffles from last night felt so far away.

I forced myself to keep up with Maddox as he blew right past the hostess stand, past the tables of people eating, to a private room in the back. It was darker back here, with the curtains drawn, and hazy. As we got closer to the head of the room, the haze thickened, into sweet-smelling smoke, colored indigo from the strips of neon that lined the room.

It made me feel a little woozy, but Maddox seemed unaffected, using a firm hand to wave it out of his face as he stopped in front of an occupied table.

I was confident the person sitting there was "Blue".

He was a large man, in a blue velour sweat suit with the jacket unzipped, displaying his hairy chest and a heavy-looking gold rope. His beard and mustache were thick, but his hair was cut low, every-thing lined so sharply it was feasible that he'd *just* stepped away from the barber. I got the feeling though that he was this immaculate every day.

His gaze came to me first, then rolled over to Maddox. He took a deep drag from the tube attached to the detailed hookah on the table in front of him, then spoke.

"Mads. Whassup?" he asked, reaching to smack hands with him.

Maddox accepted the gesture, then shrugged as he stepped back. "Typical shit."

"I got you. Who are you?" Blue's eyes returned to me, bored and waiting. I glanced at Maddox, expecting an introduction, but he only stared back.

I took a breath, then turned back. "Alyson."

"Alyson? Alyson who? I'm supposed to just know who the fuck you are off rip?"

"No." I swallowed. "Alyson Little."

"Who the fuck is Alyson Little?"

Again, I looked at Maddox for help, but all I got was a slight hitch in his eyebrow.

Asshole.

"I'm... a hair stylist. From the *Mids*. I'm looking for my little sister."

Blue stared at me while he took another hit from the hookah. He held the smoke for a moment, blowing it out in little rings that floated in my direction before they dissipated.

And then he laughed.

"You think you're looking for your sister, huh? I like that."

I frowned. "I *am* looking for my sister."

"Nah, that's what you're *supposed* to think, what they want you to think. But okay, I'll let you rock with that." He picked up a huge strawberry from the platter of fruit in front him, taking a bite. Taking his time chewing. Then, finally, "Why does it matter if you find your sister? Who is Alyson Little?"

"What?"

"You hard of hearing or something? I'on know nothing about you, nothing about your sister. You gonna tell me why she matters? Or who the fuck *you* are?"

"Blue..." Maddox spoke up, but Blue waved him off.

"Nah, she gotta answer me, Blue helps those who help themselves."

I shook my head. "But I don't understand what you're asking me, or why you're asking it. Can you elaborate?"

He scoffed. "Can I elaborate? Can *I* elaborate? Don't burn yourself Alyson Little, you're playing with fire, looking at the full fucking story, right here, right in front of you. I'm about to give you a vital tenet right here, so listen in. Listen up. You listening?"

"I nodded. "Yes. I'm listening."

"This is breaking news, aiight?"

Again, I nodded. "Yes."

"If you can't answer the question, you gotta get the fuck outta my establishment. You're not thinking hard enough, and you're blowing my vibe. You feel me?"

"I do."

"Aiight then – tell me who the fuck Alyson Little is. And tell me why finding her sister matters."

I let out a sigh. "I...*dammit*. Alyson Little is an orphan. A selfish one. Her sister is the most precious thing she has. Someone took her. And Alyson wants her back."

Another deep drag of hookah. Another stream of blue-tinged smoke rings.

"Okay, Alyson Little. I like that, I'll help you out, since you answered my first question."

"*First?!*" I snapped, but Maddox tugged me backward, behind him.

"Cut the shit, Blue," he growled. "The girl we're looking for is only nineteen years old – no more fucking games. There isn't shit that happens around here without you knowing about it, so cough it up," Maddox demanded, smacking the table so hard it made everything bounce.

Blue's eyes narrowed. "Don't burn yourself, Maddox Hatcher. You're playing with fire."

Unmoved, Maddox stared right back, until Blue's expression softened. He sat back, laughing as he finished the other half of his oversized strawberry. "You see that, Alyson Little? Mad didn't blink, I like that," he nodded.

Yes.

I'd seen it.

I'd *felt* it.

"You talking intelligent, attractive young women," Blue continued, "Then you're talking *Diamonds*, but you might not like what you find when you get there. I got breaking news for you, Alyson Little, two vital tenets – First – it's a reason we put animals in cages, you know? Everything that glitters ain't gold, and everything that's cute ain't innocent. They don't want you to succeed, so you gotta look out. Second, the Hartfords take real good care of their grass, shit looks mighty green from the *Mids*, if you know what I mean."

"I don't."

"He's saying she may not want to leave. Which is something to consider," Maddox explained.

My face pulled into a scowl. "Leave *what*? I don't know what you're talking about."

Blue laughed. "Maddox, where the hell you find this one?"

I opened my mouth to retort, but the warning look Maddox gave made the words die on my lips.

"Appreciated as always," he told Blue, grabbing my wrist to pull me along.

"Thank you," I chimed too, though I didn't understand what the information he'd given us meant. Or if he'd actually given us anything.

"Be blessed," I heard from behind us as we left the private room, and Maddox rushed me back out front.

He was already reaching for his helmet when I stopped him.

"Hey – what the hell was that?" I asked, confused.

Maddox pushed out a sigh, offering none of his usual smiles, which was a little scary. "Nothing I didn't already suspect," he answered, picking up my helmet and handing it to me. "Just needed confirmation before we moved forward."

"Move forward? So you know where my sister is?"

He nodded. "Yeah. I do."

Hope spiked in my chest, and I let it show on my face, though he didn't share my enthusiasm. "Yes!! Okay, so where are we going next?"

"To see the Queen."

E verybody wanted an audience with the "Queen".

At least, that was the impression I had upon arriving at the multi-story building Maddox referred to as her "compound". The first area we entered was set up like a waiting room, with a system where you took a number when you walked in, and waited. Maddox bypassed all of that, leading me to a guarded elevator at the back of the room. When he spotted us, the guard stepped aside, pressing the button to open it for us.

That was the moment it sunk in for me that Maddox wasn't just some guy who knew a lady who had a big house. There was a hierarchy, some political capital I was missing. I was so laser-focused on finding Nadiah that I hadn't taken a moment to interrogate who I was dealing with.

The truth was, I had no idea.

Once the elevator closed, Maddox pressed the only other button on the panel besides the one that would take us back down. He looked straight ahead, saying nothing, and I took the opportunity to stare.

The face, the tattoos, the biceps, the obvious luxury of those two braids... I was a little disgusted at how appealing I found him, and a *lot* disgusted by how that appeal distracted me from focusing on more important things.

Like what the hell was happening around me.

So much had occurred in the last twelve hours it was dizzying. Once this was all over, and Nadiah and I were back home, I'd have plenty to lay awake obsessing about, letting my imagination run. It was something to look forward to, knowing I was going right back to the mundanity of my normal life, to see none of these bizarre people again.

Most eventful day off ever.

When the elevator opened, Maddox moved, not looking back to make sure I was following. We walked into another room like the one downstairs, but smaller. This time, Maddox stopped to scribble his name down on a roll, then led me to a collection of seats, facing a raised stage. The seats he chose had a perfect view of the throne – and the person seated upon it.

Ruby Hartford.

She looked terrifying.

A black crown of hearts sat upon her head, her hair still as flawlessly styled as when she'd left my salon chair yesterday. Her matte black lipstick stood out in high contrast to her light brown face, and her dark eyelashes had the same effect. Expensive high heels adorned her feet, the shiny, spiked stiletto glinting and reflecting light as her crossed foot swung back and forth.

There was a sword across her lap.

Red blade, black hilt.

She wasn't looking at the person standing in front of her, stuttering as he argued his case. Her eyes were on that blade, fingers giving it a loving caress as she listened.

Maybe.

Suddenly, the hilt was in her hand, the tip of the blade at the throat of the man in front of her. On either side, men dressed in all black – her security – moved their hands to their own weapons.

"*Shut. Up,*" Ruby hissed, giving him the courtesy of her eyes, cold and angry. "If I have to listen to another man with another excuse, I'm cutting *something* offa *somebody* today!"

The vibe hadn't been carefree before that, but her words added noticeable tension. It had always been obvious that Ruby Hartford was someone with money, someone important. I understood now it was much more than that.

It was *power*.

She oozed it, just like the wealth I'd noticed at the salon.

"I don't give a *fuck* about your personal life. Do not come with your problems, trying to make them mine. Do you understand me?"

The guy looked about on the verge of peeing himself, but he nodded – as much as he could without pricking himself on her blade. "Y-yes my q-queen."

"I haven't spilled blood in this court in a *long* time," she said, stepping to the side and angling the sword. "Do you think the *Burrows* needs a reminder?"

"No! N-no, my queen, *please*."

"I *hate* begging," she snapped, and the man fell quiet. She stared at him with cold eyes for a moment longer, then lowered the blade. "Get him out of my face," she muttered, to no one in particular, but two of the men in black rushed forward, leading the man away.

"Next," she called, inviting the next person into her presence.

I watched her interact with three other "cases" that clearly bored her before the attendant called Maddox up. Reluctantly, I joined him, prepared to take off running when Ruby's black lips stretched into a dazzling smile. It was such a marked difference from the cold anger, then complete boredom that it was scary.

It was scary as hell.

"*Maddox Hatcher*," she purred, standing again. She glided right up to us – to *him* – with blade in hand though she was giving off the vibe of warm cookies. Her free hand went to her chest, dragging her red-manicured nails along her bare skin. "Hi. How can I help you?"

"Hi Ruby," he responded, looking her right in the eyes as he smiled. "You have something that belongs to someone else."

Her eyes widened, in genuine surprise. "Do I?"

"A Diamond. Her sister." He tipped his head in my direction, and Ruby looked at me, those emerald eyes dark and curious at first, and then, bright with recognition.

"*You.*"

I swallowed. "Yes. Me. Hello Mrs. Hartford."

"*Ms.*" She corrected. "But please, call me Ruby. I didn't know you had a sister, but I didn't know you at all before yesterday, so I supposed that isn't surprising."

I didn't know what to say, so I said nothing.

"Her name is Nadiah," Maddox spoke for me. "She's nineteen years old."

Ruby's head drew back a little as she turned back to Maddox. "One of my Knights spoke about a young Nadiah. Smart as a whip, exquisite." She looked at me. "You didn't take my offer, but she did."

"She *wouldn't*," I shot back, shaking my head. "She's getting a scholarship offer from the *Apex*, to get a degree, then a great job."

"She *has* a great job. What was your name?"

"Aly."

Ruby smiled. "Pretty. Well, *Aly*, I understand your concern, but I assure you – Diamonds never have to do anything they don't want to – many are never touched at all. Your sister is safe."

"Someone took my sister, injured, from a house where she was hiding while waiting for me to come and get her. She left a *trail* for me to follow. She didn't run away to get a job – someone abducted her."

The smile melted from Ruby's face, and a quick glance down told me her grip had tightened on her blade. She looked backward, at the Knight closest to her.

He looked like he wanted to melt into the ground.

Instantly, all her friendly energy shifted to a barely contained rage as he stepped forward, speaking into her ear.

"*Why* am I just now hearing about this," she hissed, in response to whatever he had told her.

The Knight took a step back. "We didn't want to bore you with it, my Queen."

"But you bored me with—" Ruby stopped, taking a deep breath she exhaled through her nose, making her nostrils flare. "I will handle *you* later. Bring Nadiah. *Now.*"

The Knight took off running as Ruby turned her back on him. She let out a cleansing sigh before she returned her attention to me.

"There has been a mistake," she informed me, holding out the sword for one of the other Knights to take. "Apparently, one of my Diamond recruiters used some less than desirable... less than *consensual* methods. Your sister will be returned to you, and I will deal with him. In blood."

My eyes went wide. "Oh! Oh, no, that's not nece—"

"Why on what's left of this earth do you believe it's up to you?" Ruby asked. Something in her tone led me to believe I was in danger of boring her.

I shook my head. "Nothing. I apologize. Thank you, for returning my sister."

Behind the throne, a set of doors opened, and two people came out.

The Knight that Ruby had threatened, and Nadiah.

The sight of her made my knees go weak, but Maddox caught me, steadied me, until they'd rounded the throne and Nadiah noticed me.

"*Aly?!*" she gasped. "What are you doing here?!"

She came running toward me, flinging her arms around my neck for a hug I couldn't immediately return, because... *What?*

I pulled back, looking down at her feet. "How in the world are you running?" I asked, meeting her gaze to look for any sign of *anything*.

"Huh?" she raised an eyebrow at me, looking like a mirror image of our mother – cocoa skin, big brown eyes, and full lips. "What are you talking about? And what are you doing here?"

"I'm here to *save* you," I informed her. "Bunny came to get me last night because you were hurt, and then—"

"Bunny *lied*," Nadiah interrupted, with an ire I'd never heard from her before. "I've gone out to the ruins before – all the time. She always wanted me to go further, but I wouldn't, so she'd let it go. This time she wouldn't let it go, and I followed her so she wouldn't be alone. She tricked me into that house. Those men were waiting."

My eyes narrowed. "When we got to the house, I found your trail. She tried to get me to stay there and wait while she left."

"They were coming back. She was trying to set you up too."

"Wow," I breathed. "I should've known. I should've realized something was off."

Nadiah shook her head. "She was *my* friend. I thought she was, at least. You were just being you, like always. Taking care of me."

Behind us, Maddox cleared his throat. "Uh, this is heartwarming and all that, but let's take this reunion elsewhere. I'm sure Ruby has other matters to address."

My eyes went to her, now that he'd mentioned her name. "Really? That's it? We can just go?"

A smirk spread across her lips. "Of course. I'm very, *very* big on my Diamonds *wanting* to be here, never by force. You're all free to go."

"Oh, *thank you*," I gushed, hooking my arm through Nadiah's to walk away.

Ruby's voice stopped us cold.

"But," she said, bringing a lump of dread up into my chest. Beside me, Maddox muttered "*fuck!*" under his breath. "You understand how this puts me in a bind, losing a girl. Offering restitution would be the diplomatic thing to do."

I turned to face her with my heart in my feet. "If I could, I *would*. But I have nothing to offer you. I have nothing that would be of any value to *you*."

"Oh I beg to differ," Ruby smiled. My breath caught in my throat as she stalked up, raising a hand to my neck. I fully believed I was about to get choked, but instead, she ran her fingers over the jade green kiss print Ches had painted on my neck. "It would seem that you've been moving about the *Burrows* with the blessing of that sneaky little kitty Franchesca Catlan." Ruby bit her lip, winked at me. "Not an easy honor to receive, I would think. She must've given you a nice little welcome. You have access to her?"

"Barely," I told her, honestly.

"Oh that's quite enough." Ruby lifted her hand, made a motion that brought a Knight rushing up to her, with that blade. "Take it," she said, offering the slick black hilt to me. "And *bring me that bitch's head.*"

SEVEN

I couldn't move.

Couldn't breathe.

Couldn't *believe* Ruby said what I *thought* she said, but her expression was as deadly as the blade I still hadn't taken.

Wouldn't take.

"She's not that kinda girl, Ruby," Maddox said, furthering my growing belief that he could speak however he wanted to anyone around here.

Instead of remaining on me, her cold green eyes snapped to him, staring before a smile cracked her serious façade. Not one of the calculated smirks that seemed popular in this place, but a *real* smile, borne of genuine amusement.

She's toying with me...

"Damn, Mad," she groaned, lowering the sword. "Nobody lets me have any fun around here."

I swallowed. "*Fun?*" Rage built in my chest, like a hot-air balloon. "This is a game to you?!"

Just that quickly, any warmth left Ruby as she looked to me again, her sneer dripping with superiority. "Yes," she answered. "I'm glad you've caught on. *Queen,*" she said, pointing to herself. "*Knights*" – her security – "*Bishop*" – she pointed to Maddox, and then at me and Nadiah – "*Pawns*".

Once she was done establishing the hierarchy, she turned, hips swaying as she glided back to her throne. Beside me, Nadiah threaded her fingers through mine, squeezing tight as she crowded against me.

"It seems as if you didn't appreciate my game," Ruby said, one she was seated again, legs crossed, with the blade over her lap. "So for *your* sake, I'll just say this plain – *you,* Alyson Little, can't give me a goddamn thing worth what I'm giving up by letting your sister leave here. But, I will let her go anyway, because I'm benevolent."

She stopped there, staring at me, and I opened my mouth to stammer, "*Thank y—*"

"I am *not* finished speaking," she snapped. Immediately, I went quiet. She ran a hand through her lush chestnut hair and smiled. "When I come into the salon, I don't want to hear about a *Harriet.* You will drop whatever you are doing – *whoever* – you're doing, and come to me. Understood?"

"Yes."

"And *you,*" she shifted to Maddox, whose eyebrows went up. "Make sure your *mommy* knows me wanting her head is *not* a joke. She owes me blood, and I am becoming *bored* with waiting for it. And we *know* what happens when I get bored, don't we?"

Maddox cleared his throat, nodded. "Nobody wants that."

"Of course we don't." Ruby grinned. "Get them out of my sight, before I change my mind. Take them back to Franchesca's *hovel.*" She looked at Maddox. "Make sure you tell her I said *that* too."

There wasn't time to respond.

Ruby's knights were already acting on her command to remove us from her sight, and I held tight to Nadiah's hand as they whisked us out. In what felt like just a few seconds, we were tucked into the backseat of a sleek black pickup truck, with Maddox up front, beside the driver. His motorcycle was strapped into the cargo bed.

I was teeming with questions, and he must've known. He half-turned, meeting my eyes for a subtle head shake.

I needed to keep my mouth closed.

So I did, not even talking to Nadiah, though I was dying to. Every other friend I had was gone, for various reasons that were more the fault of the world we lived in than anything else. Once Gran was gone, Nadiah would be all I had left.

She had to know I was thinking about her. Her cornrowed head settled onto my shoulder, comforting me. As relieving as it was, there was some deep part of me that still felt unsettled, like this wasn't the end I imagined it would be.

Like we weren't out of the rabbit hole yet.

Nadiah squeezed my hand, and I forced the foreboding down somewhere deep, away from my conscious mind for now.

Only for now.

"How many times am I going to answer that question before you *believe* me?"

Nadiah's words stopped my pacing.

Did I hear an edge to her voice?

Was she taking a tone with me?

After the way my last 24 hours had gone, trying to get to her?

As if she could feel my overreaction building, she stood from where she'd been sitting at the edge of the bed. We were back at Franchesca's, back in the same room where I'd woken up after venturing into that alley – which felt like weeks ago, instead of mere hours. Since climbing out of Ruby Hartford's truck, I'd been all over Nadiah, wanting to know every single detail of her time out of my sight.

I'd had my eyes on her since we got back. I barely wanted to blink.

"I'm *okay*, Aly," she assured me, answering my question once more as she tucked her arms around my waist, drawing me into a hug.

Another hug.

Nadiah was a little shorter than me, short enough for me to press my face to her tiny cornrows, breathing her in. Yes, she'd already assured me a million times she was fine, but the thing was, *I* wasn't fine.

I wasn't okay.

"We gotta go home," I whispered into her braids. "We gotta get out of here."

She pulled back enough to look at me, her face igniting conflicting feelings in me. Someone at Ruby's had put makeup on her – mascara and highlighter and lipstick, none of which were overdone – and she was in tight jeans and boots and some sheer floral top, none of which had come from her closet at home.

When *I* looked at her, I still saw a little girl I needed to protect, but I knew I was alone in that. Everyone else – especially with her dressed and made up like this – saw a beautiful young woman, old enough to work as a "*Diamond*".

"You're *sure* nobody touched you?" I asked, cupping her face in my hands as she rolled her eyes. She hadn't rushed to scrub the makeup off, so maybe she liked it. Maybe she...

"Yes, Aly," she groaned. "And I'm sure I would've noticed. They asked if I was comfortable being touched – I said no. All I had to do was talk, and flirt. That's all."

I frowned. "How the hell do you know how to *flirt?*" I asked, earning myself another eye roll as Nadiah pulled away to return to her seat on the bed.

"Reading," she answered, wearing a smirk. "Those romance novels... you don't think I dig those up and bring them home just for *you*, right?"

"Uh, *yeah.*" I shook my head. "I never see you reading anything except those thick textbooks of yours, and vampire novels and shit."

She shrugged. "Just because you don't see it, doesn't mean it's not happening. Oh, and movies too."

"*Movies?*" my eyes bugged wide. "Where?!"

"The library now. They have it set up where you have to watch alone, in a little cubicle, but it's not that bad."

I dropped into the chair where one twin had done my makeup earlier. "Wow, how the hell did I not know?"

"Because I didn't tell you," Nadiah answered. "Because the library closes before you get off work, so you wouldn't be able to go. I didn't want you to feel bad."

"I have days off though. I could've gone!"

Nadiah sucked her teeth. "Every day off, you spend budgeting, or planning, or going to see Gran, or rescuing your little sister. You do nothing for yourself."

That wasn't *supposed* to make me feel bad.

But it did.

"I don't know why you think rescuing you wasn't for *me*," I told her, letting a little smile drift across my lips. "I don't know what I would've done without you. If I hadn't been able to find you..."

"That wouldn't have happened. I was already plotting, how I could talk to Ruby, or get a message to you. Waiting on the right guy I could talk into doing whatever I wanted."

I laughed.

If *anybody* could do such a thing, I believed in Nadiah. She was so smart, so sweet, so beautiful... *so much* better than what life in the *Mids* could offer her.

"I'm going to kill Bunny, next time I see her," I spoke, looking Nadiah right in the eyes. I was dead serious. "There *has* to be some penance for this. *Why* would she do this?"

The mention of Bunny brought an instant shift for Nadiah. She'd been trying to stay upbeat, for my sake, but that hurt her.

"I wish I knew. I don't know how she would've gotten involved with something like that in the first place, let alone setting us up. I followed her out so far because she'd been weird the last few days – I didn't want to leave her alone. I was *worried* about her. She used that," Nadiah said, the tightness in her voice making me move to a seat on the bed beside her. "I don't... *get it.*"

I sighed, wrapping an arm around her. "Because you're a good person. And you will move on from this and be better. We're gonna get you home, and rested, so you can go to school, and get this scholarship, and get a great job, and never have to worry again."

"If only," Nadiah said, putting her head down on my shoulder again. I felt like more was coming, like she had something else to say, but a knock at the door interrupted it. Before either of us could say anything, it swung open, revealing Ches in the doorway.

"So," she mused, tucking her hair behind her ear. "I heard you found your sister."

"Yeah. I did," I replied, standing as she stepped in, wearing a green leather dress that molded tight to the curves of her body. "Thank you for your help."

"You're welcome," she said, though her eyes were on Nadiah, who was staring right back. "You should thank Maddox though. *Thoroughly,*" she smirked, glancing for just a second before her attention went back to Nadiah. "Young lady, you must be special, for your sister to have gone to such trouble for your safety."

Nadiah smirked right back, shook her head. "Nah. Aly is the special one. She's one of the best people I know."

"How sweet. Anybody who earns such a description can make themselves welcome in my home." Her tone was welcoming and warm, but something in her eyes... I didn't trust it. "I'm sure Nadiah was already well-taken care of at the Hartford Compound, but Aly, if you'd like to wash up, there are toiletries in the bathroom for you now, and Demaris brought clothes for both of you when we found out you were on the way back. Why don't you treat yourself to a long, *hot* shower, while I take Nadiah on a tour of the house?"

You're out of your mind if you think I'm leaving her alone with you.

"Actually, I'd love a tour myself," I lied. I didn't give a shit about her house, I just didn't trust her with my sister. "Would it be okay if I tagged along?"

Ches turned her frozen smile in my direction. "Yes. Please come along." She stepped out of the doorway, intending for Nadiah and me to follow. We exchanged a look, and then joined Ches in the hall, where she took us down the stairs, to the floor where I'd eavesdropped on her conversation with Maddox that first night.

From the checkerboard marble, to the huge, heavy-framed paintings, everything was... *lavish.* She showed us room after room of plush furniture with art covering the walls, a game room, a dining room, a ballroom, a gleaming white kitchen.

And then, in front of a closed door, she turned to us with a smile.

"I have a confession to make," she started, pressing her back to the wall beside the door. "I had my people do a little research. On both of you."

I stood a little straighter, waiting to hear where this would go. Her looking into us wasn't a red flag – she had a right to know who she was allowing to stay in her home. Though, there was nothing to find out – we were who we presented ourselves as.

But I knew Ches wouldn't have brought it up without a reason.

"And what did you find?" I asked.

"Well, you both seem to be regular girls, just trying to make it in this crazy world of ours." She grinned a little harder. "*Except* this one..." – she pointed to Nadiah – "Is something like a genius. Impeccable grades, flawless aptitude scores – up for one of those coveted *Apex* scholarships, to continue your education there. Is that true?"

Nadiah looked at me first, then back to Ches. "Well, I'm not sure I'd put it that way, but I guess it's true."

Ches nodded. "Right. And *I'm* guessing that means you'll be very interested in what's behind this door."

My eyes narrowed as she opened it, stepping back to let Nadiah in first. When she gasped, I moved a little quicker, wanting to see what had gotten that reaction...

Computers.

A whole line, in fact.

Laptops, with cords connecting to the wall and cords connecting to larger monitors than the small laptop screens. Honestly, I was shocked Nadiah was still standing in the door, instead of moving in closer to inspect. Then, movement in the room's corner made me understand why.

There was a boy.

A tall, wide-shouldered, pecan-toned, handsome boy, wearing sleek black headphones and a tee shirt with an ancient floppy disk printed on it. Ches urged Nadiah into the room so she and I could get through the door. When my eyes landed on my sister's face, the first thing I noticed was her nervous smile, and that while I was looking at *her*, she was looking at *him*.

He was looking at her, too.

Ah, hell.

"Mosley," Ches purred, wrapping an arm around the boy as she turned to face me and Nadiah. "This is Alyson Little, and her sister, Nadiah. Would you like to show Nadiah our setup?"

His eyebrows went up. "You're into tech?"

"I'm into everything," was her immediate response, and I didn't like the way that little boy's eyes lit up at the sound of that. But, before I could protest, she was already sitting down, with him way too close beside her.

Already making her laugh.

"Why don't we leave them to it?" Ches asked, hooking a hand under my elbow, which I shook off.

"I'm not leaving her. Last time she left my sight, she ended up—" I stopped myself, glancing at Mosley, then Nadiah, opting not to say something that might embarrass her. I lowered my voice, turning it into a conversation just between me and Ches. "If she's going to be in this room, so will I."

Ches lifted an eyebrow. "They're teenagers. They want to talk about this geeky shit and flirt with each other – not bone. You can relax."

"It's not just about that," I shook my head. "No offense, but I don't know you."

"Alyson," Ches started, with another one of those smirks. "Please believe me when I say, if I had any intention of harming your sister, nothing would stop me from doing it right in front of you. No one will touch her. No one will touch you, unless you want."

My eyes narrowed. "What does that even mean?"

"Must you find a threat in everything?" Ches laughed. "I was going to suggest that you shower and dress, and go downstairs and have fun tonight. I get the impression it's a rarity for you."

"I have plenty of fun," I lied. "And besides that, I was looking forward to going home as soon as possible."

She nodded. "Of course you were. But glance out the window."

Her words drew my gaze toward the thick glass pane on the other side of the room. My heart dropped at the sight of rain drizzling down the window, and I flinched as a loud crack of thunder ripped through the quiet.

"It'll be a few hours before I can have you escorted back through the ruins to get home," Ches said, from right beside me. "You're safe here. Your sister is too. Not to mention, she looks happy. No boyfriends waiting for the two of you to come home?"

I sighed. "No."

"Well then," Ches smiled. "There's no sense in you standing over her shoulder, when you've had such an eventful day. Take a long shower, relax. Get dolled up. Maddox will be back..." she added, as if that were some selling point.

"Aly." I looked up to see that Nadiah had broken away from *Mosley* long enough to snoop on our conversation. "She's right – you *never* do anything. You may as well take the opportunity."

I sucked my teeth. "You want to be alone with *Mosley*," I accused, which she shrugged about.

"Yeah. He's cute. And smart."

"You're never even going to see him again."

She smirked. "All the more reason to bask in it while I can. *And...*" she glanced at Ches, then pulled me away, all the way into a corner of the room. "Even more reason for you to do what she's talking about you doing with *Maddox.*"

My eyes bugged wide. *"Excuse me?!"*

"You're *not* hard of hearing, Aly," she sassed. "This is the stuff we *should* be able to do, at our age. You think a century ago, twenty-five-year-olds weren't going out, having fun, hooking up?"

"I *know* they were, and I know that's how they ended up with all those mutated STDs and babies!"

Nadiah groaned. "Which means you *also* know STDs – and babies, unless you're paying for fertility treatments – are obsolete. They vaccinated all of that out of us decades ago!" she hissed.

"And it would be just *my* luck that the first reoccurrence of chlamyderrea, or whatever the hell, starts with me!" I shot back, drawing a grin to Nadiah's face before we both laughed.

"Listen, Aly," she pleaded, grabbing my hand. "I want to stay here, and talk to Mosley, at least until the rain stops. If you want to sit over here, or outside the door, being a bored mother hen, I guess that's fine. *Or,* you take the chance to breathe a little while you have it."

"I'm *not* having sex with Maddox."

"And *I'm* not having sex with Mosley."

"You're not having sex with *anybody*," I countered, and she rolled her eyes.

"Whatever, Aly. I'm not trying to make you, I'm just saying. We're here. Live a little." With my hand still clasped in hers, she kissed my cheek. "I love you," she said, then stepped away to go back to Mosley, who watched her the entire time until she reached him, then gave her his full attention when she sat down.

With a sigh, I realized I was on the losing end of that argument. She was nineteen, not nine, and... what Ches said made sense, and I didn't doubt her.

If she wanted to hurt Nadiah, she didn't have to wait until we were apart.

She was cold enough to do it right in front of me.

I followed Ches out of the room, facing her once we were outside.

"Tell me why you're doing this," I said, meeting her eyes.

"Because Mosley is dying of boredom," she answered. "Every other girl Nadiah's age – *his* age – with a brain like hers, is in the Apex. Every man is into a pretty face, but some are into more. He happens to be one of those."

"And who is he, to you?" I asked, remembering Ruby's comment referring to Ches as Maddox's "mommy".

"Near to my heart," was her response. "Important to me. So, consider my introducing those two a compliment. I hold Mosley in high regard."

"And Maddox?"

She smiled. "Him too. So are you staying here, or going to indulge in some pampering?" she asked, changing the subject.

Somehow, that made me trust her words more – her not wanting to talk about it suggested there was something to protect.

That was something I understood.

"I'll take you up on that offer of a shower."

EIGHT

T he shower was a good idea.

The shower was *such* a good idea.

When I finally peeled myself from the hot spray, after what had to be at least twenty minutes, I was like a new woman. Even though I was still sore and bruised from the alley, my limbs were loose and relaxed, and I felt squeaky clean. Ches hadn't been kidding when she said someone had left toiletries in the bathroom for me – there were candles, soaps, thick body butter, none of which had been there earlier.

I took one of the body butters back to the room with me – I had a key to it now, which I'd give back once Nadiah and I left. In the meantime, I slathered myself in the best lotion I'd touched in years, put on brand new panties and a sports bra, and then went to the closet for the comfiest thing I could find, to sit alone with my thoughts.

To remind myself I didn't belong here.

It would be easy to get wrapped up in all this, pretending this was my normal life. After tonight though, it was right back to the usual – right back to...

What, exactly?

Everything I believed had been turned upside down, my entire way of life revealed to be a lie. Would it *really* be so simple to go back to the *Mids,* knowing the people of the *Burrows* were enjoying the freedom I'd only ever dreamed about?

Probably not.

Not now that this whole ordeal had ruptured my careful indoctrination, showing me everything I'd never know, through the crack.

Had my parents known about this?

Had my grandparents?

I had to believe they didn't – that they *couldn't* have – because otherwise, wouldn't they have wanted better for us? I wasn't so naïve that I thought the *Burrows* was without flaws. With a "ruler" like sword-wielding Ruby Hartford, men lurking in alleys to "recruit" *Diamonds,* and a psychopath like Ches with enough power that her "mark" – which I'd scrubbed off in the shower – gave me certain freedom of movement around here, this place had plenty of problems.

But there were restaurants.

Parks.

Stores where you could enjoy shopping without a cop staring over your shoulder – or at your chest.

The grass over here sure looked greener.

Even more reason to enjoy it while you can...

Hmm.

As I stared into the closet, my stomach growled, reminding me I hadn't eaten in hours.

And neither had Nadiah.

I searched my clothing options, deciding on a floral tee shirt dress – the least revealing thing outside of putting on the jeans I called myself saving for the trek back through the ruins. Among the heels and strappy sandals, I found a pair of simple flats, tossed there like a last-minute concession. One I was grateful for. I slipped my feet into the shoes, then went to find Nadiah, thinking of the meal I'd eaten just downstairs the night I arrived.

Once I'd found my way back to where I'd left Nadiah, my footsteps slowed. The door to the computer room was still open, and I could hear them talking – the soft tone of Nadiah's voice, the deeper rumble of Mosley's, their laughter. Instead of walking in, I peeked inside to see them still seated in the same spot, watching something on one screen while they ate from a tray of food.

Nadiah's attention was on the screen, on the food, on Mosley, but she didn't look back at the door. Mosley did though, acknowledging me with a smile before he shifted to get Nadiah's attention. I shook my head, not wanting her to know I'd come looking.

She was having a good time.

There was no reason to bother her.

By myself, I headed back around to the other side of the staircase where the entrance to the club was. I approached the guard there, not knowing what to say, but as soon as he saw me, he stepped aside, opening the door for me to enter.

So I did.

Downstairs, I let memory guide me through the crowd, pressing past throngs of people to reach my destination. Memory, plus the enticing smell of food that would probably be just as good as last time – my only chance to taste something like that before I went back to eating whatever I could afford on the meager earnings left after the bills were finished with me.

I never made it to the dining area.

Instead, my attention was arrested by the sight of Maddox and the twins, out on the dance floor. He was sandwiched between them, looking as if he were having the time of his life while the one in front – I couldn't tell which – ran her hands under his shirt, revealing his abs, and the one behind him practically crawled up his back.

They were *moving*. Dee or Dem – the one in front – turned around, pushing her ass into his pelvis as she rolled her hips, fluid motion in perfect time to the music. In a perfect position for Maddox to rest his hands at her hips, keeping her right there while the other twin took over the – required? – exposing of his abs.

I couldn't look away.

I was all too familiar with the feeling coursing through my veins. I experienced it often, watching the carefree existence in the *Apex*.

Envy.

Not grudgingly though.

I didn't know these people, had no reason to resent their happiness, or question if they deserved it, none of that.

I wished it could be me.

Hilarious.

The realization that I should look away before they caught me staring came too late. Maddox met my eyes just as I was about to return to my set path, and once he was looking at me, I was stuck right there. At first, his eyes widened in surprise, but then a slow smile spread over his face as the song faded into a different one, and he came straight to me.

"This is unexpected," he said, leaning to speak into my ear, so I could hear him over the noise. "You came to dance?"

I pulled back, putting a little distance between us as I shook my head. "No, I..." my words caught in my throat as I realized something was different about him. Underneath his hat – backward again – his hair was unbraided, a mass of glossy crinkled waves under the brim. Without the hat, I imagined it was a gloriously fitting leonine mane.

I wanted to take his hat off, so badly.

So badly my fingers itched.

He squinted at me, probably confused by my open-mouthed stare. Suddenly, his hand was in mine, and he was leading me off to a slightly more-quiet corner.

"You good? Nadiah good?" he asked, still squinting as he looked at me, concerned.

I glanced around, noting the couples we were surrounded by, who'd staked their own territory in the dark, for privacy. Privacy to do things that weren't vulgar, but right over the line for too risqué for the dance floor.

Things Maddox would probably do – or wanted to do – with the twins right now, if he hadn't spotted me gawking at them.

"Yeah," I nodded, finally answering his question. "You don't have to check on me. You can get back to your fun with the twins."

Even in semi-darkness, I could see that smirk. "Why are you saying it like that?"

"Saying it like what?"

"Like you're bothered."

"What? Bothered? I'm not bothered," I defended, in a – *dammit* – very bothered tone. "Why would I be bothered by what you do with them?"

His eyebrows went up, but he saved me the embarrassment of stating my obvious jealousy out loud. "Do you want to dance?"

"*What?* No!" My voice was too loud. I swallowed, shaking my head. "No," I repeated, at a more appropriate volume. "I can't. I never really have."

"Never?!"

I sucked my teeth. "I'm from the *Mids*, remember? We don't have the same privileges as you. The only music I grew up with was when my mother would sing, and it wasn't exactly things to shake your ass to," I snapped.

His expression softened. "My bad, I'm just surprised. I didn't mean to offend you."

"I'm *not* offended. I'm embarrassed," I admitted, dropping my gaze.

Immediately, his hand was at my chin, lifting until I met his eyes. He smiled. "Don't be. It's the easiest shit in the world. I'll show you."

Wait, what?

Before I could protest, he'd turned me around, putting his hands at my hips. He didn't pull me directly against him, but I was close enough to feel his body heat.

"Just feel the music," he said, in my ear again, leaving so little space that his lips grazed my skin. "And move with it."

I shook my head. "In front of all these p—"

"Nobody is paying you any mind. They're in their own worlds, like you should be," Maddox chuckled. "Close your eyes." When I didn't, still giving my best deer-in-headlights impression, his fingers sank into my hips a little more. "*Close them.*"

I did.

But the song was over now, with a different one filtering in – something slower.

Sexier.

I couldn't have identified the instruments, and certainly not the singer, but I didn't need her breathless words to know what it was about. I *felt* it, in my breasts, and between my legs, and all the way down to my fingertips as my arms hung awkwardly at my sides.

I had no idea what to do with them.

No idea what I was *doing*, period, and a clanging siren in my brain was screaming at me to leave, before I embarrassed myself further. I couldn't though. Stepping away from the gentle pressure of his hands as Maddox rocked me back and forth seemed like an impossibility.

I inhaled deep through my nose, then pushed the stream of air back out with my mouth, letting my overwrought mind go with it. Instead of thinking about how stupid I had to look, wondering what Nadiah was doing, thinking about how exhausted I'd be at work tomorrow, I let it go.

I did as Maddox said and focused on the music. Hearing and feeling, letting my hips sway from side to side in time with the music, letting it guide me. Maddox shifted, removing his hands from my hips, but before I could miss them, his arms were around me and he'd stepped closer, finding the beat again and moving with me.

"See?" his warm voice rumbled in my ear, amused, but not laughing *at* me. "Told you it was easy."

"*This* is," I agreed, looking at him over my shoulder. "But it's nothing like what Dee was doing with you. *To* you."

"Dem," he corrected, then stopped moving to smirk. "You're trying to do what *she* was doing?"

Heat rushed to my face. "I mean, I—"

His hands were back at my hips again, pulling my ass into him. "Bend a little," he directed, as yet another song started, this one a little faster. "And imagine you're winding up, with your waist."

"What?"

He laughed. "Just move your hips in a circle. Don't worry about the music, just do it."

I wondered if I looked as uncertain as I felt. But I did what he said because the thought of chickening out at this point was more embarrassing than trying and getting it wrong. To my surprise, once I *did* it, I realized how naturally the movement came.

"Like keeping a hula-hoop up," I said out loud, remembering one of the very few toys from my childhood – hell, on up through my teen years.

Maddox nodded. "Yes, like that. If you can do that, you can do *this*," he said, his warm encouragement lighting several fires in my body. "Do what you were doing, just find the music now."

He pulled me into him again, letting his hands drop to my thighs, resting against my bare skin as I moved. I did my best to tune out the electric warmth of his touch, focusing on the music as I let my hips move with the rhythm of whatever this was pumping through the speakers.

It was intoxicating.

My anxiety dissipated. There was no room for apprehension or shame when I felt this unrestricted, doing something that came naturally. I didn't have to think about it anymore, I *moved*. Maddox slid his hands back to my waist, keeping me close, but not contained. My hands weren't awkward anymore – they covered his, affirming the connection, or my fingers found the beat and snapped along with it, or they lifted in front, moving with me.

That glorious feeling stayed with me until I'd built up a light sheen of sweat – the kind of exhilaration I hadn't felt in forever. At least not from doing something *fun*.

That's what this was.

Fun.

Yet another sensation I could barely remember and didn't want to let go of. That resistance drove the disappointment I felt when Maddox tugged at me, pulling me away to sit down.

"So I see you've got a few moves on you, huh?" he asked once we sat down, on a tiny bench that couldn't have been meant for two people. I was practically in his lap, but I didn't mind.

I shrugged. "I don't know about that. I did what you said."

"Instructions only go so far," he countered, draping his arms across the back of the booth. "You're just a natural at it."

"A natural at a useless skill. Sounds about right for me."

Maddox chuckled, shaking his head. "Definitely not a useless skill."

"What could I *possibly...*" I stopped, noting his raised eyebrows, and the smirk wrapped across his face. "*Oh.*"

My gaze dropped to my hands as he laughed.

"You are so..."

"Ignorant? Inexperienced? Underdeveloped?"

"I would say refreshing." I peeked up to find him staring right at me, silent for a moment before he elaborated. "You're not trying to make yourself seem like something you're not, you're not scared to... hell, be scared. Or embarrassed. Or admit you don't know something, or you need help. Everybody else around here is trying to be a certain degree of badass – which is necessary in a lot of ways to survive this shit, but still, you're just being you. No bullshit."

My eyebrows went up. "Dude, I'm scared of *all* those things," I laughed. "Every single one. I either don't know how to hide it, or my *need* is greater than my fear."

"I get it," he nodded. "You're courageous."

I shook my head. "No. *No,* not at all. That's not a word I'd use to describe myself. I'm not brave."

"I didn't say brave, I said *courageous.* Bravery requires fearlessness. Courage is doing the shit anyway, even though you're scared. Or are you about to tell me it was nothing for you to hike the bridge ruins in the middle of the night and attack two big motherfuckers in an alley because you were looking for your sister?"

"When you put it like that, I guess it wasn't easy."

"Don't you still have bruises?" he asked. "Should you be down here in this loud ass music, when you had to have had a concussion?"

I raised an eyebrow. "You brought me down here last night though."

"I wasn't thinking then." His arm came down from the booth, draping around my shoulder instead, pulling me into him. "Now I am. You good?"

"Yeah," I nodded. "I'm fine."

How could I *not* be, tucked under his arm in a dark corner, my energy still high from dancing? I wasn't thinking about a concussion or tender bruises, and my hunger was long forgotten, replaced by a yearning for this closeness to go on, and on, and on, until it *had* to end.

Not a moment before.

"You're going back tonight?" he asked, eyes locked on me, giving the vague impression that his thoughts had been in the same place as mine.

I nodded. "Yeah. Nadiah has classes, and I have to go to work. It was sheer luck that I had today off, to do all of this. But I have to go back."

"*Have* to?"

My breath caught in my throat for a second, but I nodded again. "Yeah. My grandmother, my job, Nadiah's schooling, my parents' house... my whole life is there," I explained, then sighed. "A life that feels like a lie now that I know what I know. How did I *not* know the truth about the *Burrows*? It seems impossible."

"Well, you don't strike me as the type who would believe it without seeing it," Maddox chuckled. "Not to mention, the flow of information isn't free between those gates. You can only cross on official business, and your government has done an excellent job scaring the shit out of people. This isn't like it was back in the days where the internet was available to everybody. Anything not sanctioned only travels through word of mouth, and if people are scared to talk about it for fear of running their mouth to the wrong person and ending up in jail... it makes sense, when you think about it."

"All that is true, but I could get here with basically no barrier. I walked right out of the *Mids,* right into here, simply because I was following someone who knew where to go."

He pointed at me. "There it is right there though – you were following somebody who knew. Everybody doesn't know, and that's on purpose, because if too many people – or the *wrong* people - knew, they'd fuck it up. Somebody isn't careful, the APF notices, and now you're in a dragnet cause somebody couldn't keep their mouth shut."

"I guess that makes sense. It doesn't change that I feel stupid as hell though. They basically have us imprisoned, and I go about my little worker bee life, at a job I'm naïve enough to be *grateful* for, like I'm not barely keeping my family afloat," I spilled, giving much more than I'd intended when I opened my mouth. "I'm sorry, I—"

"Don't apologize for that shit," Maddox insisted, shaking his head. "Better than keeping it bottled up, and you won't get any judgment from me. Not for that."

He was staring at me so intently that I forced myself to look away. Tried to come up with something – *anything* – to say, as I stared at the moving crowd in the dark. Dee and Dem were out there somewhere, waiting for him to finish whatever the hell he was doing with me. Sure, I had his attention now, but I wasn't *sexy.* I wasn't cool. I wasn't smart, like Nadiah.

I was just an out-of-place pawn, who needed to get back to her own board.

I'd been in "Wonderland" long enough.

My intention was to tell Maddox. But I looked up at the same time he reached for me, cupping my chin in his hand – a barely there touch that damn near consumed me.

Definitely made me forget what I was about to say.

Suddenly, his lips were on mine, and I wasn't sure words

mattered at all anymore, because lips – his and mine – were made for soft brushes and long presses and subtle licks and brazen sucks, and parting for access, and everything between. I'd been kissed before, but not like this. Not with careful nibbles that set off heat between my legs, deep licks into my mouth that turned my nipples into hard, sensitive pebbles, not with an urgency that made me feel like I was on the verge of melting, in the best possible way.

But then he released me.

Pulled back, with an apology in his eyes I didn't want or need, that damn near offended me. How must he view me, to think he needed to apologize for a kiss?

"Let's dance again," I said, speaking up before he could verbalize what I saw on his face. Standing, I moved back to the floor, dancing alone. It was different without Maddox behind me, but I caught on, not thinking about it too hard. I didn't dare look back for him, focusing instead on the music, and letting my body do what it wanted.

A few moments later, I felt him behind me.

It was another of those sensual songs, and this time I had no hesitation. His fingers dug into my hips as I wound against him with abandon, ruled by the music, by pure instinct. There was no faltering, no apprehension, just the two of us moving together in tandem.

Until I felt him growing hard against me.

I wasn't sure what the hell I'd expected, but I didn't move away. That siren in my brain was going off again, but I couldn't seem to make my body listen.

Instead, I went harder.

Maddox wrapped an arm around my waist, pulling me tight against him as I moved my hips. My mouth fell open in a gasp at the sensation of his lips, then his tongue, and teeth, on my neck, sucking and biting and licking and all I could bring myself to do was angle my head to give him better access. I didn't care if he left a mark – I *wanted* him to leave a mark, something tangible to anchor the memory, even if it was just temporary.

But it wasn't enough.

Deep, vulgar satisfaction rippled through me as his hand slipped under my dress. Briefly, concern over being seen flickered across my mind, but was eclipsed by a different feeling as soon as he touched me.

Ecstasy.

We weren't even skin-to-skin.

He was touching me through the super-soft fabric of the light-weight cotton panties I wore, and it was still like being struck by lightning. Maybe because I hadn't been touched in so long, or because I'd *never* been touched by someone who elicited the feelings he did. Whatever the culprit, I was so sensitive there, so overwrought with nerve endings that in next to no time I was panting, then damn near biting a hole in my lip to keep from moaning out loud.

His mouth went from my neck to my shoulder, biting me there before he moved up to my ear. "You want me to make you cum?" he asked, just loud enough for only me to hear. My eyes were closed – I didn't know if anybody was watching, and was feeling too good to care. When I didn't answer, his arm that had been around my waist released its' hold, and then I felt his hand on my neck, his thumb curving around my jaw like a lever to turn my head. *"Do you want me to make you cum?"* he repeated, and I nodded against the weight of his palm. As if the answer could be anything else with his hand between my legs, strumming me like a guitar.

His fingers pressed harder, faster against me as he curved his body, stretching over my shoulder to connect his mouth to mine. It was a good thing too, because a few seconds later I came unglued.

I couldn't move.

Couldn't breathe.

Wasn't sure I was conscious, with my heartbeat roaring in my ears, and my eyes shut so tight I saw stars. I moaned, long and loud, but Maddox swallowed it with a kiss that seemed to drag out the tightness in the pit of my stomach, and intensified the blissful feeling between my legs.

After a few moments, I pulled back, breathless and weak in the knees, only upright because of the hold Maddox had around my waist. Now that I wasn't dancing, now that I was coming down from my high, the thought of looking him in the face mortified me. I did it anyway though, *needing* to see if he was laughing at me for being as easy of a target as I felt like now.

Of course, he wasn't.

Still, I staggered back a little as the lights came on, and I saw how many people were around us. It was easy to be bold and brazen in the dark, when everyone was focused somewhere else, but in the light, I couldn't believe what I'd just done.

With someone I barely know.

"Aly..." Maddox spoke, stepping toward me with a clear intention of taking me by the arms. I backed away though, turning to dart through whatever openings I could find in the crowd until I made my way back up the first stairs, and then the second, and then to my room.

As I fumbled to get the key from where I stashed it in my bra, my wet panties stuck to me, reminding me of what I'd done. I abandoned the door to my room, going to the bathroom instead to wash up, leaving the underwear in the laundry bin beside the door.

In the mirror, my eyes landed on my neck – I'd been marked. Not even ten minutes ago I'd wanted this, and now all I wanted to do was scrub the evidence off.

What the hell is wrong with you, Aly?

I wasn't this girl. One with no inhibitions, no regard for what people thought. I was regular old Alyson. The one who had no fun. Who went to work, and paid bills, and did what was required.

Alyson Little was *responsible.*

Swallowing tears, I left the bathroom, peeking to make sure Maddox wasn't there before I darted to my room, key in hand. I slipped inside, flipping the light on and going for the stash of panties to snag a fresh pair to put on.

"There you are," I heard from behind me, nearly jumping out of my skin as I pulled the underwear past my thighs.

I looked back to see Nadiah sitting up in bed, under the covers, rubbing the sleep from her eyes as she yawned.

I must have woken her up.

"I brought you a sandwich and stuff," she said, her eyes still only half open as she pointed to the dresser – where I was standing. "But you weren't here when I came back, so I washed up and went to bed. It's still raining. But Ches says she has people keeping an eye out for it stop, so we can go back."

I cleared my throat as I made sure my dress was down. "Um... awesome. And thank you for the sandwich."

"You probably ate with *Maddox*, huh?" she grinned.

"What? No. I went to get something to eat, but then I got distracted. So like I said, thanks for the sandwich."

Her smile broadened. "Distracted by *Maddox?*"

"Dammit, Nadiah, give it a rest," I snapped, regretting it as soon as it came out of my mouth, but saying nothing to take it back. It wasn't that I didn't *want* to talk about it –though I *didn't* want to talk about it.

I couldn't.

"Fine, Aly. Sorry."

"Don't be. I'm sorry for snapping at you. I'm just exhausted, and ready to go."

Nadiah's hurt expression slid to sympathy, as she waved me toward her. "Okay, well, you may as well come lay down. We can't go anywhere until the weather clears, so get some rest. I won't complain if you bring the sandwich."

I laughed and shook my head. "I don't have an appetite, but I *will* come and lay down."

Just like when we were kids, sharing a room in the house we were in now. Just like then, we giggled as we snuggled under the covers together, tuning out all the horrible shit enough to feel normal.

It was soothing, and familiar, and easy to cling to that, instead of worrying about our future in the *Mids*, and wondering how Harriet would react about me taking her client. Instead of thinking about Maddox.

I laid on my side, smiling as I listened to Nadiah gush about how cute Mosely was, and how smart he was, and how nice he was, and how he'd kissed her on the cheek when they parted. This was how life *should* be for her, at nineteen, and I hated it couldn't be this way all the time.

But then I pushed *that* away too.

And let her happy stories lull me to slumber.

NINE

There was this saying.

Something about death and taxes being the only sure things. Even now, when we didn't have America in our pockets, this was still true.

Somebody was getting paid off somebody else.

Sometimes there were those who thought they could get out of it.

Sometimes I had to pay them a visit.

I hated that shit, unlike some other soldiers, or whatever the hell Ches was calling us this week. I had no repressed anger to burn off anymore. Violence and intimidation didn't make my dick hard anymore.

It felt like a dangerous place to be – what did it mean for you when constant indulgence of all your dark, unrefined tendencies just wasn't enough anymore? Where did you go from there?

I didn't want to end up like others I'd watched, on a constant cycle of sex, drugs, fights, and alcohol, always engaged in something to avoid thinking about anything.

Feeling anything.

This was the place for it if sedated excess was your thing. If you wanted to drift, numb, through a world made purely of your own imagination, until it consumed you, we had just the things for it.

Tempting, sometimes, but I never indulged in more than a few too many shots of whiskey – the pills and shit weren't for me. Alcohol was mood-altering enough, and in the moments where it wasn't an option, I got comfortable with a feeling too many people around here were hellbent on chasing away.

Boredom.

That was what I felt strongest as I listened to Wally's crooked ass try to talk his way out of the payment I was supposed to be retrieving. It was always an excuse with this motherfucker, and I'd been listening for damn near fifteen minutes while he wove an intricate web of bullshit to explain himself. As if I didn't know the money he owed Ches was locked up in the back right now.

"Are you done?" I asked, interrupting when I knew he wasn't. He'd talked all the *polite* out of me.

Wally's eyes went wide for a second, but he recovered, running a hand over his smooth bald head, then along his bushy mustache. "My apologies, young Maddox – have I talked your ear off?"

My only response was to shift positions, moving from leaning against the wall to standing on my feet, fists clenched on either side of me.

That made his eyes go wider.

"Now hold on just a moment," he stammered, moving on to fingering one of many buttons on his olive-toned suit. "I've known Franchesca for years and years. Certainly she can show grace for an old friend who's fallen on hard times?" he asked, with a syrupy grin.

My gaze landed on his fingers, glittering with diamonds, then shifted around, taking in the obvious opulence surrounding this motherfucker – opulence Ches had not only allowed, but helped facilitate.

"That's why she sent me," I told him, remaining stone-faced.

"Instead of one of those hotheads who would've already smashed your shit up by now. Cut the shit, Wally. You took over territory from Bill after he 'fell' off the ladder, and you've raised prices on your product – an unapproved price hike at that, but Ches let you rock. So enough excuses. Enough bullshit. Just run the money, that's all."

"How about a negotiation?" Wally asked, still intent on pressing his luck. "With so much changed, wouldn't it be wise to revisit terms? Perhaps a lower percentage rate? Everyone still wi—*Ahhhh!*"

All of Wally's bluster disappeared as soon as I closed the distance to snatch him up by the collar. "I have a proposal for you," I growled. "Pay what you owe, and I won't smash your fucking head in. You get to stay in business. Ches gets her money. I get to go back to doing anything except looking at your ugly ass face. What do you say, Wally? How about that? Sound good to you?"

I had his collar pulled so tight that his face was turning more of a maroon shade than his usual brown, but he nodded. Satisfied, I dropped him into a heap on the floor so he could scramble to his office to do what he should've done in the first damned place.

Pay to play.

It was the way of the world everywhere, but especially here. There was plenty of freedom to be had if you knew which rules to follow.

Ten minutes later, I was back on my bike, pleased that I hadn't had to pull anything from a holster to get my business handled. I dropped my packages off at the office as usual. Got my payment as usual. Went straight downstairs to the bar, like usual.

Usual, usual, usual.

Fuck.

I miss Aly.

"Damn, she didn't even give you any, did she?" Mosley asked, dropping into a seat beside me.

I frowned at him, knocking back the remaining liquor in my glass before I spoke. "What the hell are you talking about? Did I say that shit out loud?"

Mosley chuckled, accepting a drink of his own – only me, him, and the bartender would know it was just soda, no liquor. "Nah... you've just been moping around here since they left, so I assumed."

I grunted, but didn't deny it – *wouldn't* deny it, not to him. My mood *had* been sour for the two or three days since Aly had made her presence felt, then dipped.

She hadn't been bold about it either.

Nah, *bold* was not a word I'd use to describe her, and that wasn't a critique, or a criticism – just a fact. She had other qualities I much preferred.

"You gonna do something about it?" Mosley asked, and I grunted.

"Something like what?"

"Like going to see her," he suggested, but I could tell by his tone, by the steady press of his gaze that there was more behind his words than just a friendly suggestion.

I met his gaze, searching. "Why would I do that? That girl isn't trying to have shit to do with me."

"Only because she doesn't know you that well yet. I bet you could change her mind."

I stared at him a little longer, and it clicked.

"Change her mind... and deliver a message to her little sister?"

Mosley tried to keep his expression in line, but he couldn't help it – a grin broke across his face, and he dropped his head. "Fine. Yes, I want you to give Nadiah something for me when you go."

"*When?*"

"Yes, when," he repeated, his tone confident. "I haven't seen you this pressed over a woman since..."

"Don't say that shit, Mos," I warned, with a fresh drink halfway to my lips. "Don't you fucking do it."

"Chill, Mad," he smirked, as I poured the liquor down my throat. "I'm not going to remind you how bad you used to have it for Ruby Hartford."

I choked, sputtering as the whiskey burned in my lungs. "What the fuck did I say?" I snapped, though the goofy look on Mosley's face made it hard to be mad.

"Man, Ruby is the finest woman in the *Burrows*, hands down – everybody wants her, there's no shame in that."

"It's not about shame," I scolded him. "It's about loyalty. Ches hears you talking about Ruby, you'll learn what I'm talking about."

"Fine," he shrugged. "Back to Nadiah and Aly. When are you going?"

I sucked my teeth. "Who said I was going anywhere? I don't know *where* in the *Mids* they live, and I'm not trying to get caught out there figuring that shit out either."

"That's easy enough to find. We can put some *Apex* scouts on it."

He probably already knew.

"You pushing this shit hard. She must have made an impression on you."

Mosley grinned, biting his bottom lip as he nodded. "Man, did you *see* her?"

I did.

Nadiah was a cute girl, and she was smart, so I understood his attraction. I wasn't concerned with her though. Even if she hadn't been what I considered too young for me, I was much more interested in her big sister.

Alyson was beautiful.

Deep brown skin, big expressive eyes, round nose, full lips on a heart-shaped face that exuded a certain purity.

Innocence.

But not immaturity.

I wasn't thinking about her face anymore now, but of her as a whole. Naivety could read as vapid, but that wasn't Aly, not at all. As much as she didn't know about the world beyond the *Mids*, she caught on, and adapted. And just like I'd told her the night before she left, she was courageous. She had heart. Lots, which was a quality in short supply around here.

And she wasn't jaded.

That was rare.

And so fucking attractive.

"Why don't *you* go," I dared him, though now that he'd planted the idea in my head, I couldn't shake it.

Mosley frowned. "Nah. Too close to the *Apex*. I haven't been back since... you know. What if I'm brainwashed or something? The closer I get to my old den, the stronger the mind control."

"Sounds like a bad excuse," I joked, even though it wasn't. I didn't want Mosley any closer to the *Apex* than he had to be, which included the *Mids*. It had been hard enough getting him out the first time. If they got him back, they weren't letting him go again.

Then I'd have to fuck shit up.

"What is it you're trying to give Nadiah?"

A different person may have been embarrassed, but Mosley grinned as he pulled something from his pocket, putting it on the table between us.

"What the hell is this?" I asked, picking up the tiny device and turning it over in my hands. My eyes widened as I recognized the battery plugged into it, with an indicator light blinking green. "Is this a rechargeable battery pack?"

Mosley nodded. "Yep. Solar, so it's undetectable. I gave her a loaded MP3 player, but you know the battery will only last so long. I want her to use it forever."

Chuckling, I ruffled a hand over his hair. "Look at you, with your romantic gifts and shit. You're really digging this girl, huh? Even though you probably won't see her again."

"This is why I need you to take her this charger, man. No matter who she meets in the *Mids*, I'll always be the one who gave her the gift of music. Who's gonna top that?"

I shook my head. "Nobody."

"Damn right. So you're gonna do this for me, right? Keep that flame burning for me?"

I frowned. "You been watching those movies again?"

"Just answer the question Mad," he deflected, barely keeping a straight face.

"I'm not about to make any promises," I told him. "Maybe you and Nadiah hit it off, but the last time I saw Aly, she ran. I feel like that was a sign she wasn't that fond of me."

Mosley's eyes narrowed, and he scooted forward on his barstool, casting his gaze around the empty bar before he spoke. "Or *maybe* you scared the fuck out of her because you couldn't keep your hands to yourself?"

My eyebrows lifted as I picked up my empty glass, wondering when the hell I'd taken the last drink. "Yeah, maybe. Even more reason to *not* show up at her door. If she's afraid of me, how the hell do you think she will react to that?"

"Maybe she'll think it's romantic?" Mosley countered, though we both knew that shit was weak. More likely, the best course of action was leaving her the hell alone.

Even if it didn't sit well with me.

The pager at my hip went off, letting me know my presence had been requested, by the only person with the power to do such a thing. I grabbed the charger and pocketed it, then tossed a few bills on the bar top for my drinks.

"No promises," I reminded Mosley, who was grinning way too broadly for me to be confident he understood. "I'm taking it in case."

"Of course," he agreed, not losing any of that smugness. "I'll get you that address just in case."

━━━━━━━━━━

Ches wanted me to meet her in the garage.

I already knew what that shit meant, so I dragged my feet getting there, not caring that taking my time might piss her off.

She'd deal.

Not that I liked to make pissing her off a habit, but Ches knew the day-to-day dealings with her soldiers wore on me – she knew I'd rather stay away. But just like with Wally, she'd called me anyway, because she knew I got shit done. However old this stuff got to me, I'd come when she called, out of a sense of duty.

Loyalty.

The kiss print tatted on my neck wasn't there for nothing.

I could hear them before I walked through the doors, loud chatter punctuated by the occasional shout. When I stepped in, it took my eyes a moment to adjust to the stark white light in the garage. Under its illumination, everything from the rows and rows of gleaming bikes to the varying shades of skin and hair and fabric were all tinted green – a small detail that only helped feed Ches' obsession with the color.

She wasn't here yet.

When my heavy footsteps got close enough to catch their attention, echoing off the thick concrete walls, the chatter quieted to nothing. I lifted my chin, acknowledging everyone at once and being careful not to make any specific eye contact – the last thing I needed was any of these motherfuckers, man, woman, non-binary, *anybody*, thinking I thought they were special.

I didn't.

They were all part of that *sameness* I was so sick of.

I made my way to the black Jeep that anchored the space – Ches' Jeep – and took a seat against the front bumper, ignoring the stares. I crossed my arms and was damn near ready to close my eyes when I felt someone approaching me.

Jab, Bandz, and JuJu, none of whom I felt like being bothered with.

They were – somehow – the self-appointed superiors of the other generals. It amused Ches, so she let it rock, as long as they deferred to me. They annoyed the shit outta me sometimes, taking their position so seriously, but they were good at it. Natural leaders, and there was never a need to question where their loyalties centered.

They'd die for Ches.

Anybody in this room would... or they'd die for daring not to.

"You know what this is about?" JuJu asked, sweeping her long weave over her shoulder, with the same long, pointed nails that Ches favored for herself. She idolized the woman, wrapping herself in things that could've come straight from Ches' closet. "She paged everybody."

Jab looked around, his lips moving as he counted the bodies in the room. "Everybody except the street kids accounted for."

"Somebody has to keep eyes out," Bandz chimed in, taking a long drag from an ancient electronic cigarette. I remembered seeing it in Mosely's lab, one of his restoration projects.

Now that they'd spoken, all their eyes came to me, waiting for input I didn't have. I'd learned years ago that interpreting the moves Ches made wasn't my specialty, so I didn't try.

I just showed up where I was supposed to be.

They were still looking at me when the object of everyone's curiosity entered, wearing a jeweled bikini top and leather mini skirt – jade green, of course. JuJu squealed, gushing on a whispered breath about how good Ches looked. Jab and Bandz agreed, but it wasn't her outfit and hair that impressed them.

I figured the way she looked was at least 20-50% of the reason people followed Ches, just depending on the day. Sure, she offered safety, a sense of belonging, a chance for survival, and access to excess – those things comprised most of their loyalty. But, honestly , ninety-nine percent of this crowd wanted to be her, fuck her, or both.

And then there were those like me, and Mosley, who knew her before she'd become *the* Ches. To us, she was family.

"Hello little ones," she sang, addressing the group as she came to stand beside me. She met my eyes, saying without speaking that she wanted to see me after this, alone. "I have bad news."

JuJu, Bandz, and Jab all stood a little straighter at those words, a reaction that the other pursued. I stayed where I was, wondering what bad news she could have decided not to address with me first, before bringing it to everyone.

But I knew she had her reasons.

She *always* had her reasons.

"There's been an act of aggression," Ches said, her tone almost scarily calm. "Division Eight."

My mind went to Kimberly Tremaine, and her ongoing feud with Ches. I had my suspicions, but I'd never gotten a straight answer about the source of their disdain for each other. Whatever it was, it ran deep, and God help anybody who got between them.

"When do we ride out?" Bandz asked, already pulling his gloves from the strap at his belt.

Ches rewarded him with a smile, but shook her head. "There's no need for that yet." She turned to the group. "I don't want to hear about any of you in Division Eight causing any trouble – this is a provocation we will *not* respond to, because we're better than that," she declared.

The group nodded along with her words, not picking up that she was leaving out what was obvious – this wasn't some noble speech about nonviolence, it was a delay. Time to think about it and make plans. To retaliate when it was least expected – and she *would* retaliate to whatever this "act of aggression" was, and she wouldn't show any mercy, and it wouldn't be traced back to her.

It wasn't her style.

"The reason I'm telling you this, is to encourage diligence. We have enough danger on our hands with the *Knights* playing fast and loose with the boundaries, and not to mention those hooligans from Division Four."

Oof.

Dee and Dem would've rolled their eyes about that jab – they were from Four, which was nice as hell – one of the few places that still had clean beaches and the *best* rum money could buy these days. But Ches didn't like us over there because Ches was beefing with Sula Archer.

Because Ches beefed with everybody who didn't do what she wanted.

"Whatever you do, be *safe*," Ches insisted. "I don't want to bury anybody. I've done enough of that, okay?"

"Consider it done," Jab told her, with a little salute that earned *him* one of those treasured smiles.

"Maddox."

No further instruction necessary.

I peeled myself up from my seat, following her to the private elevator at the front of the garage. As soon as the doors closed on us, she dropped the zen bullshit, turning with flared nostrils.

"Those motherfuckers blocked my shipment," she growled, her hands hooking into claws in the air as she paced, frustrated. "A whole fucking truck of product – *poof. Gone!*" She pulled herself together when the elevator opened into her office, making sure it was empty before launching in again. "How the *fuck* am I supposed to run a business if I can't get products?!"

I took a seat at the edge of the desk. "What was it? Where was it coming from?"

"Spices. From nine."

"*Ouch.*"

"Yeah. Fucking *ouch*," Ches muttered, raising a high-heeled foot to kick her chair, sending it tumbling to the floor. "*Ugggh!*" She whipped around, turning with blazing eyes. "I want Kimberly Tremaine's heart. On a platter."

"And Ruby Hartford wants you. You move on Tremaine, you *know* what will happen," I responded, paying no mind to the cutting nature of her gaze. Ches could be mad all she wanted, but facts were facts. Ruby only let Ches breathe because of a commitment her husband had made – he'd promised her space to conduct her business, and Ruby had honored that. But expanding territory, attacking other Division heads, wasn't part of the deal.

Ruby was *dying* for Ches to break ranks first, just itching for Ches to give her any reason to become an aggressor. Just like it wouldn't surprise me for Ches to claw Kimberly Tremaine's heart out herself, I was confident about Ruby's hatred. All she needed was a nudge, and she'd be at the front door with that goddamn blade to claim a certain head.

Ches knew it too.

And it burned her the fuck up.

"Then *let it happen*," she bluffed, looking around for something else to kick over or destroy. When she found nothing – at least, nothing worth the mess – she flopped down on the couch, fuming. "This shit makes me look weak. I can't let it stand. Tremaine is only fucking with me because that over-inflated *bitch* Sula put her up to it."

Nah.

It was more like, Kimberly Tremaine was fucking with her because *Dre* Tremaine had spent more nights in Division Three, in Ches' bed, than he'd spent at home with his wife. I didn't see a need to point that out though.

"Listen," I said, moving from the desk to take a seat near her, on the arm of the couch. "I've got contacts with APF, a couple of guys I trust. Let me see what I can do, aiight?"

She rolled her eyes. "I have contacts with APF too."

"*Your* contacts will tattle to Ruby. Mine won't," I told her, nudging her leg with mine, which made her shoot me a scowl.

"Fine. But don't think I don't know this isn't just an excuse for you to go to the *Mids* to see that little starry-eyed girl. You're not slick, Mad."

I smirked. "Never claimed to be."

"Uh huh." She sat up, hooking her hand under my chin to cup my face. "You be careful. You hear me?"

"Always."

Her grip tightened – not in intimidation, with worry – "I'm serious. You know how I feel about my people. Especially Mos. Especially *you*. If something happens to you, you know I'll burn down everything the Earth hasn't already taken back."

I tossed an arm around her shoulders. "Yeah. I know. I told you though, I'm *good*. Always."

"Uh huh." Her tone was harsh, but she returned my embrace. "You make sure you don't let that damn girl get you in any trouble."

I frowned as I stood, already planning my trip to the *Mids*.

"Alyson Little, get me in trouble?" I sucked my teeth, shaking my head as I moved for the door. "That shit ain't possible."

TEN

I stood at the coffee machine, wondering what would happen if I drank it all.

If instead of my proper serving, I picked up the whole damn container of needed caffeine, cradling it to my chest while I sipped with a straw, *daring* anybody to come near me or try to take it away.

A girl could dream, right?

Instead of doing any of that, I followed the rule, taking my tiny ration and sitting down, hoping to have the break room to myself. I *needed* it. So, so bad.

My eyes drifted closed as I took my first sip, savoring it. Before I could take another, I heard too-familiar footsteps. When I opened my eyes, Lori was standing at the other side of the table where I was seated. Arms crossed. Frowning.

"Not working," she sniped. "How unsurprising."

For a week now, Lori had been throwing this same barb, not caring how ridiculously unfair it was. My days off were supposed to be *mine,* and were the only times I didn't show up to work. For whatever reason though, Lori had taken exception to my not being available at her beck and call, and would *not* let it go.

Nadiah and I had returned home from our little adventure in the *Burrows* with four hours to spare before I needed to be at the salon for my shift. While Nadiah settled in, I'd opted to check the phone messages first, in case there was anything from Gran. There was – her checking in about Nadiah while being careful of her words. But there were also several messages from Lori.

I listened to all four, alarmed at how they evolved – *devolved* – from a curt but polite request for me to take a sick stylist's place, to veiled threats against my job because I wasn't returning her calls.

It wasn't okay.

Even if I *had* been in the *Mids*, there was no guarantee I would've been home for those messages, not with a sick grandmother in assisted living. And if that weren't the case, it still didn't give her the right to make demands of my private time.

But I needed this job.

That was the *only* thing that stilled my tongue, saving Lori from the verbal lashing I *so* wanted to give. Vaguely, I wondered if I would be so moved by any of this before my trip to the *Burrows* had opened my eyes.

Probably so.

The difference now was that I knew I had other options.

Harriet breezed into the break room wearing a smile that faded as soon as she saw Lori. Her – artificially – gray tresses swung around her face as she whipped her head back, pretending as if the sight of Lori was like a blow to the chin.

Well... not *exactly* pretending.

My face must've given something away, because Lori turned fast, attempting to catch Harriet in the act. She was already done with her silliness though and was pulling out a mug to stand at the coffee machine herself.

Lori rolled her eyes, then turned back to me. "I want you on the floor as *soon* as your break is over."

"Aren't I always?" I retorted, before I could catch myself. Lori's eyes bugged wide – she *wanted* to say something ugly back, but there was no denying the truth of my words.

I was *always* here when I was supposed to be.

I *always* did my best, which was twice as good as most of the other stylists here.

I didn't complain, I didn't give her attitude, I had steady clients who loved me – I was an ideal employee, all the damned time. I understood that she'd been in a bind being a stylist short, but it was nonsensical to take it out on me. And if she said *one* more thing at this moment... I would snap.

But she didn't.

Her nose scrunched, and her top lip curled, but her mouth didn't open. She turned and stomped off, and Harriet turned with wide eyes as she set her coffee ration in front of me. "Should we refer to you as Alyson Little, slayer of dragons?"

Laughing, I shook my head. "She and her hot breath will be back. Forget her. I want to know how Nessa is doing on those... you know."

The restrained smile that passed over her lips told me everything, but she still leaned in to gush, "Working like a *miracle*, thanks to the good people of Division Two."

"Good," I told her, putting a hand to my chest. "I'm glad it worked out."

"They better had," she giggled. "Imagine if I'd bailed on an appointment with Ruby for nothing? Thank you again for doing that for me."

"It was nothing."

Just like every other time she'd brought Ruby up, I said as little as possible, dreading the inevitable moment she'd find out she'd essentially been replaced. It had been a week since I styled Ruby, which meant she'd be back in the next few days. I had done nothing wrong, but it sure as hell felt like it – so much that I barely glanced at the promised coffee ration she'd slid in front of me, knowing it would feel like lead in my stomach.

"I've gotta get back out there," I said, rising from my seat. "Wouldn't want to keep Sargent Lori waiting."

Harriet laughed, retrieving the coffee for herself. "I mean, if you aren't going to drink it..."

"Please, go ahead," I told her, heading toward the exit.

"Aly, hold up," she called, and I stopped, turning to her. "You seem... I dunno. *Something* is different with you."

I swallowed. "I don't know what to tell you. Same old Aly."

She shook her head. "It's fine, keep your little secrets," she teased. "You'll tell me when you're ready. Just know *I'm* ready, okay?"

I laughed. "Noted. Thank you."

"You're welcome," she called after me as I headed back down the hall.

I didn't know what made her think something was different with me – I'd thought I was putting on a good façade.

But apparently not.

As much as I was trying to pretend everything was normal, that I didn't know what I did, that everything was okay... it wasn't.

And I wasn't the "Same old Aly".

━━━━━━━━━━

"**N**adiah, are you ready to go?!" I called one more time as I slipped my feet into my shoes. My previous two inquiries had been ignored, so when I still didn't get a response, I grabbed my jacket from the bed and headed down the hall to her room.

This time a week ago, I'd been heading out with Maddox in hopes the mysterious "Blue" could help me pinpoint my sister so I could bring her home. Now, I was trying to get her *out* of the house to go see our grandmother.

I rapped on her door, and when I didn't get an answer, I opened it anyway, smiling when my gaze landed on Nadiah. She was putting on shoes too, but was too enthralled by the music pumping into her ears – and singing along - to notice my presence. The thin navy cords peeking out of her braids gave it away.

To get her attention, I waved my arms. Her eyes got big, then a slow, embarrassed grin crept across her face. "Sorry," she said. "Were you trying to talk to me?"

"Just seeing if you were ready to go. I hate to tear you away, but..."

"Granddaughter duty calls," she finished for me, with a nod. It wasn't just "duty" to either of us, but making it an obligation ensured it didn't get lost in the vast depths of our other priorities. I watched as she pulled the wired earbuds from her ears, taking care to treat them with all the delicacy of an antique – which is what they were, really.

Many *Apex* residents had an implant which allowed music to be called up directly in their heads. Others, without the implant, used "seeds" – a tiny device that clung to the skin like a sticker, broadcasting for only that person. Both options were only for those who could afford it – unlike the *Burrows,* where music had been available to everyone.

Nadiah tucked away her treasured gift from Mosley, a tiny neon blue music player that ran on a battery. In the back of my mind, I was dreading the day that battery would go out, knowing it would break her heart. In the meantime, I was just happy about how happy *she* was. She wasn't moping about not being able to see Mosley, just reveling in having met someone so exciting, who'd been able to show her something new.

I was hoping some of that energy might rub off.

Unlike her, I was feeling moody and agitated – because *I* had been engaged in more than just innocent flirting. It hadn't been enough to just enjoy the dance lesson Maddox had given, or just his company, or just leaving it at the kiss.

No.

It had gone so much further – so far that I couldn't shake the memory. The comfort of his body wrapped around mine, the heat and pressure of his hand, the rasp of his tongue, the scent of his cologne... it was all on a loop in my brain, playing in high definition at inconvenient moments.

Like when I was headed out with my sister to visit my grandmother.

I shook my head as if that would help drive away the inappropriate playback.

"Let's get on the road," I encouraged Nadiah as she slid her drawer closed. "The earlier we get there, the more time we can spend before we have to come back – I'm trying to avoid being out late. you know how it gets."

Nadiah's head bowed. "Unfortunately."

A few minutes later we were on our way, sticking close as we headed for the bus stop. I usually wouldn't splurge, but Ruby's huge tip from last week gave me enough breathing room to make our trip a little more comfortable.

Once we got there, I was glad I'd made that choice.

From the second we walked in, I knew something was up, just from the way the receptionist greeted us. Her bright smile didn't reach her eyes, and instead of pointing us down the hall to Gran, she asked us to wait, while she paged the nurse.

My frustration and anxiety only built as we sat down, waiting and waiting, and waiting more. Beside me, Nadiah was panicking a little, her hands shaking as she peppered me with questions I didn't have answers to. *What's going on, why is it taking so long, do you think Gran is okay?* I wished like hell I knew, but this wasn't some fairytale where I could just close my eyes, make a request, and have it fulfilled.

When the nurse came out, one look at his face made pressure bloom in my chest.

"Aly, Nadiah, I'll be honest with you," he started, looking between the two of us. "It does not look good for your grandmother, and I'm sorry to have to tell you that."

Shaking my head, I met his gaze. "Then *don't*. Tell us what in the world changed from two days ago when we talked to her on the phone. She was fine!"

"She wasn't," he countered, his tone grim. "She hasn't been, for a while. Even with the treatments."

"*How is that possible?*" I blinked, hard, trying to hold back the tears building behind my eyelids. "We've been here, been around her, she—"

"Aly, people lie. To preserve the feelings of their loved ones, people lie around here *all the time*. The numbers don't lie though."

"That's your answer to this? That my grandmother is a liar? You're telling me that everything I've sacrificed—"

"Aly," Nadiah spoke, putting a hand on my arm. When I looked at her, her eyes were wet with tears. "We knew this was coming. She *hasn't* been looking good. Remember, you wondered if they were actually treating her?"

I did.

That didn't mean I wanted to accept it.

"You're the relative everyone here wishes they had on their side," the nurse said. "You've done the best you could by her, and we'll keep treating. Keep trying. But at her age, the level of kidney function just isn't enough to keep up with the demands of her body anymore. Unless a transplant is an option for you..."

I laughed.

Right in his face.

I wasn't trying to be rude, but I thought about how taking the bus to get here had been a splurge. I was barely affording the most basic of treatments, so a transplant- the surgery, the aftercare, the mainte- nance- was out of the question.

"I'm sorry," he said, and I shook my head.

"No. You've done nothing wrong," I assured. "Um... can we see her, at least?"

He cringed. "She's sleeping right now. Can you come back in a few hours?"

Only if we want to get snatched off the street on the way home.

"No," Nadiah answered for me. "We won't wake her. We need to *see* her."

For a moment, he said nothing, just looking between us. Then, with a sigh, he nodded. "Okay. But only for a few minutes."

Fine.

Something was better than nothing.

I wasted no time gathering myself and Nadiah to follow him down to Gran's room, where he opened the door to allow us in, but didn't join us.

She looked so small.

Not that she'd ever been a large woman, but now she seemed tiny, like the bed and stark white linens were swallowing her. Her thick white hair was neat as always, braided into a crown around her head. That was soothing, even if just a little – arthritis had taken over Gran's hands, stripping her of the ability to do it herself, so one caregiver had to have done it for her.

She was being taken care of.

But it didn't matter.

It would not save her.

I would not save her, as hard as I'd tried. No wonder she'd been so adamant about me stopping the treatments. They were bleeding me dry, but not helping.

"I got the official offer," Nadiah said, just above a whisper. My eyes lifted to meet hers, confused for a second before I realized what she was talking about.

The scholarship.

"I found out yesterday, but I was waiting so I could tell you both," she continued, her hands gripping the railing at the side of the bed. "This was supposed to be a happy moment."

"It still is," I insisted, approaching her side of the bed. "*Still.* That's *wonderful*, Nadiah." I cupped her face in my hands. "I am so, *so* proud of you, and so is Gran. And so are mom and dad."

Nadiah shook her head, pulling away from my touch to turn back to Gran. "I'd rather hear that from them."

Yeah, you and me both.

She'd been so young when they died. Barely a teenager. One of my most vivid memories of my mother was a conversation about Nadiah – about the things she'd need me to help teach her. Mama had thought the lessons would come easier from me, since Nadiah studied me back then, modeling everything I did. If I was pouty, so was she. If I was in a good mood, so was she. If I forced myself to accept the mournful state of the world without complaint, so did she.

But we were adults now.

I'd done the best I could, with Gran's love and support, but the bottom line was, we weren't Nadiah's parents. They'd been prematurely stripped away when she was a child – when she still had that certain elasticity that only children have.

She felt the loss differently now.

With years to understand the depth of their absence, the things they'd never gotten to pass along, the things we never got to tell them... I knew because it wasn't the same for me either. For Nadiah, it was harsher now, grief with its edges sharpened by the reality that soon, we'd be saying goodbye to our grandmother.

For me, it felt inexorable.

In the back of my head, a tiny voice nagged, reminding me that *this* was the natural progression. Especially if we loved them, people died.

All I'd succeeded at was delaying the inevitable.

"Well, *I'm* proud of you," I reiterated. "Even if that's not enough."

"That's not what I meant. Your opinion means *everything.*"

I wrapped an arm around her waist, and she returned the gesture, resting her head on my shoulder. "When are you supposed to report for classes? Will you have to travel every day, or are they putting you in a dorm?"

Straightening, she shrugged. "I don't know yet. I haven't

responded with my acceptance."

"What are you waiting on? You *will* accept, right?" Her expression was blank, giving nothing away, but the delay in her response made me uncomfortable. "Nadiah…"

"What?" She lifted her hands. "It's not a light decision."

"You've been busting your ass for *years* to get one of those invitations – on what planet is this not the easiest decision you've ever made?"

She scoffed. "Um, the one where my grandmother is gravely ill? The one where chasing an *Apex* degree means leaving you here by yourself? The one where a week ago, we found out that the *APF* is lying about the *Burrows*, so who knows what else?"

Ugh.

All of those were sensible, so I latched onto what was easiest to dissect. "You shouldn't let worrying about me hold you back," I told her, shaking my head. "I'm a big girl Nadiah, I'll be okay. This is your chance to live *so* much better than we've ever been able to."

"Maybe," she countered. "But at what cost?"

"Nothing you can't afford," I hissed back. "If Gran passes, what do you have to lose?!"

"*You*, fool!" She rolled her eyes at me, grabbing her purse before she headed for the door, over me for the moment.

I sighed, glancing to where Gran was still peacefully sleeping, oblivious to her grandkids' whispered arguing. Knowing there was nothing more for me to do, I got my things and followed Nadiah out the door, finding her waiting at the entrance for me.

"You know," she said, scowling, before I could open my mouth, "I get that you're the caretaker. You work, and you sacrifice, and you protect. That's your role, I get it, and I cannot explain enough how much I appreciate you for it. But I know it's selfish. I know you don't do it just for us, it's for *you* too, because you don't want to be alone in the world. And that's fine, Aly, I swear it is. But you don't get to be selfish by yourself, okay? Just like you need me, I need you, too. I'd appreciate if you stopped acting like you're not supposed to matter."

With that, she pushed through the front doors, leaving me again. I took a moment to swallow her words, trying not to be irritated by them, but the truth was, I never considered what I might mean to Nadiah, or Gran. I knew they depended on me – I knew they loved me, because we were family, and I wasn't horrible, so why wouldn't they? Maybe it was a strange distinction to make, and a stranger thing to overlook, but... I knew I was important to them, just didn't consider that I might *matter*.

It never crossed my mind.

Catching up to Nadiah didn't take much, and neither did grabbing her around the waist to make her laugh. Once that was accomplished, I fell into step beside her. We settled into silence – not comfortable, not uncomfortable, just *there*, with both of us lost in our own thoughts. I felt I could safely assume Nadiah was consumed with her *Apex* scholarship, or Mosley, or both, with a healthy dose of worry about Gran. I was worried about all of it, especially now that she'd brought up a point I hadn't considered before.

Was that *Apex* scholarship as desirable as I thought?

Before seeing the *Burrows* for myself, it had always been a motivator.

Go to work because if you can't pay the bills you'll end up in the *Burrows*.

Don't lose your job, or you'll end up in the *Burrows*.

What you're experiencing right now? It's just existing, not living. But it could be worse! You could be in the *Burrows*.

And there was always the easy answer to convincing Nadiah to do her "boring" schoolwork when she was younger and swayed by threats.

"If you don't put that book down and do your schoolwork first, you'll end up in the Burrows!"

But all that was before.

Before I knew how we'd been lied to, how the *Apex* and APF had stripped a successful rebellion from public conversation. But there *had* to be people around here who knew about it – the Burrows were too close for all of us to have simply taken the government's word for it... right?

Right?

I wished I'd asked Maddox how long ago the revolt had happened – I wanted dates, and details, I wanted to know everything.

I wonder if Gran knows about any of this?

I'd resolved to ask her about it next time I got her on the phone, and was about to ask Nadiah if Mosley had mentioned it to her when she took off running.

"Hey!" I shouted after her, putting all my speed behind catching up to and stopping her before an *APF* officer noticed. "What the hell is going on?!"

"Arleigh!"

I frowned. "What? What is that?"

"*Bunny*," Nadiah huffed. "Her real name is Arleigh, and I just spotted her for the first time since I've been back. She and I need to have a conversation."

From the fire in her eyes, a beat down was more likely than a talk, but my feelings weren't much – if any – different. Her little friend had some explaining to do.

"Which way?" I asked, nodding when she pointed.

Instead of the pell-mell running Nadiah had wanted to do, we took a different, less noticeable approach. This part of the *Mids* – close to the *Apex* – was nicer – more buildings, better stores – but there was a steady police presence that was best avoided. We snuck around the back of the bank of buildings were Bunny had gone, picking our way through the alleys. I stayed ahead of Nadiah, risking myself as the one to peek around the buildings until we hit pay dirt.

Bunny was waiting for someone, at a corner.

I motioned for Nadiah to wait for me, and to be ready to run. Once she nodded her understanding, I took a deep breath and then took off around the corner, snatching Bunny from behind, with a hand over her mouth to keep her from screaming until I had her pulled back into the alley, in a doorway hidden by a rusty dumpster.

"You *better not* scream," I told her, dumping her to the ground.

She shot back up to her feet, but Nadiah was right there in the way, cutting off any chance of escape. "You're not going *anywhere*, bitch."

"Nadiah," Bunny pleaded, her tone panicked as she glanced around. "Please. I can't... I don't have time for this right now. I need to—"

SMACK.

My eyes – and Bunny's – went wide as Nadiah slapped those words right out of her former friend's mouth showing her disinterest in what Bunny "needed".

"The only thing you need to be worried about is explaining why the hell you tried to set me and my sister up," Nadiah hissed.

Bunny shrank back, holding her face where Nadiah's blow had landed. It wasn't enough to hide the red handprint darkening her light brown skin. "It wasn't like that!"

"I think it was *exactly* like that," I snapped. "You showed up at my door and *lied* about my sister being hurt. You tried to keep me there in that house. You pretended you didn't know where my sister was. So you tell me more about how it *wasn't like that.*"

"I didn't have a choice," she insisted, choking on the words as tears trickled down her face. "I *swear*, I didn't want to do it!"

"There's always a choice!" Nadiah advanced on her again, but I grabbed her arm, keeping her back. The girl was already on the edge of a meltdown, there was no telling what might happen if Nadiah hit her again.

"What do you mean, you didn't have a choice?" I asked.

Bunny's eyes came to me, grateful for a chance to explain herself. "My mom, and my brother. They took them to the factories, in Division Ten."

No...

"That's a lie," Nadiah snarled. "I was just at your house! I saw them...weeks ago." A little of the anger that had bristled earlier evaporated. "Okay, I haven't seen them in weeks. But you said nothing about it."

Bunny's gaze dropped. "Because I couldn't. If you'd known something was up..."

"She wouldn't have followed you," I finished, shaking my head. "So this wasn't an impromptu lie, you planned this. *Nothing* you say is going make this any better. My sister has been nothing but a friend to you, and you do *this*?" I snapped, shouldering my way past Nadiah to put my hands around Bunny's throat. "*Why?!*" I asked as I squeezed, ignoring the contradiction of expecting an answer from someone you're choking.

This time, it was Nadiah with the cooler head, pleading with me to let her friend go as she tried to peel my fingers from her neck one by one. "Aly, *please*. You're better than this."

I shook my head and tightened my grip. Because of this girl, I'd almost lost my sister. Could've lost my life, which would've affected Gran too. She'd traded my whole family for herself. "Not today."

"*Every* day." She stopped trying to get my hands loose and faced me instead, with pleading eyes. "I want to hear what she has to say. I want to know why. *Please?*"

Shit.

I shoved Bunny away from me with a grunt, staring with cold eyes as she dropped to the ground, sobbing. My hands were shaking as I stepped back, alarmed by my sudden rage. Aside from those guys in the alley – which hadn't gone well for me – the last time I'd been in a physical fight was...

Whenever the last time was that I'd had to protect my sister.

Apparently, that was a sensitive issue for me.

"Arleigh," Nadiah called, crouching in front of her friend, trying to calm her down enough to speak. "Tell us what setting us up did for you? You said you didn't have a choice. Why?"

Bunny sniffed. "The guy, the recruiter for the *Diamonds*. He knows somebody in the APF who arranges travel. As payment, he needed two 'quality' recruits."

"Aly and me," Nadiah said. She pushed out a sigh as she straightened to stand, and Bunny nodded.

"So you were trading us, to get your mom and brother back?" I huffed.

"No," she denied, shaking her head. "Not to get them back. Getting them back was impossible. My mother owed too much money from when my father was sick."

Nadiah's eyes narrowed. "So then for what? What transport were you using us to pay for?"

"To take her there," I answered. "So they could be together."

"*What?*" Nadiah snapped. "The factories are prison camps. Why...?"

"Because it's better than being alone. At least I'd get to see my mother."

"You weren't alone," Nadiah argued. "We were friends!"

"You're an amazing friend, Nadiah, but it's not the same thing. You don't understand."

"Why, because I don't have a mother anymore?"

She didn't answer.

Her non-answer was an answer though.

"I *can't* miss this ride," Arleigh insisted, looking back and forth between me and Nadiah. "If I do, then I'll never..."

"Go."

Nadiah's eyes went big, angry that I was letting Arleigh go. She blocked her at first, but I shook my head. As much rage as I had about the situation, the *fact* was that Nadiah and I were fine. It had scared us, but we walked away with no lasting harm. We had each other still, and Gran as well for now.

Bunny had no one.

With nostrils flared, Nadiah stepped aside, and Arleigh took off, running back in the direction where she'd been waiting.

"I can't believe you're letting her slide, after what she did. She sold us out, Aly!"

"To get to her family," I countered, turning to face my baby sister.

"I know you're angry – you have every right to be. I'm angry too. But you know what, if *you* were somewhere and I couldn't get to you, or if it was Gran – I would step on anybody too. Without a second thought."

"That doesn't make it right."

I huffed. "It's *not* right. It's horrible. It's ugly as hell. But look around us, Nadiah. Do you *see* the world? It's *not right, horrible, and ugly as hell* too. Can you blame people for adapting?"

"For adapting, no. For using people – for betraying your friends. Hell yes. You won't convince me she deserved any grace."

"I'm not doing a great job of convincing *myself*," I admitted, with a wry laugh. "Not ten minutes ago, I had my hands around her neck. I'm not ready to throw the girl a parade. I just don't want either of us to be on the side of the *wrong* thing. Standing in her way didn't feel right."

"So which is it, Aly?" Nadiah asked, frustrated. "Are we adapting to the world, or doing the right thing?"

I shook my head. "I don't have that answer. I'm sorry."

"Don't be." She sighed, coming up to hug me. "I know you're the nice one. The "right" thing is in your nature. Definitely thought I'd converted you when you choked her though."

I laughed, but it turned into a sigh. "Yeah, all this new information is bringing out the worst in all of us. Life was simpler before we knew the truth."

"We'll be okay though," Nadiah assured, the brightness of her smile almost making those words believable.

"Yeah," I agreed. "We will."

Because I'd do my damnedest.

Sure, maybe life *had* been simpler with the wool over our eyes, but I'd take clarity over an illusion any day. I was only one woman, so I had no plan – or desire – to lead a revolution, or anything like that. But now that my eyes were open?

Something would change.

ELEVEN

Ruby was coming in today.

I was glad I didn't have any chemical services sched-
uled, because my hands had been shaking all morning.
Dropped tools, clumsy parting, multiple scissor corrections – it *had* to
be obvious to everyone that something was going on with me.

Still, I was taking the coward's way out by not telling Harriet
about Ruby. When pressed, I explained away my clumsiness with
worry about my grandmother – not a lie, but not quite the truth
either.

I *was* concerned about Gran.

Today I was just *more* concerned about losing my job.

Ruby's appointment for today was a standing one, already on
Harriet's book. As the time for that appointment ticked closer, my
anxiety got worse and worse, hitting a peak when Lori approached
Harriet, pulling her aside to speak about something in a whispered
tone before they both turned.

If looks could kill.

After a moment, Lori stalked away, and Harriet turned back to
her station. It only took me a second to realize she'd packed her things

back up, but before I could say something, the tablet at my station chimed.

I had a new appointment.

All my others had been shifted.

"Harriet!" I called after her, following her into the supply station. "Listen, I—"

"You could've just told me," she snapped, rounding on me. "What would've been so hard about that? We've talked *how many* times since you took that appointment for me? Wait... *that's* why you haven't been accepting my coffee, isn't it? Because you feel guilty?"

My shoulders dropped as I nodded. "I'm *sorry*. I didn't say anything because yeah, I feel guilty. And I didn't know if Ruby would *actually* want to come to me again, just because she said she would. I know how stressed you've been with Nessa being sick, and I didn't want to add to that."

"But you can take money out of my pocket without a second thought?"

I shook my head. "No, it's not like that. At *all*. When she asked at first, I declined, because I'd *never* do that to you. But then I didn't have a choice."

Harriet rolled her eyes. "You don't think I know that? Nobody says no to Ruby Hartford."

"So then why are you pissed at me, if you know?!"

"Because I have a sick kid, and I need that money! I know – you have a sick grandmother, and you need the money too – we *all* have problems. I get it. But I'm still pissed. And I'm gonna *be* pissed, for a few days. You're the homie, Aly, but get the hell out of my face, okay?" she said, dumping the small tub of supplies for Ruby's hair into my arms before she stalked off.

It was a kind gesture – she could've turned it all in, forcing me to gather it all myself, which was normal protocol.

So maybe she did just need time.

That only *barely* made me feel better.

Once again, here was a situation where someone lost, in a game of survival. Harriet had a whole family to worry about, including a sick little girl who hadn't had the chance for a full life yet. She *needed* that money. Had probably come to depend on it since she'd been Ruby's regular stylist for years.

But there was so much I might do for Gran with a boost like this. Better therapy, better medicine, make her more comfortable, put her to rest with some dignity when the time came.

And it wasn't like it had been left up to me.

If I refused Ruby as a client, there was no doubt in my mind Lori would fire me – she'd already been gunning for me anyway. I thought about messing up, so Ruby wouldn't want to use me, but the thought of *purposely* ruining hair – especially hair as glorious as hers – made me feel sick to my stomach. Not to mention, *that* would be a fireable offense too.

I hated being in this position.

However.

My *feelings* weren't stopping anything, and Ruby would be here soon. So instead of letting myself wallow, I moved on, preparing everything I needed for her steam conditioning treatment and a simple style.

In what seemed like no time, she was walking through those doors, just as beautiful and imposing as I remembered. She smiled at me in the mirror, her guards flanking the area just like last time.

"Ms. Little, so we meet again."

"You requested me," I reminded her, as I started on her hair – freeing it from the sleek ponytail she'd walked in with to coat her strands in a pre-conditioning treatment. "I'm sure you're used to having people at your fingertips, waiting for their commands."

She smirked.

"Does that bother you, Alyson?"

My stands stopped moving as I thought about it, then shook my head. "No. It doesn't."

"*Really*. Why is that?"

I shrugged, running the detangling brush through her strands as the moisture reverted them back to their coily state. "I like the idea of women with power. *Black* women, with power," I admitted. "It feels like a win, even if..."

Her smile deepened. "Even if the woman herself isn't quite *nice*?"

"I was going to say even if she isn't *perfect*. No one is."

"Well that's true," she agreed. "But I'm not very nice, either."

I didn't know how to respond to that.

So I didn't.

I moved her to the sink, going on with the treatment for her hair while she conducted business on the phone or talked with her guards. Mentally, it was easy for me to check out – focusing solely on my task, getting it exactly right.

My hands weren't shaking anymore.

Now, they moved with certainty – with confidence. Drama or not, I was damn good at what I did. An assertion Ruby seemed to agree with as she surveyed her glossy, ultra-moisturized strands in the mirror.

"This is the best my hair has looked in years, Aly – I hope you don't feel you did anything wrong by being a superior stylist."

I swallowed hard, meeting her eyes in the mirror. "I'm glad you're satisfied."

"Of course you are. Now – the style?"

"Oh! Yes, have you decided what you'd like? The appointment doesn't specify."

She nodded. "Yes. A simple crown braid. I have an event to attend."

Oh.

I could do that in my sleep.

I grabbed my comb, my brush, edge control gel, made all the preparations, and then I began the braid.

And then my eyes welled up with tears.

You'd better not, I scolded myself, trying to hold back the inconvenient emotions that had sprung up out of nowhere. It was a *terrible* time – the worst possible time – to be reminded of my Gran, sitting in a chair at the facility while I stood behind her and did this same thing to *her* hair.

The same braid she'd taught me to do, but could no longer do herself.

"What's wrong with you?" Ruby asked.

When I met her gaze in the mirror, her eyes were narrowed, digging into me like lasers, but I shook my head. "Nothing."

"That's a lie. I don't like lies. So tell the truth."

I let out a huff that only made it harder to hold myself together. "It's personal. It has nothing to do with you."

Her eyebrow went up. "Okay, so we arrive at the truth, but no details. Fine. I do *not* tolerate unexplained tears – it makes me think you're weak, which fortunately for you, wasn't the opinion I held. Inexperienced, sure. Ignorant of the world around you, unsurprising given where you're from. But *weak*... oh Aly, I expected better."

"I'm not *weak*," I hissed, with enough venom that her guards stepped forward, but Ruby smiled.

"Then what *are* you?"

"*Heartbroken*," I admitted, with way too much cracking in my voice. "This style. It's my Gran's favorite, and she's dying. Since you want to know *so fucking bad*."

That was too far.

I knew it.

She knew it.

The guards knew it.

But she didn't snap.

She looked me right in the eyes, through the mirror. "Grandmothers are very important. Especially good ones. How is your mother?"

"Dead."

For a second, something like actual emotion flickered in her eyes, but she shuttered it. "Okay. They're *especially* important when we don't have our mothers anymore. What's wrong with her?"

"Her kidneys."

"Is she being treated?"

I nodded. "Yes. The best I can afford."

"Good. *Good.* You're a good kid, Aly. I know this because you will give me the name of the facility where she's being treated."

This time, *my* eyebrow went up. "Why?"

"*Why?*" she smirked. "Because I like racking up favors from people I think have potential. Finish my hair. I have places to be."

I picked up my comb and finished.

But now, my brain was swimming with questions and confusion, wondering what the hell Ruby was plotting. I was on auto-pilot, hands moving on muscle memory, but it must've been good enough still, because Ruby put another stack of too much in my hand as a tip before she breezed out.

For a few minutes, I could only stand there – my mind was still reeling. Once that moment passed, I counted out the money Ruby had given me, splitting it in half before I stepped out of the private station where I'd been working.

I went straight to Harriet.

"*You do not have to do this,*" she hissed at me, as soon as she realized I'd slipped a handful of bills into her pocket – my escape was too slow. "Ruby has a right to switch stylists, and *you* have a right to accept any client that comes to you. You *earned* this, Aly. You don't have to give it away."

I thought about the conversation I'd had with Nadiah not even two days ago – adapting to the ugly to survive, versus doing the right thing. I shook my head.

"I know I don't *have* to, but I should've given you a heads up. I should've given you time to adjust, and I didn't, and it wasn't okay. This is me trying to correct that. Some, at least."

Harriet sighed, then peeked into her pocket. "I get that, and I appreciate it. But you have responsibilities too, and giving away your whole tip... I can't let you do that."

"It's not all," I assured her. "I split it."

"What, 80-20?" she looked in her pocket again. "You must've put in work, because this 'split' is more than my usual tip. I *have* to give you some of this back."

"No, you don't. Just consider it a thank you."

After a moment, she nodded. "Okay."

I t was hard to sleep sometimes.

Tonight was one of those nights where I couldn't seem to shake off the plaguing thoughts of the last few days. Between my grandmother, Arleigh, Ruby, Harriet... somehow, everything felt more unsettled than usual. It wasn't as if I'd ever felt particularly safe before, but this was different.

It was one thing to be acclimated. Growing up in the Mids, my parents had made sure I knew the rules – not just the laws, but the stuff that wasn't written anywhere, wisdom to follow to stay as far out of reach of danger as I could. There had been a certain comfort in that – not staying out too late, not going to certain parts of town, not hanging with certain people, no drugs, no alcohol.

I knew all the right things. And I *followed* those things, and I passed it down to Nadiah as best I could.

But with what I knew now, everything was in limbo.

Did we *really* have to ration electricity? Were those communication panels listening, recording everything in our houses? Why was there a barrier between the *Apex* and the *Mids*, really? Why had they sterilized us, really? Did the other divisions do this?

I was pulled from my thoughts by a series of loud thumps that damn near made me crawl out of my skin. I sat straight up, staring around in the dark, trying to discern the source.

Maybe it was just Nadiah...

Instead of going with that thought, I crawled out of bed to investigate.

"*Nadiah?*" I asked, in a loud whisper, as I pushed her door open. "Was that you?"

No.

It wasn't.

Because Nadiah was sprawled across her bed, snoring, with those damn earbuds blasting in her ears.

Shaking my head, I switched her music off to preserve the battery just a little longer before I snuck back out of her room, trying not to wake her. I was pulling her door closed behind me when I heard the same sound again, but now I could tell it was coming from my kitchen.

Coming from the back door.

Shit.

It was way too loud to be someone breaking in, and that was dangerous anyway. At this time of night, the *APF* shot first and asked questions later, so it would have to be a stupid criminal to risk that to break into *this* house.

So what the hell is going on?

The quiet lulled me into the kitchen, to the door. There was a window there, covered with blinds my mother had been obsessive about preserving – no peeking out, wearing down the cords. If we wanted to look out, we were supposed to *open* them, but I wasn't about to do that now, not when I didn't know what was on the other side.

Thump, thump, thump.

Before I could help myself, I'd let out a yelp as I scurried away from the door where someone was *knocking*. As if it weren't past midnight.

"Aly, open this door before I get shot please? I can hear you on the other side."

My eyes went wide.

Against my better judgment, I moved back to the door, yanking the cord to open the blinds. It was dark, and a little hard to tell, but... yeah.

It was *him*.

Maddox was outside.

"Aly," he called again. "Open the door."

Right.

My hands were shaking as I undid the locks and pulled the door open, letting him slip past me into the kitchen. I locked it again before I turned to face him, meeting his eyes since his gaze was already locked on me.

Damn he looks good.

"Maddox?"

We both looked toward the entrance to the kitchen where Nadiah was standing, half-awake and confused.

"Nadiah," he greeted, tipping his head. "What's up? I've got something for you, actually."

He pulled a leather backpack from his broad shoulders, unzipping a specific compartment. Nadiah approached, curious, as he pulled out a little bundle and put it in her hands.

Even in the semi-darkness of the kitchen, I could tell her eyes lit up.

"Mos wanted me to give you that," he explained. "He said you'd know how to use it."

"He got it fixed," Nadiah gushed. "That's so *cool*."

"Uh... what is it?" I asked, speaking up.

"A solar charger, for the battery on the music player. So I can use it forever."

My eyebrows went up. "Wow."

"I *know*, right?! He's so romantic," she sighed, then looked back to Maddox. "Thank you for bringing this."

He gave her a nod. "You're welcome. Have fun."

She rushed off to her room, leaving me alone in the room with Maddox again. I wasn't sure if I was good with that or not. The short time since I last saw him had done nothing to dull my memories of that night in the club, and those same feelings came roaring back now. Anxiety and arousal tangled into a knot in my stomach.

"So you came all the way here to bring her that charger? You must've owed Mosley a big favor."

Maddox grinned, shook his head. "Nah, I needed to come out here anyway, handle some business."

Of course.

Business.

"Plus it gave me an excuse to check on you."

My lips parted. "... Check on *me*? Why?"

"Why not?" he shrugged. "You had a lot tossed your way, all at once. Had to be overwhelming, right?"

"Yeah. I guess."

"So..." he leaned onto the counter, framed in the sliver of moonlight streaming in from the window. "How have you been?"

The "polite" answers played in my head – the ones I gave my regulars at the salon. The ones you gave the people who didn't really care to hear the answer, who were only asking because it expected.

"I've been fine."

He stared at me – *through* me – and then shook his head. "No you haven't."

I sucked my teeth. "You know, you're the second person to call me a liar today."

"So you should just tell the truth."

"Neither one of you *knows* me, to call me a liar."

"Maybe you're more transparent than you think," Maddox offered with a shrug. "And maybe we'd like to know you, and that's why we're asking questions."

"Why?"

His eyes widened. "Why what?"

"Why would you want to know me?" I clarified. "I'm not very interesting."

"I wouldn't agree with that."

I huffed. "The twins probably would. How would they feel if

they knew you were here, questioning me, instead of at the club with them, or whatever. Do they know what you did with *me* at the club?"

"Not exactly, no. I wasn't aware it was supposed to be public knowledge."

"Well, I don't know how it works in the *Burrows*, but usually when you're sleeping with someone, they'd care to know if you were doing things with other people."

"I think you already know Dee and Dem aren't about that kind of thing."

"What kind of thing?"

"Possessiveness."

"And you think *I* am?"

He smiled. "Aly why don't you ask me what you want to ask me?"

"What makes you think I have something to ask you?"

"Common sense."

I swallowed, hard. "Fine. The twins. Are they your girlfriends, or something? They are, right? And they're okay with you having a little plaything on the side?"

That amused look on his face only deepened, to the point that he laughed, shaking his head. "You've got that all twisted, Aly. If anything, *I'm* the plaything on the side."

My eyes narrowed. "What?"

"Dee and Dem don't have romantic feelings for anyone except themselves. We've known each other a long time – we're really good friends. I'd kill a motherfucker over them, and they'd do the same - and extend that same protection to you, if I asked. Do we have fun sometimes – that's our business as grown, consenting adults, but I think you already know that answer is yes. What else would you like to know?"

Great question.

I wasn't sure why I'd brought them up, other than an easy way to get the attention off myself. Only, that had backfired, because now I looked like some jealous weirdo, all wound up over some guy I'd met not even two weeks ago.

Why the hell should I care what he was doing with the twins? I'd never planned to see him again, and as he'd said – it wasn't my business.

"Can I take your silence as a *no?*" he asked, moving to step closer. "Does this mean you're done deflecting, and ready to give me a real answer?"

"A real answer to *what?*"

"How have you been?"

"I've been horrible," I answered, honestly this time, though I didn't mean to. I couldn't catch the words before they came tumbling out of my mouth. "My grandmother is dying, Nadiah is waffling on a scholarship that could change her world, Ruby Hartford is inserting herself into my life, and my boss hates me. Oh, and, everything I thought I knew about society might be a lie. So there you have it."

Since everybody wanted to press me today, they could accept whatever spilled at their feet.

Or not.

Either way, I felt a little better having spoken it aloud.

I was so preoccupied with my thoughts I hadn't realized Maddox was approaching until his arms were around me. He completely enveloped me, arms tight around my shoulders, my face pressed against his chest. It caught me so off guard I stiffened at first, but then I melted.

The steady, comforting warmth of his body felt too good not to.

"I'm sorry you're having a hard time," he muttered into my hair, and I had to close my eyes, squeezing them tight to stem the sudden urge for tears. It wasn't as if Nadiah, Harriet – hell, even *Ruby* – hadn't offered words of comfort, or a shoulder to cry on. I was hard pressed to accept it because I wasn't that girl. I didn't cry, I didn't get emotional – I swallowed it. Maybe I thought about crying, or I *almost* cried, but then instead I sucked it up, and I got shit done. Tears and talking things out took too much time. Too much *energy*.

Neither of which I had to spare, when there were things to do, things to take care of.

But maybe, just for a second, since I barely knew him anyway, and he was leaving soon, and his arms felt like a comfortable place to call home... maybe I could take a moment to let it all go.

Just this one time.

My hands were pinned between us, so I couldn't return his embrace. Instead, I pulled handfuls of his shirt into my fists as tears rolled down my face, and he didn't move. He held me a little tighter as I cried, and my stress slipped away. After a few minutes, I felt his hand under my chin, tipping my head back to point my face toward his.

He said nothing.

Just picked up a dry towel from the stack on the counter, using it to clean my face. It was a simple thing – the simplest of things – but so nurturing that it made my chest hurt.

When he put the towel down, he kissed me.

So, so softly at first, like he was testing the waters – making sure I was okay. I pressed into him, seeking more. *Needing* more. And that was all the invitation he needed to devour me. His tongue probed the seam of my mouth, seeking entry I eagerly gave. His hand tangled in the braids at the base of my head, gripping and holding me in placed as he licked and explored, taking my breath away before he pulled back, finishing with another soft brush of his lips.

"Do you feel better now?" he asked, prompting my eyes to narrow.

"Because you kissed me?"

He laughed. "No. Because you let it all out."

"Oh. *Oh.* Yes, actually," I replied. "Thanks for letting me ruin your shirt."

"Just a little salt water," he shrugged, offering a lazy grin I couldn't look at too long. "Although, you had a little snot going on too..."

Immediately, I stepped back, embarrassed, but Maddox was laughing as he caught me by the elbows, pulling me back into him.

"Chill, Aly. I'm just teasing you."

"That doesn't make it less embarrassing."

"You embarrass way too easy," he countered. "And have a habit of running away from it."

Obviously, he was referring to that night in the club, which was the *most* embarrassing thing. I didn't want to think about it when I was alone, so I had no desire to recount it in front of him.

"Does *anybody* like staying embedded in situations that make them feel bad?"

His teasing expression melted into concern. "I made you feel bad?"

"*No*," I shot back, immediately. He'd made me feel the exact opposite of bad. As far from bad as you could get. The aftermath though... "It wasn't you, it was... I don't know. I don't know how to explain it."

"You ran off like I scared you."

"You *do* scare me. I've never met anybody like you."

"The feeling is mutual. But you got pissy when I said I thought you were interesting."

"Because I'm *not*."

"And I disagree with that. So tell me, where do we go from here?"

I shrugged. This time, he didn't catch me when I disengaged. "You came to check on me and bring Nadiah the charger. You've done that."

"Are you kicking me out?"

"I don't know what reason you'd have to stay."

"We talked about this already, I thought." He pushed his hands into his pockets. "I want to know more. What is your boss tripping about? What did Ruby want? Is there anything you can do for your grandmother? What scholarship is Nadiah up for?"

"Let's say I tell you all these things. Then what? I've spilled my guts and then you leave, and I never see you again?"

"It doesn't *have* to be that."

"Doesn't it though?" I asked. "You don't live here – you only came for *business*."

"I never said I *only* came for business," he corrected me. "And either way – I'm here now. I could be here again, another time."

"*Why?*"

"Damn – what is with you and that question?" he asked, laughing, as he leaned into the counter with his hip.

I frowned. "What's with *me*? No, what's with *you*?" I threw my hands up. "You're... handsome, you're smart, you're strong, you're dangerous. The tattoos, and the motorcycles, and the take-no-shit persona. You're sexy. You're *cool*. You probably have the women of the *Burrows* all over you. Why are you *here*?"

It wasn't about self-esteem – I was confused. The twins made sense for him. Hell, I didn't know the details of their relationships, but even Ruby or Ches would make more sense, even with the age differences. I was the polar opposite of those strong, sexy, confident women.

What the hell did he want with me?

"So you think you're not cool? That's our disconnect here?" he asked, eyes narrowed, waiting for me to respond. Or maybe not, because he kept talking. "You are beautiful. Smart. Strong. Dangerous. We had this conversation already, but I'll say this again since you forgot, but you left the *Mids* in the middle of the night, in the dark, to come for your sister. Attacked motherfuckers twice your size, with nothing but an improvised weapon and heart. I've watched you not let fear make you shrink and give up. You work hard to take care of your family, and I haven't heard you complain about it. All this shit I've mentioned? *That's* sexy. *That's* cool. Why the fuck *wouldn't* I be here?"

I dropped my gaze.

I didn't know how the hell to respond to that without embarrassing myself, so I didn't. I walked off with my face hot and ears ringing and heart galloping so fast it was a wonder it was still in my chest.

I went to my room, thinking a chance to breathe a little air that wasn't filled with his energy, his scent, would help me think more clearly.

It didn't.

Probably because when I looked up, Maddox had followed, and was standing in the open doorway of my bedroom.

"So no answer, huh?"

Ugh.

I rushed toward him, pulling him inside and closing the door before the deep tenor of his voice pulled Nadiah into our conversation. She was probably asleep again anyway, with those damn earbuds, but still.

"Take your shoes off on the carpet. I'm trying to keep it nice."

He responded immediately to that request, removing those heavy boots and placing them beside the door.

"This is your space, huh?" he asked, flipping the light on without asking. The room was fine – I *liked* this room, had done a good job of making it my own instead of feeling like I was sleeping in my parents' room. But no one had really been in here before.

"Yes," I answered, holding my breath as he approached the desk. There were at least 200 ink pens there, sorted into various cups and tins and mugs. I treasured every one. As the *Mids* became more and more digital, like the *Apex*, pens had become obsolete. Checks weren't accepted anymore, and I suspected cash would disappear soon.

In the meantime, I was holding on to this one relic – handwriting and paper sketching were both useless skills my father had taught me. Two things I held close, but rarely showed anyone. If Maddox had taken notice of the pens, there was no doubt in my mind that the sketchbook would be next, and if he picked *that* up I might die.

That thought was still lingering when he turned with a smirk. "I'm not going to open your sketchbook, Aly. You can relax."

I let out the breath I'd been holding. "How did you...?"

"Well, you about sucked all the air out of the room," he chuckled, as my face heated yet again. "But even if you hadn't reacted, shit like that is personal. You can show me if you want to, another day."

"You sound sure we'll see each other again."

"Just a gut feeling," he countered, with another grin. He sat down at the edge of the desk. "But you seem sure we won't. Which, if that's what you want, I'll respect that. I told Mos you might not be that happy to see me."

I've thought about you every single day though.

"What makes you say that?"

His eyebrows pulled together. "That you *literally* ran from me in the club. Well, a lil bit ago you said it *wasn't* me. So are you freaked out by orgasms or something?"

He wasn't being a creep. There was no innuendo. It was just a question. An honest question, a casual one, though it was anything *but* casual to me.

"No."

It must not have been convincing, because his eyes narrowed more. "That wasn't your first one, was it?"

"Of course not!"

The skepticism playing across his face didn't let up. "Your first because of someone else though?"

"I told you I wasn't a virgin."

"That doesn't have shit to do with the question I asked," he countered. "And if you say you're not, then okay."

"*I'm not.*"

I wasn't.

I'd had a boyfriend, in high school. His family was moving away – transferred, to another division. Before that, we'd been content with our clumsy teenaged kissing and groping, but had never gone further than that.

Until he was leaving.

Then, we went all the way.

And then he was gone.

"It's not something that matters," Maddox tried to assure me, shaking his head. "We can talk about something else."

He said it didn't matter now, but I still remembered his teasing that first night we met.

"Typical good girl from the Mids, probably never even had your cherry popped."

I'd denied it then too, because *technically* I had.

Eight or nine years ago.

It wasn't something I thought about often – at least not with someone else. I was familiar with my body – knew how to make an orgasm happen for myself, if I was too stressed or anxious to get to sleep. But when Maddox touched me, that was something else.

Something *better*.

"You wanna talk about your job? Didn't you say your boss was giving you drama?"

"No," I responded, stepping up to him. "I mean yes, she is, but I don't want to talk about that."

"Fine. What do you want to talk about?"

Nothing.

Definitely not any of the shit that was stressing me out. I had no reason to expect he'd be around later, but he was here *now*. The perfect temporary distraction from everything that ailed me.

This time, I kissed him.

Nervously.

Clumsily.

But he accepted me with open arms and minimal teasing, and hands at my waist to pull me closer, and soft nibbles and slow licks. Like he was *savoring* me.

That made it feel so easy.

Easy for me to get lost in that kiss, easy to get intoxicated off mutual desire, easy to be a little bold.

I pushed his jacket off his shoulders.

No, it wasn't a *big* move, but it was something – enough that I felt gratified when he shrugged it all the way off, tossing it behind him before he pulled me in closer. Kissed me deeper, harder. Stoked the fire he'd started in me that night at the club, that never had burned out.

Before I could second think it – *over* think it – I let my hands fall to the waistband of his jeans. I had the button undone, and was going for the zipper when he pulled back, his hands covering mine.

"Aly, what are you doing?"

I met his gaze. I was nervous as hell, but backing down wasn't an option, not from here. Not for me. "You *know* what I'm doing."

"Yeah, but do *you*?"

"If we do this, you won't have to ask that question anymore, will you?" I countered. "No choice but to believe I'm not a virgin, if you've been inside me."

He dropped his gaze for a second, shaking his head before he brought his eyes back to mine. "Aly, I will not have sex with you so you can prove you're not a virgin."

"That's not why."

"Okay I'm listening. Why then?"

I pushed out a sigh as I drew my hands away from his. "*Because*, I need this. And I need you to not make me explain that, I need you to... wait..." I stepped back, as it dawned on me. "Unless you don't want to this."

Shit.

How had that not occurred to me?

Sure, he thought I was cute, and thought I was sweet. So he'd kissed me, okay. That was a far cry from wanting me in *this* way.

Not compared to who I knew he'd been with.

"Aly, don't," he insisted, catching me as I turned my back to him, not wanting him to see the humiliation playing across my face. "It's not like that."

I pulled away, avoiding his touch as I moved across the room, wishing I'd stayed in the kitchen the first time. I could use an escape route now.

"Hey." His voice was firm now, and so was his touch as he forced me to turn and face him. "What the hell is happening right now?"

"Well, *I* am about to go to bed, and you are going back to the *Burrows*, or something. I don't know."

"So you're kicking me out?!"

I shrugged. "I don't know what I'm doing, Maddox, but I don't feel like talking anymore, and I'm not about to *beg you* to fuck me!"

"Nobody is asking you to beg for shit, Aly! Damn, I'm trying not to end up being something you look back on and regret."

"It's too late for that."

Did he think I would look back on being rejected after I threw myself at him with a smile? Did he think there was happiness, instead of mortification, behind the gloss in my eyes?

"Just *go*," I insisted, pulling away from him. "Or, if you need to lie low for a few hours or something, you can crash on the couch. Thank you, for coming to check on me, and for bringing Nadiah the charger, and for letting me cry. Thank you."

"Aly..."

"It's fine. It's *fine*, Maddox, I promise."

That was a lie, but I'd say anything to get him to just leave, *please.* Before I embarrassed myself any further. I grabbed his jacket from the desk, putting it in his hands before I turned back, intending to climb in my bed and bury myself under the covers. I'd only made it a few steps before Maddox hooked an arm around my waist, turning me back in his direction to crash his mouth down over mine.

Yet again, this was different.

Not the sweet and comforting, or the slow and savory, this was *urgent.*

Whether I could breathe seemed of secondary importance to him, and I quickly realized it didn't matter much to me either. I wanted to kiss and be kissed exactly like this, clumsy and hot, tangled tongues and bruised lips, with his hands gripping my ass so hard I was up on my toes.

But...

"I don't want this, if it's out of pity," I said, half-breathless, as I pulled back. "I want this – *need* this – but not if you're only doing it because you feel bad for me."

Maddox smirked, shaking his head as he grabbed the hem of the tee shirt I'd thrown on with a little pair of shorts, after my shower earlier. I was suddenly very conscious of my lack of underwear. He pulled it over my head, tossing it away, then went for the hem of the shorts, bending to tug them down my legs.

When he straightened, he bit down on his lip, giving me a look that made my knees feel weak.

"Trust me, Alyson – what I'm about to do to you doesn't have shit to do with pity."

The tiniest bit of panic crept up my spine as he eased me backward, toward the bed. "What are you about to do?"

He smiled.

"Sit down."

My knees bent on their own.

From my seated position I watched, riveted, as Maddox undressed. He was just as beautiful as I expected, all lean muscle and tattoos and magnificent dark skin.

Fear kept my gaze above the waistline, trying to avoid the unavoidable. I couldn't help it though – my eyes landed there as he ambled toward me after he'd put his clothes in a little pile, hard and swaying in front of him like it was guiding him.

Maybe it was.

He pushed me backward and climbed on top, kissing me again. And again, and again, before he made his way to my neck, sucking, biting, licking. I pushed up onto my elbows to watch, enthralled, as he made his way to my breasts. My mouth was open, barely breathing as he circled my nipples with his tongue, teasing them into hard, sensitive peaks.

And then his mouth was on me.

Sucking, hard, creating a pull I felt all the way down to my toes. My stomach clenched, and my fingers did too, snatching up handfuls of the sheet as he did the same thing on the other side. He kept on like that, back and forth, using his fingers to tug and pinch and tease when his tongue and teeth were otherwise occupied.

And then lower.

I was panting as his lips moved over my stomach, the soft rasp of his facial hair tickling my skin as he went. *So* badly, I wanted to close my eyes – the visual *and* the physical sensation were too much. But I couldn't look away – I didn't *dare* look away, not even when Maddox glanced up with a smirk that made another tremble run down my spine.

And then his mouth was on me again.

It felt like his tongue was *everywhere*, licking and slurping and moaning into me, as if I'd been prepared just for him. He hiked my thighs up over his shoulders, spreading me open wide as he buried his face in me, lapping and licking and closing his mouth over my clit and sucking and licking more, and...

Shit.

It was everything.

Not enough, and just right, and too much, but with his arms locked around my thighs I couldn't get away from it. I snatched my pillow from up near the headboard, biting down and pressing it into my face to keep from screaming as I orgasmed. Maddox kept going, and going, and going, until the tension left my body and I couldn't do anything but lay there, pillow still covering my face, wondering what in the world I'd gotten myself into.

I didn't have long to think about it.

Maddox snatched the pillow away as he made his way back up my body. He wiped his face with the back of his hand, grinning as he lowered himself on top of me to press his lips to mine.

"Are you *sure* you want to do this?" he asked, as if I weren't soaking wet, as if he weren't hard against my stomach, as if his face wasn't coated with *me*. Still, it was a valid question, among others I was trying hard to suppress.

I said *yes* anyway.

And then he sank inside me.

Tried to sink inside me.

Shit.

Shit.

Shit.

"*Relax*," he urged, trying to push, though my pussy didn't seem to have gotten the memo about what we were doing here.

I *tried* to relax, I did.

But the more I tried, the more I couldn't, and the more frustrated I became.

"Hey." Maddox caught my face between his hands. "Don't get upset."

"*How?*" I pushed out a sigh, then let my mouth fall into a pout. "This is so..."

"*Don't* say embarrassing," he laughed, knowing it was *exactly* what I was reaching for. But instead of letting me grasp it, he kissed me. And kissed me again, and again, and so good that all I could focus on was keeping up, until very, *very* suddenly, he was inside me.

All the way.

Filling me up.

I shuddered as a wave of pain spiked through me, but it was gone just as quickly as it came. Maddox didn't move – he kept kissing me, distracting me, as my body stretched to accommodate him. And then, he moved his mouth to my ear, chuckling in a low, warm rumble.

"You're *definitely* not a virgin now."

Any other time, I would've laughed – it was a perfect thing to say, in what *I* felt was a perfect moment, but Maddox moved, and the friction took my breath away.

It was so, *so* good.

He was careful with me, I could tell. Slow, measured strokes as we molded to each other, kissing and caressing and squeezing whatever we could touch. The wetter I got, the faster, deeper, he went, until we'd built up a rhythm, and I was taking all of him.

Then, he went harder.

My feet pressed to his chest, or spread out wide, or hiked up over his shoulders. Idyllic pressure built and built and *built* in my core. I closed my eyes as he wrapped my thighs around his waist, moving in closer to devour my mouth once more. His arms locked around my body, holding me tight as he slammed again, and again, filling me up as a familiar tension built in my limbs until...another round of bliss.

He growled into my neck as he pushed into me one final time, his hips pumping as his body worked through his orgasm. I didn't open my eyes until he collapsed on top of me, his weight feeling like the only thing keeping me connected to the bed.

Otherwise, I was sure I'd be somewhere near the ceiling, floating.

I was *high*.

After a few minutes, he rolled off, onto his back, grinning at me. When I returned his smile, he reached over, pulling me on top of him.

"Come on, *Not-a-Virgin-Aly*. Show me what else you've got."

TWELVE

I'd never been a "stay the night" kinda dude.

Even at the height of when I was *really* out there, I did what I came to do and moved on.

Maybe that was the difference.

I didn't come here for this.

Hell, I wouldn't be that convinced the shit had happened if it weren't for the fact that Aly's nude body was draped against mine while she slept, oblivious to the fact that I was staring at her. Probably unaware I was there at all – a state I hated to interrupt to bring her back into the reality of what had happened between us last night.

There was no scenario where she wasn't embarrassed.

By her own doing, of course.

As far as I was concerned, there was nothing embarrassing about her – that awkward greenness she was so ashamed of was a positive quality to me, taken together with everything else. I couldn't do anything about how she saw herself though. Metamorphosis of thought was something you had to embrace on your own – well, by choice or by force, and I for damn sure wasn't about to force.

Not when I had shit of my own to figure out.

"*Hey*," I murmured, giving her a gentle nudge. She felt good against my side, soft, and warm, but I had to get out of here before the sun came up or I'd be stuck in the *Mids* until night fell again. It took a little urging, but Aly finally awoke.

Her lids were still shut as she sat up and stretched, baring the perfect handfuls of her breasts. The lamp beside the bed was still on – albeit dim – bathing her in a soft golden light as she swept her braids behind her shoulders.

It was quite a picture.

Like something that belonged on display in one of the *Apex* museums.

Especially once her eyelashes cracked open. With sleepy eyes, she stared at me in the dim light, as if she were deciding if she was still dreaming or not.

Suddenly, she snatched fistfuls of the covers, pulling them around her to hide her nudity.

I smiled.

"I've seen it all already anyway, *Not-A-Virgin-Aly*," I teased her, enjoying the way my words made her eyes go wide. "You don't have to hide it. See?"

I climbed out of the bed, further scandalizing her with *my* nudity as I ambled over to where I'd left my clothes. I picked up the whole bundle, dropping it all on the desk to sort through it. When my gaze went back to Aly, she was staring.

At one area in particular.

"It's like that every morning," I explained, prompting her to avert her eyes as I pulled my boxers back on.

"Do you *have* to be like this?" she asked, keeping her gaze planted on the ceiling.

"Hard?"

She scowled. "*No.*"

"Oh. Blunt then."

"*No.* Crude."

My smile came back as I finished with my jeans and tugged my shirt over my head. "You telling me you don't like it?" She didn't answer. Didn't have to. "Yeah, I thought so."

She still said nothing.

Just rolled her eyes as she climbed out of the bed too, not releasing the covers until she *had* to, if she wanted them to stay on the bed. Her movements were stiff as she went to her drawers – she was forcing herself to do this, feigning comfort she didn't feel, to prove a point I assumed.

Probably not the one she thought she was proving, but admirable either way.

"You're going to have to dress a little warmer than that if you're coming with me," I told her, when she came to stand near me in nothing but a tee shirt and shorts.

"You know I'm not going with you."

I did.

She'd refused already, in the wee hours of the morning, after she'd told me everything that was going on. The only thing holding her and Nadiah here was their grandmother, which I understood – and respected – but still.

Things *were* changing in the *Mids*, and not for the better.

"Then why did you get out of bed, *other* than to show off?"

She bit down on her lip, trying not to smile. "To walk you out. To be polite."

"Oh okay, gracious host, I got it." I pulled my jacket on, then raised an eyebrow at her. "Lead the way."

Back in the kitchen, I picked up my backpack from where I'd left it on her counter. As soon as I did, the weight of it reminded of something.

"Hey – this is for you," I told her, pulling the bundled package from the bag, and putting it in her hands. "Open it," I urged, when I realized she intended to just stare at it.

She gave me nervous eyes before she put it down on the counter to undo the packaging. When she got it open, the gasp she let out told me my information had been correct.

"How did you know?" she asked, breathlessly, as she held the bag of coffee up to her nose. I grinned as she inhaled deep.

"Mos, actually," I admitted. "He talked my ear off about Nadiah, and I guess she must've mentioned to him that you were a big fan. I meant to give it to you last night, but then we got sidetracked. There're instructions there for the coffee press thing, but all you need is hot water. And I hope the powdered creamer is okay, I couldn't travel with the real stuff."

"It's perfect," she gushed. "A luxury, honestly. I don't know what to say."

"You ain't gotta say shit," I told her. "But *now* you don't have to worry about Lori down your neck about coffee rations, or agree to do hair for another tyrant to get a little extra. You've got your own."

She laughed.

A sound I hadn't heard often enough in the time I'd known her, because there was always something fucked up going on. I'd seen the fear, the despair, the anger, the confusion, the uncertainty. But the things I'd seen *now* – ecstasy, peace, happiness – I filed in my mind, resolving to see more of that, less of the other stuff.

"Thank you," she said, her eyes glossy as she put the coffee down on the counter. A second later, there was no space between us, and my face was in her hands, and she was up on her toes in her bare feet, pressing a kiss against my lips.

I wasted no time taking over – an arm around her waist to haul her against me, to get her closer, and my tongue in her mouth. She didn't shrink away either – she kissed me right back, moaning and practically fucking purring, making it impossible to end it.

So I didn't.

I put her little ass up on the counter, stepping between her legs to deepen the kiss. I wasn't sure when I'd see her again, so I had every intention of making an impression – a sentiment she must've shared. This time when she went for my belt, I didn't stop her.

I tugged those shorts off her.

A moment later, I was inside her.

Pants around my ankles, one arm draped under her knee to keep her open for me, the other hand clamped over her mouth to keep her from waking her sister up. Her teeth sank into my fingers as I stroked her, and my teeth sank into her exposed neck before I sucked her there, hard.

Leaving something to remember me by.

It took next to no time for her to melt around me, in a gush of wetness that brought me right along with her. I planted myself as deep as I could go, gratified by her muffled cries of pleasure and her fingernails digging into my hips as I emptied into her, with my face buried in her neck.

When I caught my breath and looked up, she was smiling.

Already, she knew how damn good she was.

I couldn't do shit but grin back.

By the time we got cleaned up again, it was *really* time to go, and I was cutting it close. Still, just before I left, I stopped to pull the backup pager I carried from my pocket, making sure my main number was programmed into it before I put it in Aly's hand.

"I don't have time to explain, but I'm sure Nadiah can show you how to use this, okay? If anything happens – if you feel even a *little* unsafe – you use it. I've got you, okay?"

Her eyebrow lifted. "All the way from the *Burrows*?"

"Doesn't matter where I am – if I say I've got your back, I've got it. Okay?"

"Okay."

One more kiss.

We shared that, and then I had to move along, before I ended up with an APF bullet in my head. Couldn't help anybody like that.

"**S**oooo... how did it go?!"

I did a double-take as I walked into *my* place to find Dee and Dem posted up in front of *my* window, smoking *my* weed... and in *my* business. I made a big point of looking around, making sure they understood I was trying to figure out what the fuck they were doing in here.

Even though I knew what the fuck they were doing in here.

"Cut the drama, Mad," Dee told me, passing the rolled cigarette to her sister. The usual double-down from Dem never came – the marijuana mellowed them into normal speech patterns.

"Did you de-flower sweet Alyson, or no?" Dem asked, eyes low, scanning me as I passed her.

"He did," Dee called to her, following me past one of the partitions that separated my studio apartment into designated areas. "He smells like pussy."

"Ooooh, is she like, your girlfriend now?" Dem peeked around the wall too as I stripped out of the clothes I'd traveled back in.

"*Relax,* goddamn," I groaned, talking to both as I headed to the bathroom with them still following me.

"We've been worried about you – couldn't get dressed this morning, and all you've got to say is *relax?*"

"You *should* be – you helped yourselves to my stash, I see." I glanced back to find them both hanging in the bathroom doorway. They *were* way more dressed down than usual – matching leggings and hoodies, no makeup, just the same oversized hoops.

"Perks of having a key," Dee grinned. "You make us worry, you supply the relaxation."

Dem giggled. "Those are the facts. And since we know your dick is reserved now..."

"Who said that?"

I asked, and they both laughed at me.

Right in my damn face.

Dee came closer, into the bathroom, sniffing at me again. "*Yuuup.*

Nigga, your *face* smells like pussy, which means you were *allll* up in there."

"And we *know* you don't do that on the regular, even though you love it," Dem chimed in. "Only when it's *special*," she teased, and then she and her sister broke out in giggles.

"Can I take a fucking shower in peace?" I asked, flipping the water on.

"It's your place, do what you want," Dee laughed. "We'll be out here finishing up, and when you're done, you can tell us about Aly."

"I'm not telling y'all *shit*," I countered, but they were already gone, their laughter traveling down the hall.

I shook my head as I climbed in the shower, washing away stress, sweat, and... sex. Wondered if Aly was doing the same thing, miles away, getting ready for work.

My cue that yeah, this shit was *very* different.

I forced my mind to something else as I cleaned myself up – business. I'd pulled strings and call in favors to get Ches her spice delivery, but she would not like anything else I had to report.

But... most people didn't like hearing about their fuckups.

Between divisions, your power lived in different layers – money, which was tangible, and the easiest to increase, which made it less valuable than the intangibles. Fear, respect, reputation. Ruby, as an example, had it all, albeit inherited from her husband, who'd held the throne before she did. In some situations, that would've left her power diminished, but it was a known secret that Ruby had been the one to send him to his maker, after years of bullshit. She'd done it bloody too – no poisoned drink, nothing like that, and she did that shit to send a message.

She was done being fucked with.

Ches was different.

She and Ruby were built from the same blueprint – deadly and fine. For all her faults though (if you considered them that) Ruby had a reputation for fairness. She kept her word, held up her end of deals – now, you might get used, or end up with the short end of the stick, but it would never be because she was getting over on you on some slick shit. It was *your* bad for not asking questions or reading the fine print, but terms were terms, and Ruby respected them.

Ches could be on some other shit.

She too was done being fucked with, but she'd picked up the role of being the fucker. Literally, sometimes.

It was how she'd gotten any power in the *Burrows* in the first place – from the late Baron Hartford – and *I* believed that shit was Ruby's last straw, with both.

She and Ches had been friends.

Good friends.

That was how I'd first met Ruby, as a teenager, and developed my crush. The two of them were thick as thieves, but I saw now what I couldn't back then. Ruby had been in it for genuine friendship – she loved Ches, and made sure her friend had everything she needed. Initially, that feeling had been reciprocated, but at some point for Ches it became about the access to power.

It was why Ruby hated her now, but wouldn't put that red blade through her chest and call it done. On some level, deep down, Ruby probably still loved the friend she'd had all that time ago, and never did replace. Besides that – she had principles. Baron Hartford gave Ches her power, and without a direct act of aggression, it couldn't be revoked. Ruby had the resources to eliminate Ches, sure, but if it alienated her followers and put a crack in her reputation – and exposed a weak point – it wasn't worth it.

Especially considering that with the way Ches was moving, she would destroy herself, without Ruby having to lift a finger.

Within our division, she was fine, everything was business as usual. Outside of that though, people talked – about her reneging on deals, switching rates at the last minute, betraying alliances.

About her taking what – and who – didn't belong to her.

Whether all of it had merit – and I hated to admit it, but a lot of it did – the shit was getting around, and it was affecting her business. People didn't want to work with her, not just because of personal issues but because of appearances. They didn't want a relationship with her reflecting on *their* businesses, more than they were afraid of her screwing them over.

Not only did this take away her negotiation leverage, it made shit dangerous. Once upon a time, "Franchesca Catlan" demanded a certain amount of respect, but not when word was that she didn't have any allies and couldn't be trusted. With the loss of respect came the loss of fear, and with loss of fear came the loss of safety, especially for our people who were posted in those other divisions.

It was *Ruby's* name holding this shit together. Even if they weren't her people, she was within her rights to retaliate against aggression because they were from her division. Whether she *would* was up in the air, but nobody wanted to take that risk. Nobody was stupid enough to want Ruby as an enemy.

Almost nobody.

I shut off the water, knowing I'd put off the inevitable long enough. I finished up in the bathroom, then tossed on a tee shirt and fresh sweats. Dee and Dem were in my kitchen, and the smell of breakfast drew me in that direction.

"Do *not* put your hand in my plate!" Dee scolded as soon as I stepped in, and I drew my hand back, because I damn sure was about to swipe a strip of bacon. "Your plate is over there," she pointed.

"Thank you," I told her, and I smacked her on the ass as I passed to get to where she'd directed. I stopped in my tracks when both let out loud gasps. "*What?*" I asked, on high alert, already reaching for a familiar compartment under the counter.

"Hands to *yourself,*" Dem admonished, jabbing the spatula she was holding in my direction. "Aly would *not* be pleased."

I frowned, confused as hell for a second until I realized she was referring to me smacking Dee's ass – something that had been more reflex than anything.

"Oh, *shit.*"

They were right.

It was nothing to me, and despite their reaction, nothing to them too. We'd known each other for years, and had been sexual, but that interaction wasn't. I knew that, so did Dee, and so did Dem.

But.

If Aly had been in the room, to her it may have looked like something different.

"Wow – look at his face, he's so worried."

"He's in love."

"It's so adorable."

"Over the top."

"When is the wedding, Mad?"

"Do you need us to help you pick a ring?"

"Are you moving to the *Mids* or is she gonna live here?"

"Did you get her pregnant, Mad? I know they sterilized us, but still."

"When is the baby coming, Mad?"

"Is it a boy? Will he be wearing a hat?"

"*Goddamn it,*" I groaned, fighting the urge to laugh. I couldn't encourage that shit or they'd never stop, and it would be worse when they weren't high anymore, cause I'd have to hear the shit twice.

"We're just *teasing,*" Dee giggled. "But it *is* cute that you're concerned about her comfort level like that. It's super cute."

"The *cutest,*" Dem agreed.

There it was.

If their high was wearing off, it meant I'd been back long enough that Ches would wonder where I was with my report. I endured their teasing through breakfast and then they went on their way while I dressed to leave my place. There was no denying how good it had been to escape to another world – Aly's world – for a few hours.

Now though, it was time to get back to work.

S he was too quiet.

Long ago, I learned that nothing good was happening in her head when Ches stopped speaking, and got that vacant look in her eyes.

Sometimes she was plotting.

Other times, her mind had taken her to another place – a place of hellish pain she'd fought tooth and nail to drag herself from. I knew because she'd brought me with her.

Those things were equally undesirable.

"Ches..." I spoke, firmly, trying to pull her from her trance. Her hands were folded together in a neat stack, her shoulders were relaxed, her face in a placid expression – all working together to perform the appearance of calm, though she wasn't.

Suddenly, she pushed out a deep sigh, her long green nails drumming a staccato rhythm on her desk's smooth finish.

"You know what the problem is here, right?" she asked, the first words she'd spoken after I delivered the news that though her delivery was coming, it would be her last with that supplier. As I spoke, it was obvious that my words were just making her angry – at everyone except herself.

"Yeah – you don't like to listen," I told her, unphased by the look she shot me.

I was not afraid of Ches.

As a teenager, she'd rescued me from something I couldn't have gotten myself out of. People I couldn't have gotten away from on my own. She'd risked her own freedom to ensure mine, before she knew me.

Because it was the right thing to do.

In another life –though it wasn't *so* long ago – Ches had been a social worker. The first and only friendly face I'd ever seen in the place I was sent after my parents died – a place I was convinced had the specific purpose of leaving you dead inside.

Ches was *too* much of a bright spot.

So those people swallowed her.

Did the same things to her they did to us.

Maybe worse.

But she survived.

We both did.

Spilled necessary blood and burned that fucking place to the ground.

I still remembered, still had the scars, but this was a different life. An entirely separate existence, where anybody that came for me *now*, had to come with death in mind – mine or theirs. But otherwise, I didn't mess with anybody. I didn't have to operate from that place anymore.

Maybe her trauma ran deeper than mine. Maybe she'd given too much of herself to have anything left for decency and all the other things that tyrants found optional.

Other people were right to be afraid of her, but *I* was not.

She saved me when she saved herself, yes.

But I'd repaid that a hundred times over.

"*The problem,*" she snapped, opting to ignore my input, "is that I've been too nice. These people think they can do whatever, say whatever, act however, because I haven't been ruthless enough."

"That's what you took from what I told you?" I asked, sitting forward. We were in her office, which bore no signs of the destruction she'd wrought not even a week ago, when she first got word she wouldn't be getting her shipment.

She tipped her head. "What else should I take from it, Maddox?"

"That your ass needs to *chill*," I urged. "Everything was good last year – business was thriving, you were hap*pier*. Then this year comes around and you start just doing shit. Pissing people off."

"That's how power *works*. Sometimes, you're going to piss people off."

"You're pissing the *wrong* people off, Ches. You're not gaining power – you're losing it. And you need to be more worried about damage control than you are about acquisition, or you're not gonna have *any*."

"Oh *please*, Maddox – your new pussy already got you going soft?"

I sat back, letting out a dry chuckle. "I've been trying to warn you something like this would happen since before I knew Alyson Little existed, so don't deflect this shit on her. Or *me*. We're talking about *you*."

"How about *you* remember who the fuck you're talking to," Ches growled.

I shrugged. "How about you *tell me* who the fuck I'm talking to, cause I don't know who the fuck *you* are," I shot right back. "The Ches that earned *my* loyalty, the one *I'm* willing to ride for, would be smarter than this. For the longest you've been cold, calculated – fine. I can rock with that. But the shit you're on now is just reckless, and *that* is something you won't fucking drag me into."

"How *dare you?!*" Ches pushed up into a stand, her sharp claws digging into the desk. "I *made you* little boy – you don't tell me what you will and won't do!"

I stood too, meeting her glare with one of my own. "You're right, Ches – you made me. Into a grown ass man. You wanna go at it, okay, we can go. Call your goons in here, call your army, call everybody, and I'll drop every motherfucker you put in front of me. *That's* what you made. Remember that every time you say that shit."

Her eyes narrowed, blanketing her rage because she knew I was right. I was the absolute *wrong* one, of every single person who followed her, she wanted to turn away.

It would take a lot more than this though.

"I should have left you there a little longer," she whispered, and I didn't have to wonder for a second where 'there' was. "Maybe you'd be a little more grateful now."

I blinked.

Years ago, I'd wanted to believe she wasn't capable of this kind of vitriol, but here it was. *This* was Ches.

A terrified, shattered woman, hiding behind inflated bravado.

"Yeah," I told her, smirking. "Maybe you should've."

I turned to walk off – I didn't have shit else to say to her. But like most narcissists who'd just finished spewing the ugliest of their innermost thoughts, she was right behind me, hanging on my arm, wanting me to hear her out.

"Something is happening in the *Mids*," she blurted, darting between me and the door. I could shove her aside, but Aly was in the *Mids*, and Nadiah. If they were in danger…

"I don't know what yet," she continued. "But I've heard whispers – from connections in the *Apex*," she added, sensing my doubt. I couldn't move around in the Apex though, not like other places, so I wasn't as informed as she was.

"Something like what?"

"I don't know," she repeated. "But there will be territory available. Resources. I need to claim some of it if I ever want to get from under Ruby's shadow. I *need* the power, Maddox. I've fucked up, I know. I *know*. But I need you. If all these other people are turning against me, as you say – I need you now, more than ever, if I'm going to do this."

I scoffed. "Then fucking act like it."

I moved her out of the way – not roughly, but not gently either – so I could yank open the door.

"Where are you going, Maddox?!" she called after me, and I shook my head.

"Where do you think?!" I snapped, not turning around.

I was going where I *always* went I needed to decompress, and between her and Aly – for polar opposite reasons – I needed that shit today.

I was heading to the cages.

THIRTEEN

Mmmm.

I was a little obsessed.

Either with the coffee or with Maddox, I couldn't say, but in the week since he showed up at my back door, I'd found a new favorite morning routine: I made myself a cup of coffee – hazelnut flavored, with sweet vanilla creamer – and sat at my kitchen table sipping it slowly, eyes closed, while I replayed, in painstaking detail, Maddox's head between my legs.

It was a *great* way to start my day.

"You look happy," Nadiah chirped as she breezed into the kitchen, book bag in hand. "Been a trend, since Maddox showed up to get you together."

I drained the last of my coffee. "Get me together?"

"*Mmmhmm.*" She smirked, taking a bite from the toast I'd prepared for her before she did a double-take. "Is there butter on this?"

"Yep," I told her, standing up. "I thought it would be nice."

What it had been was a splurge. Even so, buttered toast had been one of her favorite things back when our parents were still alive. It hadn't been a regular thing, but still – they'd made it happen.

"It *is*," she replied, beaming. "You should get laid more often."

"Nadiah!"

She shrugged. "*What?* I'm jealous, honestly."

"*Jealous?*" I asked, putting my washed mug on the counter. "Meaning...?"

"Meaning, you got laid, and I didn't – don't act like you don't know what I'm talking about."

"Oh I will definitely act like my teenage sister isn't talking about 'getting laid'."

Nadiah laughed over another mouthful of toast. "I'm *barely* still a teenager, Aly. I'll be twenty in a few months – far from a kid."

"I do not want to hear this."

"Too bad," she giggled. "If it eases your mind any – I'm not having sex with anyone. But if – *when* – I ever get back into a room with Mos? I'm definitely—"

"Go to school please!" I spoke up over her, making her laugh again.

She shoved the rest of the toast into her mouth, spreading bread crumbs all over my cheek as she planted a kiss on me. "Give Gran a kiss for me."

"A much cleaner one, sure," I called after her as she left.

And then it was my turn to go.

Nadiah had classes today, but for me it was a day off, which meant I could get back to Gran. We'd managed phone calls, but seeing her in person was high on my list of priorities, since our last attempted visit had gone awry. I was *determined* to see her today.

My determination paid off.

When I arrived at the facility, not only was she awake, she was out of bed, relaxing in the covered garden. With the way everything had gone after the earthquakes and storms and the long list of other disasters that precipitated the current state of the world, plant life had suffered. Keeping a garden now was a luxury – I'd realized a while ago that most of the plants out here weren't real. But there were enough living plants mixed in with the intricate fakes to make it feel like you had stepped into another world – a time back when forests and trees dominated the landscape that made what was now *Division 3*.

I could understand why she gravitated here.

"Gran," I greeted her, when the attendant led me to where she was swaying back and forth in a rocker. She looked up at me with a placid smile, her eyes clouded with confusion for a moment before they flooded with recognition.

"*Mari*," she grinned.

Okay.

So maybe not.

"*Aly*," I corrected her. "Mari's daughter."

Gran's face wrinkled into doubt, and she laughed. "Mari, you too old to be playing pretend. Sit down and look at this with me, help me figure this out."

I sat down where she'd directed, on a nearby bench, and let out a heavy sigh. It had been a long, *long* time since she'd gotten me confused with my mother, and then it only took a gentle reminder.

Must be a side effect of the new medicine...

Yes.

The "new" medicine that was suddenly available to my family, at the same price as the other one. It couldn't reverse the damage, or give her any more time, but it was – at least – supposed to make her more comfortable, without making her loopy, or tired, like the other one.

Very convenient, that it was an option, after the conversation I'd had with Ruby Hartford.

I wasn't complaining though.

I wouldn't dare.

As long as she wasn't in pain, I had no real interest in questioning their systems, though I realized that was how these fucked up policies and procedures worked. And that went *so* far beyond this facility.

They relied on people's hesitance to make things worse for themselves, our fear of losing our comfort. We'd shut up and take a *lot,* as long as there was someone else who had it worse – as long as we lost nothing we thought we deserved.

As long as *we* were the ones with the advantage.

But I could worry about my complicity later.

Gran was out of bed.

"You see this plant right here? I don't think that shit is real, Mari!"

"Me either," I told her. "Look – the leaves don't come off!" I tugged at one of the plastic leaves, and Gran's eyes went wide.

"Stop it girl," she scolded, waving my hand away as she looked around, making sure none of the attendants were nearby. "You gone mess around and get in some trouble you can't get out of, I keep trying to tell you and Leo. Can't be doing that with those girls to take care of. Mess around and have the APF looking around again."

I frowned.

Again?

"What are you talking about?"

She pursed her lips, setting off lines and ripples around her mouth. "You know what I'm talking about. Those meetings and crap got you thinking you and your lil friends are gonna save somebody. Save the *world,*" she croaked, half-cough, half-laugh. "You make sure you don't get your ass shot. Or get those kids hauled off to one of those work camps."

What?

"Gran. *Gran...* I'm not Mari. I'm Alyson, Mari's daughter. I need you to tell me what you're talking about."

"I'm not doing this with you today, you're not fooling anybody girl," Gran scolded, waving me off. "I know my child."

"Okay. Okay," I told her, in a soothing tone. "We can talk about something else then. Can you..." I glanced around myself this time, ensuring our privacy. "Can you tell me about the revolution in the *Burrows?*"

Gran rolled her eyes. "Oh *God,* this again little girl? You're damn right I can tell you – I can tell you that your little meetings don't give you death tolls, do they? They don't tell you about all the people that died, or got tortured, or went to prison for that foolishness!"

"Foolishness?" I countered. "Cause it looks a lot like *freedom*."

"You're free now! And *safe*."

"We're *not*," I hissed. "Not either of those things."

"Don't you talk back – you're not too old for an ass whipping."

I slid along the edge of the bench, getting closer to her, as close as I could. "Listen to me – I *need* you to tell me what kind of meetings you're talking about?"

"What meetings?"

Goddamnit.

"How long you been here?" she asked, when I didn't answer about the meetings. "Where's Nadiah?"

My eyes narrowed. "Nadiah had classes today. Remember?"

"Oh. Yes, I guess so," she answered, though her expression had shifted from her anger a moment ago, to confusion now.

"Gran, who am I?"

Her frown deepened. "What kind of question is that baby, you're my granddaughter. You're Alyson."

I sat back, blowing out a sigh. "Right. But when I first got here, you thought I was mom."

Gran's mouth cracked into a smile. "You look like my Mari. Especially with those braids. Pretty as a peach, just like her."

"Yeah, you've told me that," I replied. "But you mentioned something about her going to... dangerous meetings. About saving people, or something like that. What is that about?"

Her smile melted away, her expression turning solemn as she shook her head. "That ain't nothing for you to worry about. Trouble you don't need, okay?"

"Don't tell me that. I'm not a little girl anymore, okay? Why do you always get so tight-lipped when I ask you about them?"

"Who?"

"*My parents*." I sighed again. "I feel like there's something you're not telling me, and there's not a lot of time left. There's *no* time left, Gran. You were worried about mom and dad – worried about them getting shot, about me and Nadiah getting taken away. I've *never* heard this before now, but I need you to tell me what it's about. What were they involved with?"

"*Trouble.*" She fixed me with a glare – familiar, immovable. "I promised to protect you – to keep you from getting involved. I may be on my death bed, but I kept it together this long – I ain't about to break it now."

I huffed. "Ignorance is not protection – it's a disservice! Do you think Nadiah and I are *better* for not knowing there was another option out there for our lives? Do you think we're *free*, here? Safe?! We can't even have a goddamn party! Can't have too many people in the same aisle at the market at the same time! We're just *cogs*. Keeping the wheels of the *Apex* turning while they live in fucking luxury and I have to make a hard decision to buy a stick of butter," I growled. "We could've had a *life* in the *Burrows.*"

Her head snapped up. "Who told you that?!"

"I've seen it for myself," I told her, earning wide, horrified eyes as a response. "If you don't want to tell me, *fine*. But I *will* find out."

"You know what they do to people who ask questions," Gran hissed, albeit shakily. "They smack them down – which is what they will do to you – to *us* – if you pursue this."

"*Then tell me what you know.*" I got down in her face, pleading, hoping she could see the desperation in my eyes. "There's no need for me to go looking, when *you* know things! Things you have hidden from me long enough."

"No. *No*," she said, determined.

Only... I was determined too.

I hadn't come here for this – I hadn't known *this* existed. But now, because of her, I did. And there was no way I was going to just let it go.

I stood, looking Gran in her tired eyes. Any guilt I felt over going back and forth with her this way, I swallowed, because this wasn't okay.

We *weren't* safe.

We *weren't* free.

But we could've been.

Or maybe not.

But we could've had a choice.

Instead, we'd lived years and years in fear, not knowing there was another way of life. I didn't fault her for trying to protect us, but the truth was, I didn't *feel* protected at all.

I felt swindled.

It was one thing for the *Apex* to do it, but my flesh and blood?

"Fine," I told her. "Then come what may."

I turned to leave and didn't look back, stalking down hall after hall to get back to the entrance. I was almost there, turning the last corner, when I walked right into someone heading the way I'd just come.

"Shit, sorry," I muttered, stepping back to regain my footing. It wasn't until I looked up, eyes focused, that I realized I knew the person rubbing her elbow to quiet the sting of our collision. "... Isabelle?"

The woman frowned, bringing her eyes back up to mine. Her frown faded once her eyes lit with recognition. "*Alyson?* Girl, I haven't seen you since..."

"Graduation," I filled in for her, nodding. "It's been a long time."

At least six or seven years. I'd attended high school with Isa, and hadn't seen her since then – she was from a worse part of the *Mids* than I was, close to the *Burrows*.

"It has," she agreed. "Do you ever see anyone else from our class?"

I shook my head. "Not regularly, no. I've seen people in passing over the years, but everybody is working all over the place, or got to another division, or...got taken away."

Isa let out a deep sigh. "Yeah. What are you doing *here* though? At this facility?"

"My grandmother," I explained. "You?"

"My father." When my eyes went wide, she nodded. "Yeah, it's pretty messed up. He hadn't been right since my mother passed though, and now he's just been worse and worse. Dementia."

My shoulders sank. "I'm so, *so* sorry Isa."

"Thank you. We always want to see them as invincible, and strong, but then you realize they are just as fragile and human as you are. Maybe more."

Her bag had been hanging limp over her arm, and must have been sliding lower as she spoke. When it dropped, the contents spilled all over the floor.

I kneeled to help, snagging a tiny, worn paperback she'd dropped. That was Isa, always, with her nose in a book.

It was a memory that made me smile.

Before I could glance at the title, Isa had snatched it from my hand, tucking it away in the confines of her bag, and piling everything else on top.

"It was my mother's," she explained, shaken that I'd seen it, though I didn't understand what the hell I was looking at. "From her rare collection. I shouldn't have it out, but—"

"You don't have to defend yourself," I told her. "I think it's cool, to still have old books like that, that weren't confiscated."

She nodded. "Yeah, well they tried. My mother was just great at hiding them."

"Do you know if you have anything that's about a revolution?"

Isa laughed. "Uh, yeah. Tons of stuff about all different—"

"—in the *Burrows*."

Her words died on her lips.

"Aly..." Her voice was quieter now – tense. *Scared.* "I think you know that's not a topic—"

"I do. I mean, I figured. And I don't want to get you in trouble or anything, I—"

"I get it," Isa nodded. "But if the wrong person heard you even *asking*... it's that bad. Especially now."

My eyes narrowed. "What do you mean, *especially now?*"

"Rumblings," Isa said. "People are getting frustrated." She smiled. "I know you, Aly, you keep your head down, focused, so you don't see it. But it's there. Just an undercurrent, but still."

"No, I know what you mean. I know that the *Apex* has been feeding us lies. I know the *Burrows* isn't what they've made it seem."

Her eyes lit up. "Good. But don't get yourself in trouble. They're not known for mercy."

"Yeah," I nodded. "I know."

"For what it's worth, most of the books are too damaged to do anything with. And of the ones that aren't, I haven't seen any that are about... your current interest," she said, adjusting her words because of a nurse passing by with a group of visitors.

"Thank you," I told her. "You've still given me plenty. I won't hold you up from checking on your father."

She sighed. "Yeah, I'd better move along. My *husband* doesn't like when I'm off on my own too long."

"Husband?!"

Not that it was uncommon, but Isa had always been more interested in books than boys back in school, so it threw me a little, though we weren't teenagers anymore. And the derisive inflection she'd put on the word...

"Yeah," she groaned. "Not my choice."

"*What?!*"

"No! *No,* not like *that,*" she clarified, shaking her head. "I had a say in the matter, I just couldn't afford to take care of my father. So I did what I had to do. Some rich *Apex* bastard who I luckily haven't had to *do.* Yet. He's been too busy terrorizing."

"*Isa...*"

"It's not as bad as it sounds. *Really.* I got what I needed, and he doesn't touch me, so it's a good set up. I'm okay."

"You're sure?"

She smiled, pulling me into a hug. "Yeah. I gotta go – I'll see you around."

"Of course," I told her, though I wasn't that sure.

I walked out of the care facility with my mind reeling, with way too much information. I spent the entire trip back to my house with my head on a swivel, absorbing the details of everything around me. Usually, I was so focused on not being followed, not giving anyone the wrong idea – tunnel vision, for mine and Nadiah's protection – that I didn't *see* my surroundings.

Now I did.

The worn and raggedy streets and buildings, the graffiti, the faded posters, the kids younger than Nadiah, begging on the streets between being chased by APF officers. People, not unlike me, ignoring it all, just trying to go about their day without making eye contact, lest they invite trouble.

I couldn't believe I'd ever bought into the lie that we deserved this life. That we could work our way to better.

No.

This was all they ever planned to give us.

Anything more would have to be taken.

S omeone was knocking on the door again.

This time, though, it was at the front door, not the back, and not to mention still daylight outside. Nadiah and I were putting dinner together, both intending to go to sleep early to accommodate the busyness tomorrow would bring.

When the knocking – pounding, really – started, both of us looked up, then at each other, for a possible explanation. Nadiah shrugged, and I moved to the front door, wiping my hands as I went. I put my eye up to the peephole, then scrambled backward, almost tripping over my feet.

Shit.

Shit.

Shit.

I'd been warned to be careful, warned not to ask questions.

Warned to stay out of trouble.

And yet, the *APF* was at my door.

The conversation with my grandmother had just been this morning, and already, here they were.

Shit.

"*Nadiah!*" I hissed, then turned to find her right behind me.

"What?" she asked. "Who is it?!"

I took a deep breath. "It's the police, okay? Listen – I need you to hide. And get the pager Maddox gave me. It's in my room, in my top drawer. Get it and then go out the window. Go to the safest place you can think of, and contact him, okay? And then wait for him to tell you what to do next."

"Aly, you're crazy if you think I'm about to—"

"They're here for me, Nadiah." The pounding started again, more urgent, more demanding this time. I squeezed her hands. "If you stay, they'll take both of us. If you go... maybe we can get help. Go. And close the room door. I'll occupy them."

"Aly, seriously—"

"*Now, Nadiah!*"

She huffed and puffed about it, but she went. As soon as I heard the bedroom door close, I opened the front, halfway expecting to be greeted with a backhand for having the nerve to make them wait.

That didn't happen.

Instead, the *APF* officers stood back, making way for another man to step through. He was tall, and broad, dressed in the traditional stark, spotless white of people with status in the *Apex*. He looked down his nose at me – clearly agitated. His eyes were a cruel, terrifying gray that froze me in place, staring at the dark, jagged scar that bisected an otherwise handsome golden-brown face.

"You are *not* Nadiah Little."

Nadiah?

"*Where* is she?" the man asked, in a tone that invited obedience, and promised nastiness for anything else.

I swallowed, hard, readying my mouth to tell the lie that she was anywhere but here.

Before I could, she spoke.

"I'm right here. Who are you, and what do you want?"

My head whipped around and there she was, standing defiantly at the kitchen counter, arms crossed.

"Adam Bishop. National Security."

Nadiah's eyebrows went up, just slightly. "You mean *Apex* National Security."

"Obviously."

What the hell is happening right now?

"How can we help you, Mr. Bishop?" I asked, turning back to him. "What are you doing in my home?"

His nose curled into a derisive little snarl as he glanced around, then back. "*You* can't help me. Your sister, however, can."

"How exactly?" I countered, not backing down. "She's barely an adult."

"She was offered a scholarship. Aerospace technology and robotics. She was identified by her university as having an affinity for it. Therefore, the *Apex* has proffered the privilege of continuing her studies with us, where she'll have access to better resources, limitless informational materials, and the opportunity for real life, hands-on experience," he stated, sounding like a brochure.

Like propaganda.

"Hands-on experience?" I spoke up. "Don't you mean, the *Apex* wants to put her to work? The privilege isn't *hers*. It's *theirs*."

His nostrils flared. "It is a more than generous offer."

"I don't accept," Nadiah said, with certainty. I'd asked her about the scholarship a few times since she'd revealed the official offer, but time had made me less convinced it was a good idea.

This little visit sealed it.

"Excuse me?" Bishop asked, anger flashing in his cold eyes.

"She said she doesn't accept your offer," I told him, even though he damn well knew what she said.

His unsettling gaze slid to me as a slow, chilling grin unfolded across his lips. "That you believe this is optional is the funniest thing I've heard all day."

"What?" Nadiah and I echoed, both struck off guard by those words.

Bishop stepped back, full-on smiling now as he headed for the door. "Tomorrow morning," he said. "Present yourself at the *Apex* gate to be checked in, or I will come and get you myself. And I promise – I won't be as pleasant as I was today."

And then he was gone.

Just strolled out, as casually as if he'd come by to ask to borrow a little sugar as a neighbor, not like he was leaving turmoil in his wake.

I slammed the door behind him, bolting it closed before I turned to Nadiah.

"Pack a bag – we're leaving."

Nadiah huffed – not defiantly. Defeated. "And going *where?*" she asked. "They probably already have people watching the house, there's no way we're getting past them. And if we do where could we go? You think we'd make it all the way to where, the *Burrows?*"

"I don't know, Nadiah!" I snapped. "But I know I am *not* turning you over to these people without at least trying. This isn't just about you getting an *Apex* degree – they want you there to put you to work on... something. Something they can't figure out by themselves, so they need to add you and your brain to the mix, so they can further whatever fucked up agenda they have going. But I will tell you this – if they want you without a fight, they're gonna have to kill me."

"Do you think that's a deterrent? You think they care about you sacrificing your life for mine?"

I shook my head. "No. Not at all. But I know I won't be able to live with myself if I don't *try*. Go pack a bag."

Her shoulders dropped, but she did as I asked. That was all I cared about for the moment anyway. Sending her off to collect whatever she could fit in her backpack gave me a chance to stand still for a moment, to process what was happening.

Too much.

Too fast.

I pushed out a deep breath and forced my feet to move, digging out a backpack from my closet. I only bothered with a bit of clothing in the bag, knowing it would be the least of my concerns over the next few days.

Necessities only, I chided myself, as I grabbed the things I might need from the bathroom. Nadiah's things were already gone from there, and I found her in the kitchen, digging through the cabinets for non-perishable snacks to shove in her bag.

Like those damn "cheese" balls.

Those had kinda been the start of everything.

The awakening.

"*Ah!*" Nadiah shrieked, startling both of us.

"What?!" I asked, as she closed her eyes.

"Nothing, sorry," she said, sliding a hand into her pocket. "Well, not *nothing*, it's the pager. I forgot it was in my pocket, and it vibrated."

My eyebrows went up. "It vibrated? Like with a message?!" I asked, taking the tiny device from her hand when she held it out.

"SOS received. Answer the knock at the back when it comes and follow instructions. He'll get you out."

"This is from Maddox? You paged him?"

Nadiah's head bobbed. "Not when you first told me to – I came out when I heard my name. But when you sent me to pack the bag, I reached out. I guess he took a bit to get something arranged."

"But he's sending someone. Okay. Okay, this seems a little less awful now," I said, pushing out a deep breath. "Okay. Okay...okay. *Shit.*"

"What?" Nadiah stepped in front of me, eyes wide. "What is it?"

"*Gran.* We can't just leave without her. We can't abandon her here."

She nodded, again. "Right. But we can't take her, either. Like we literally *can't*, not without a discharge order, and she's sick, Aly." She let out a deep, shuddering breath as her gaze dropped to the floor. "Okay, lets page Maddox back. Tell him it's fine. We eat dinner, we go to sleep, and in the morning I report for duty. It'll be fine. I'll be fine."

"Have you lost your mind, Nadiah?"

"No, I have it right here," she countered. "I'm using it, instead of letting us push forward with an idea that will get one of us hurt!"

I scoffed. "We're already hurt, Nadiah. Already terrified. Already on the edge of falling into line, defeated. There is no part of me that believes they will ever let you walk out of that place once you're in."

"They could've taken me today," Nadiah argued. "Or any other time. They're letting me come in by myself."

"Under threat of having you brought in anyway," I growled. "Yes, they are still holding on to the edges of civility now – giving you the appearance of a choice in the matter – just like that scholarship. My best bet is that they didn't want to be seen dragging you out of here because it's bad PR."

"So what would you have us do? Huh? What is the right answer here?"

"*Not* making this shit easy for them, at least! I don't want to leave Gran here alone either." I let out a hard breath, remembering how I'd left things with her that morning. Everything that had gone unsaid. "Lets call, okay? She deserves to know what's going on."

I hadn't told Nadiah about that conversation yet – I'd intended to bring it up over dinner, knowing she could help me hash it out. But in the back of my mind, I couldn't help wondering about the words she'd spilled when she thought I was Mari.

Specifically, the concern about my parents getting in trouble with the *APF* again.

Again.

That meant that my mother and father had been on their radar before, for reasons unknown. It couldn't have been too serious, or we'd all have been carted off, but it still left a lingering question.

Were Nadiah and I marked?

Had we *always* been?

"Okay," Nadiah agreed. "We can call. How did she seem when you saw her this morning?"

"Talkative."

If she found my reply strange, she didn't say so, just moved to where that interactive panel was. I took a seat at the counter while she dialed, dropping my head into my hands. For the past few weeks, I'd been thinking the trip into the *Burrows* to retrieve Nadiah was the most excitement my life would ever see.

What a shitty thing to be wrong about.

"What the hell?"

Nadiah's exclamation brought my eyes to the screen just in time to see it flicker out, before it could connect to the care facility. That had never happened before, and the timing was too convenient for this to be any coincidence.

Sure enough, as I stood to move to Nadiah's side, the screen flickered again, filling suddenly with Adam Bishop. Those steely eyes narrowed as he lounged backward into the obvious comfort of a luxury vehicle.

"Going somewhere, ladies?" he asked. "Looks like you're heading out."

Shit.

I didn't have to move my eyes from the screen to know he was referring to the jackets we'd donned, because we *were* heading out.

"Just going to see our grandmother," I lied, without an errant blink. "We were calling ahead."

"You've already seen her today, haven't you?" Bishop's gaze didn't falter. "You signed in at the care facility just this morning."

"Alone, yes. But as I'm sure you know, she's not in great health. Nadiah wanted to share her good news about accepting the scholarship."

Beside me, Nadiah tensed, and I willed her to keep her cool. On sight, it was easy to recognize that Adam Bishop was a dangerous man, and a smart one too. Even the slightest falter, and he'd see right through this – already shaky - ruse.

"This late in the day? It would be nightfall before you arrived, and more dangerous later. I could send someone to escort you," he offered, in a honey coated tone I knew not to believe.

"No, you're right. We can just tell her the news over the phone and celebrate another day. We're hanging up now, so we can call the care facility. If you can turn off whatever rerouting service you've placed on our panel, we'd be grateful."

Bishop stared for a long moment, then smirked. "No. No, I don't think so. We'll be seeing you ladies soon."

The screen went black.

"Okay, we're getting the hell out of here," I told Nadiah, snatching my backpack from the counter to pull it on. "*Now*. Get your bag."

This time, she didn't argue. She picked up her bag to zip it closed and then followed me to the back door. I took a deep breath, glancing at Nadiah to make sure she was ready to do this. Whatever the hell *this* was. She nodded, and I opened the door.

To an APF officer standing on the other side.

FOURTEEN

My heart stopped.

For longer than a heart is supposed to go without beating.

At least, that's what it felt like.

Time stopped too – *nothing* moved, nothing made a sound, I couldn't bring myself to blink.

"*Aly.*"

That didn't come from behind me, from Nadia. It came from the black-clad man in front of me, as he lifted the wind guard on the mask all the *APF* officers wore, revealing brown eyes that were warm.

And *familiar.*

"Are you coming or not?" he asked, his voice too muffled by the mask to make a connection in my mind.

I didn't need it though.

The eyes were enough, though I hadn't looked into them since the night I offered someone my body for the first time.

"*Prince,*" I breathed, hardly believing he was standing in front of me, in an *APF* uniform, at that. "What are you doing here?"

"Saving your ass," he replied. "Adam Bishop will be back at your door, in..." —he raised his arm, checking the display on his wrist – "Eight minutes. Throw some shit in a bag and let's go."

"We already have bags," Nadiah chimed.

"Even better. Follow me."

"Wait," I hissed, holding up my hands to stop her. "We can't just follow him! My high school boyfriend shows up at our back door after who knows how many years and this shit doesn't seem like a trap to you?!"

Not to mention "conveniently" running into Isa...

"Aly, chill – Maddox sent me. He put out feelers, and I happened to be here, so I said I'd help. *Seven* minutes now. Are you coming, or not? Maddox is my boy, but I'm not about to let you get us killed."

I let out a breath, looking back and forth between him and Nadiah before I nodded. "Fine. Let's go."

He reached into a pocket, pulling out two large black satin scarves.

"Cover your hair, then follow me."

It only took a glance at Nadiah to realize what he meant was, *"cover your braids"* – the easiest way to make us less distinctive. We did it, and then followed him, sneaking up to the main road behind our house. He escorted us up the sidewalk past other *APF* officers and civilians, leading us to a marked *APF* vehicle. The alarm on it chirped as he unlocked it, then gestured for us to climb inside.

I didn't breathe until we were all in, and he pulled onto the road.

Once he was driving, he tugged his mask down, displaying the face I recalled all too well – just older now. Gone was the baby-smooth chin and sparing mustache – he had full blown stubble now that made him look like a *man*.

Not the boy I remembered.

"So you joined the *APF*, huh?" I asked from the back seat with Nadiah, trying not to sound as bitter about it as I felt. I was hoping he'd tell me this was just an elaborate costume, that he *wasn't* one.

But he nodded, meeting my eyes in the rearview mirror. "Yeah, *Division Eight*. At risk of sounding like an apologist though, you should know, the *APF* isn't the same everywhere. These mother-fuckers in *Three*... I wouldn't trust us either."

"As long as you understand," I muttered, looking away from him to check our surroundings, on all sides. I didn't know where he was taking us, but it wasn't towards the ruins, or the wall that separated the *Mids* from the *Burrows*.

"Thank you for helping us," Nadiah said, pushing her knee into my thigh as a way of scolding me. And maybe she was right – maybe I was being rude, but as far as I was concerned, these were extenuating circumstance.

"You're welcome, Nadi," he told her, shooting her a grin in the mirror. "Man, last time I saw you, you were in elementary school?"

"Middle school," she corrected. "Still a long ass time ago."

"Right," he laughed. "I guess y'all have had some adventures since then, if you know Mad."

"How do *you* know Maddox?" I redirected, glaring at him. "You're a *Division Eight APF* officer – how the hell do you know an enforcer from the *Burrows*?"

"*Aly!*" Nadiah hissed, kneeing me again, which I ignored.

"It's a fair question," Prince conceded. "I know Mad because I needed extra money. He needed information, eyes on the ground, somebody in a position to do a favor here and there. We could help each other out."

I snorted. "So not only are you a cop – you're a *dirty* one. Got it."

"Call me what you want, but you'll call my family alive," he countered, with a shrug. "It's the world we live in – I've done what I had to do to make sure my people were taken care of, and I wouldn't take it back. Not ashamed, either."

I pushed out a breath, letting his words process before I responded. "Sorry. This is all just throwing me for a loop. Today has been a lot to absorb."

"I can imagine," he agreed. "And I get that you're scared, but you don't have to fear *me*. I will get you two out of here, then get back to where I'm supposed to be, before somebody notices."

Nadiah leaned forward. "Where are you supposed to be?"

"Patrol. We got called in as reinforcements, something about increased unrest around here. Officers from all nine other divisions got diverted here – I was one."

I chewed at the inside of my lip, thinking about what Isa had mentioned earlier – the *undercurrent of frustration* among the residents of the *Mids*.

Was that what the increased police presence was responding to?

"You're not going to end up in trouble, are you?" I asked.

Prince shook his head. "Not if I can help it."

He pulled off the main road, heading down an alley where he parked in the lot of a warehouse. He instructed us to stay in the car while he pulled a huge side door open, then drove the car inside, leaving us there again while he pulled the door closed, bathing us in darkness. When he got back, he gave us flashlights.

"Come on," he said, motioning for us to follow him through the abandoned building. Flashlights in hand, we did as instructed, following him down a ladder into a defunct, dry drainage system. "Okay," he said, once we'd both made it down. "You're on your own from here."

"*What*?!"

Nadiah was the one to say it, but I echoed her sentiments. I had no idea where the hell we were, and though the bright concrete reflected the flashlights enough that we weren't enveloped in darkness, it was still creepy down here.

Really creepy.

"You *cannot* be loud down here," Prince warned, his voice low. "There's an echo. By now, Bishop has every cop in the *Mids* on high alert, looking for you. I don't think anybody will come searching the tunnels, but just in case, you need to be moving. *Fast*."

"We don't know where we are," I said, grabbing his arm. "What are we supposed to do?"

Prince grinned. "That's right, sweet little Aly, never would come exploring out here with me," he said. "I found these tunnels back in high school – too scared to take it all the way myself, but I know now that it opens in the *Burrows*. Follow it this way," he pointed. "Don't take any turns, just stay straight."

"Okay, how will we know we're there?"

"A couple of years ago, I marked it – from the *Burrows* end. A big red 'B' in spray paint. Can't miss it."

I shared a look with Nadiah that must have been a little *too* worried, because Prince took me by the shoulders.

"Listen – I know we're not seventeen anymore, you got a new man now, all that – but I promise you, I would not send you down this tunnel if I wasn't confident you'd make it where you're supposed to go. And if you don't believe I'd do it for *you*, know I'd do it for Mad. Ain't nobody trying to get on that nigga's bad side, trust me."

I shook my head. "It's not that. I mean, this tunnel isn't welcoming, no, but it's... everything. *This is too much.*"

"But you've got it. If you don't have it for yourself, I *know* you've got it for Nadiah, so there you go. Get your sister to safety."

Him putting it that way put an infusion of steel down my spine. Even if I wanted to be a coward, or sit here and whine, the fact remained that Nadiah wasn't safe in the *Mids*, not anymore.

We had to go.

"Are you going to be okay?" I asked, and he nodded.

"Yeah. The tracker is stripped off that car, and I'll toss this gear somewhere – it's not mine anyway. Mine is with my car, but I've gotta get back to it. And y'all need to go. *Now*."

"Okay."

I turned away, but he caught me under the chin, taking a second to examine my face.

"Damn," he muttered. "Still pretty as hell. Prettier. You know I hoped you would get ugly, right?"

My face pulled into a frown. "What?!"

"It made it easier to have to leave," he laughed. "Moving away from you broke my little teenage heart, but I convinced myself you would get ugly as you got older, so it wouldn't hurt so bad."

"So you're *still* the same damn fool you always were, is what you're telling me."

He grinned. "Exactly."

"So," I asked, stepping back as he dropped his hand. "Are you heartbroken all over again now?"

Prince bit down on his lip, giving me a once-over before he grabbed the first rung of the ladder to get back to the surface. "Maddox is a lucky motherfucker. I'll leave it at that."

"Bye Prince," Nadiah called, as he headed back up. Once it was just me and her, she nudged me, with a little smirk. "You're gonna get in trouble. Flirting with your boyfriend's friend who happens to be your ex-boyfriend."

"Maddox is *not* my boyfriend," I said, starting down the tunnel. "And I wasn't flirting."

"*Denial* is more than just a river in what used to be Egypt, I see," Nadiah teased, catching up to walk beside me. "You know *damn* well—"

"We have *much* more important things to talk about. *Quietly*," I reminded her. "Like, how we're going to get to Gran, like what the *Apex* wants so badly from you, like how our parents used to attend secret meetings that might get them in trouble with the *APF*."

"Wait, *what?*" Nadiah asked, eyes wide as she stopped moving. "Where in the world did you find that out."

"Gran," I told her. "This morning. She thought I was mom, so she started talking. Rambling, really. And then after she realized I was me, we kinda went back and forth a little."

Nadiah coughed. "*You.* And Gran? Back and forth?"

I nodded.

"Okay...," she followed my urging to move again, but only after one more declaration. "Talk. And tell me *everything*."

I should have asked how long the tunnel was.

Not that we had any real way of keeping time, other than estimating the fatigue in our lower backs and heaviness of our legs.

Judging by *that*, we'd been down here for hours.

When Prince told us to "keep straight", I couldn't help wishing he'd explained that "straight" was relative. The dark, winding tunnel kept forcing shifts, taking us back and forth in what at least seemed like one general direction, as long as we avoided the branching paths that would turn this little adventure into a maze, when it was already difficult enough.

As dry as the tunnels had seemed at our entry point, we'd long discovered that wasn't the case throughout. In more than one place, we'd had to trudge through unidentified filth, deep enough for our boots to sink in, too wide to step over. The foul odor was enough to make us thankful for the dinner we never had eaten – it meant there was nothing on our stomachs to throw up.

The inverse of that meant we were running on fumes, and afraid to be already breaking into the stash in our bags, because what if we were already lost?

What if we were stuck?

An odd sensation made me stop moving to glance behind me. I moved the beam from my flashlight around, my gaze intent as it bounced off the walls, illuminating the thick gauze of cobwebs we'd just passed, the layers of dust we'd disturbed, and nothing else.

"What is it?" Nadiah whispered, looping an arm through mine.

I shook my head. "Nothing. Let's keep going."

So we did.

For at least another hour, until the beam of Nadiah's flashlight flickered, threatening to leave us even more in the dark.

I wasn't sure what was worse – less light, or the reality of the faltering shaft of light, turning shadows on and off, creating an illusion of movement that made my anxiety spike.

"Just turn it off," I urged, when I couldn't take it anymore. "There's enough light from just one, and we should preserve battery anyway. Should have thought of that before."

Nadiah agreed, nodding as she switched it off. "I don't think either of us expected to be down here this long. We've gotta be almost there by now, right?"

Before I could reply, something reached my ears – something less than human, echoed in the dark. I put a finger up to my lips, urging Nadiah to be quiet. After a minute had passed with nothing, I shook my head, giving my sister a sheepish grin before I opened my mouth to admit that I had imagined it.

But no.

There it was again.

Louder.

Closer.

"Nadiah, *run.*"

She didn't question it.

She took off, and I was right behind her, my heart feeling like it was getting ready to explode out of my chest. The sound came again, half-screech, half-growl, multiplied as it bounced and repeated through the tunnel.

"No. *No!*" I screamed, snatching Nadiah by the arm as she slowed down, dragging her with me until she found her footing again. I didn't know what the hell was behind us, but I *knew* we'd come too far for me to turn it down now.

We have to be close. We have to be close.

I kept repeating that to myself as my lungs screamed for oxygen I couldn't slow down long enough to give. We turned a corner, and relief sank my shoulders.

Light.

My eyes were bleary with sweat, but I could see it, way, *way* in the distance.

We were almost there.

All my exhaustion caught up with me at that moment, slowing my feet to a lazy stroll. It was quiet around us now, like we'd outrun whatever the hell was behind us. I didn't have enough left in my tank to keep my adrenaline from switching off.

I'd used up everything I had.

"I need to catch my breath for a second," I explained to Nadiah, who was panting and sweating too.

She grinned at me and wrinkled her nose. "Fine, lazy. I *guess* we can slow down for a few minutes for you."

I laughed at her teasing even though it made my throat burn – highlighting our glaring oversight of not packing any water.

"We're pretty sucky survivalists, you know?" I said, calling on sheer will power to force my legs to move.

Nadiah looked to me, face still pulled into a smile – a smile that shifted to an open-mouth gape of horror, just before someone – some*thing* – grabbed ahold of my backpack, pulling me backward.

"*No!*" she screamed, diving toward me as I tried my best to untangle myself from the straps of the bag. She swung the flashlight at something I couldn't see, and must've connected, because a moment later, a deep, wounded scream echoed through the tunnel.

It wasn't like *anything* I'd ever heard before, like freezing cold claws across the skin.

"*Run!*" I screamed at Nadiah, as my shoulders slipped free from the straps. I'd thought I was out of energy, but I found enough from somewhere to snatch up the flashlight I'd dropped and take off behind her.

A hand around my ankle stopped that.

"Just *go!*" I insisted, to my horrified sister as she turned, watching me go down. I hit the ground hard as a growl reverberated around us, and Nadiah came sprinting in my direction, ignoring my plea.

And then, there was a different sound.

A loud, splintering *bang*, that lit the whole tunnel for a second and left my ears ringing. The hand around my leg relaxed, but didn't move, and I didn't either.

Couldn't.

Somehow, through the ringing, I heard the pounding of heavy footsteps – heavier than Nadiah's. She was crying – sobbing – but I couldn't will myself to get up, or open my eyes. I was *so* damned tired.

All I could manage was a groan as someone pulled me up from the ground, balancing me in their arms.

"*Aly*. Aly, hey. Aly, I need you to open your eyes for me."

That voice... and that touch...

I found something, from somewhere, and used it to peel my eyelids open for just a moment, just long enough to confirm what my body knew.

Maddox.

———————————

Gran.

She was the first thing that came to mind when I came awake, in the soft, warm comfort of a bed, eyes still closed though I was conscious.

I was safe.

Nadiah was safe.

But Gran, I wasn't so sure about. My brain flashed to that intercepted call, then continued down the path of worst-case scenario to wonder if Adam Bishop were cruel enough to use her for leverage.

I was sure I already knew the answer to that.

I'd expected to wake up in the same bed I'd used last time I was in the *Burrows*, but this felt different. *Smelled* different.

I opened my eyes, giving in to the insistence of sunlight streaming through a window on the other side of the room, filtered only by a sturdy screen that separated the bed from what appeared to be a much larger space.

This is where Maddox lives.

Flickers of the night before played in my mind – walking for what seemed like forever, then running, being grabbed, then the gunshot. I hadn't been lucid enough last night to name it for what it was, but I knew now. Knew Maddox had been the one to pull the trigger, had carried me a long time to get out of those tunnels.

Knew he'd been the one to hold me up under the hot spray of a much-needed shower.

I was sore now, my whole body aching as I maneuvered out of the bed. An oversized tee that wasn't mine draped me in super-soft cotton, but a quick peek between my legs confirmed I was wearing my own panties – clean ones, one of the pairs I'd stuffed in my bag.

Which meant it had been recovered.

Good.

I peeked around the screen, my eyes scanning the room for Maddox. I didn't see *him*, but he was everywhere in the cool, eclectic furnishings of the apartment. The exposed brick, the worn leather furniture, barstools at the kitchen counter scuffed to a smooth finish. None of it was shabby, but it was broken in, giving his home a comfortable vibe that let my shoulders relax.

And honestly, it flattered me, more than I would ever admit out loud, that he'd brought me *here*.

Complaint from my bladder drew my attention away from finding him to finding a bathroom, which didn't take much, with the way the space was laid out. I was standing at the sink, washing my hands, when the door swung open again, and a half-asleep Maddox stumbled past me, his eyes still closed as he stepped up to the toilet.

"Good morning," he muttered, pulling himself free of his boxers. A moment later, I was listening to him pee.

I averted my eyes back to my reflection in the mirror. "Good morning."

He finished before I could find a towel to dry my hands, then came to the sink to wash up too. I was still standing there, incapable of asking where to get what I was looking for, when he reached behind the mirror, pulling out a dry towel and holding it up between us.

"How are you feeling?" he asked, as I accepted the towel, patting the moisture from my hands.

"Fine," I told him. "Where is Nadiah? Did Prince make it back safe? We need your help, to get our grandmother out of the *Mids*."

Instead of immediately answering, Maddox wrapped his arms around my waist, pulling my body right up against his. "We'll get to all of that – *after* you tell me how you're feeling. *Really*."

I sighed. "Sore. And tired, like I could sleep for days. But relieved, too. To not be in the *Mids* anymore. More than that though, I'm anxious about my grandmother. And Nadiah. And Prince."

"I checked in with Prince," he assured me. "Don't worry – your high school sweetheart is just fine."

My eyes went wide. "He told you about that?"

"Why wouldn't he?" Maddox shrugged. "Nadiah is with Mos. They both insisted, and last night didn't seem like the time to press the issue – especially when they're both grown."

I rolled my eyes. "Whatever. As long as she's safe."

He smirked. "Yeah, Mos ain't letting *shit* get between him and your sister. She's in good hands."

"Fine. And what about Gran?"

I braced myself.

Delivering good news about Prince and Nadiah had come easily, but I already knew Gran would be a different story. She was ill, and in a secure facility much too close to the *Apex/Mids* line to sneak her out, even if she could discharge.

"You owe Ruby Hartford an arm and a leg."

My eyes went wide. "*What?!*"

"Yeah," he nodded. "I got in contact with her after Nadiah sent that message, because I knew it was beyond my reach. You told me

Ruby seemed to have a soft spot about your grandmother, so I took a chance. I don't know what kind of strings she pulled, but your grandmother is safe at the *Hartford* compound."

"The *Hartford* compound... meaning she's *here?* In the *Burrows?!*"

He nodded again. "Yeah. You say the word, we'll swoop Nadiah up, take you to see her."

"You're *serious?*" I pressed, and he laughed.

"Yes, I'm serious. I'm also serious about you eating something before we go – y'all were in that tunnel for damn near six hours, and Nadiah said you hadn't eaten before you started."

The news about my grandmother had lifted the weight from my shoulders, replacing it with a blanket of relief. Now that I knew my people were safe, there was room for other discomforts – like hunger pangs.

"Were you in here the whole time?" I asked, following him out of the bathroom, into the kitchen, where he directed me to sit down.

"Yeah, I was passed out on the couch. You wouldn't have seen me unless you came all the way over here," he told me, gathering things from a full refrigerator and full cabinets.

Luxuries.

In just his boxers, with his hair loose – and sexy – he made breakfast for us, immersing me in the aromas of scrambled eggs and bacon, and fresh tomatoes – a delicacy, as far as I was concerned. I pulled my gaze away from that visual to investigate the dull ache in my ankle.

I almost wished I hadn't looked.

I sucked in a breath at the sight of the dark bruise that wrapped the lowest part of my shin and spread lower. The bruise itself wasn't so bad – it was that it was a clear handprint, blue-black against my skin.

"Looks nasty."

I glanced up to find Maddox standing over me, a plate in each hand. He put one down in front of me, placing the other at the next seat before he went back to grab something else I hadn't had in a long, *long* time.

Orange juice.

"What the hell was that thing?" I asked him once I'd taken a deep gulp. He put a pitcher of water out too, pouring me a glass I downed in one long drink, making up for last night's lack of water.

"That *thing*?" he said, as he sat down.

I nodded. "Yeah, that thing that grabbed me. The thing you *shot*," I reminded him.

A grim, close-mouthed smile turned his mouth up. "Wasn't a *thing*, sweetheart. It was a *who*."

"What?!" Suddenly, all that liquid was like lead in my stomach. "You're telling me that the growling, and screeching came from a *human*?"

He sighed, sitting back. "Yeah. You live underground long enough, the lines get blurred."

"*Live* underground? Why would anybody do that? And why the hell did Prince send us down there if it sounds like you knew there was danger?"

"There *shouldn't* have been," Maddox answered. "Those people go down there to get away from the world, or escape, or hell, I don't know. What I know is that they rarely bother anybody unless they feel threatened, even though the tunnels are *their* territory. They stay away from the main vein you and Nadiah were supposed to be on."

My eyebrows went up. "*Supposed*?"

"Yeah. You guys got turned around somewhere, somehow, but you were way deeper than you were supposed to be when we found you. It should've taken a couple hours, max, for you to make it down here. When you didn't, we came looking."

"So *that* was the light we saw up ahead? A flashlight?"

"Yeah." He sighed. "Man, you don't understand how relieved I was when we spotted your light. I wondered why you were bouncing it all over the place, and then I realized – you were running. And then you were down on the ground."

"And then you shot *it*."

He nodded. "Calculated risk. Mos had insisted on me taking this night-vision gear shit he'd found in some military surplus boxes. It paid off. It was too far away to get a good shot in the dark otherwise, and I had to act fast. *Very* fast."

"I'm glad you did. Even though I feel bad," I told him, as he picked up his buzzing pager from the counter to check it. "Because I guess we were in *their* territory. Strangers, stomping through their home—"

"Nah," Maddox waved me off. "You know earlier, when I said y'all got turned around "somehow"...?"

"Yeah. But I don't remember any place where that could have happened, except this one spot that was collapsed, but that was something that looked like it happened ages ago."

He shook his head. "Nah." He held up the pager. "Just heard from the scouts – that section was just recently collapsed, and on purpose. It would've been hard to tell in the dark. Apparently they've decided not to allow passage that way anymore. They didn't feel a need to tell anybody."

"Wow... is that a big deal?"

"Not really – not used enough to consider it a real loss. The only reason Prince sent you that way is that it was better cover – coming over the ruins would've been too open, and trying to get you through a division checkpoint would've been suicide. Nobody wants to be underground without a damn good reason – like it being the last option. Ches will turn it into a big deal though."

Ugh.

Just the sound of her name agitated me.

"Eat your food," Maddox urged, changing the subject. "Then you can get ready, we can grab Nadiah, and go see your grandmother."

I nodded, taking a deep breath before I looked down at the plate – the freshest food I'd had since the last time I was here.

"Yeah. Sounds like a great plan."

FIFTEEN

I should have known Ruby would live like this.

Seeing her at court, on her throne, was one thing, but her home was another.

Vast double-doors had welcomed us into the front entrance – an extravagant display of black-and-white marble. Twin staircases led up to a landing – pure black, adorned with blood red carpet that spilled down the stairs to the entry. On one side, the banister at the end was carved into a life-sized chess piece – a handsome king, wearing a fearsome expression. On the other side, a beautiful queen, bearing a remarkable resemblance to the woman we were waiting to greet.

Floor-length windows lined the circular entry, flanked with red embroidered panels that seemed to pour from the ceiling, pooling on the floor in arranged piles. It was all impractical, and gorgeous.

"Well. The two of you are just *glowing*, aren't you?" Ruby asked, from the landing at the top of the stairs. "I know Maddox has gotten ahold of you, and *you*," she aimed at Nadiah, "Are right about the same age as Mos, right?"

Speaking of gorgeous and impractical.

"Hello to you too, Ruby," I said, standing from the plush velvet benches where we'd been instructed to wait. Maddox had brought us here, but hadn't come inside – something I'd have to ask about later. For now, I had one purpose.

Checking on my grandmother.

Ruby smiled at me as she headed down the 'queen' side of the stairs. "Forgive me – I don't mean to be immodest. I'm just happy for you – good dick is an age-old remedy that not everyone has the good fortune to discover."

"We are *not* discussing this with you Ruby, we're here to see our grandmother," I told her. "Just point us in the right direction, and we'll be out of your hair."

"Of course." I didn't see her give any cue, but a maid stepped out from somewhere. "Nadiah, Pamela here will show you to your grand-mother's room. Aly, you and I have things to discuss first."

"Go ahead," I assured my sister with a nod. "I'll be there in a minute."

Nadiah hesitated a moment, then followed the maid into the depths of the house, while Ruby moved forward, into my personal space.

"Since you brought up hair, I've got a bone to pick with you, Alyson Little."

I raised an eyebrow. "What might that be?"

"Well, going to the salon to have my hair done was one of the highlights of my week. I *despise* the *Apex,* but my position requires a certain level of attendance there."

"Your position?"

She nodded. "Diplomatic, inherited from my late husband. You didn't think peace between the *Burrows* and *Apex* was just kept on its own, do you?"

"Honestly, I hadn't considered it."

"No one does. They think I go flitting off to the *Apex* just for the hell of it, not realizing that it's *my* influence that keeps their experimental drones out of our skies, and the *APF* out of our backyard. They see the throne, and the blade. But none of the politics of it all.

"So that's what you are? A politician?"

Ruby sat down on the deep red bench, with all the elegance of a woman who knew a crown belonged on her head. "I feel like *politician* is such an ugly word, when you consider the history. There's a reason the election system failed, and the power ended up in the hands of those who were strong enough to simply take it."

"Are you suggesting that the current system is better? Where the world is ruled by rich sociopaths?"

Ruby threw her head back and laughed. "Oh, honey, the world has *always* been ruled by rich sociopaths. Some of us are just less awful than others."

"And where do you fall, Ruby? On which end of the spectrum do you land?"

"That's a hard question to answer – there are several to consider. Egocentric to altruistic. Passive to sadistic. Virtuous to malevolent. Materialistic to charitable. Cruel to kind. It goes on and on, and any combination, along with the right rhetoric and charm... can rule."

"That's not an answer."

Her hair fell in smooth, bone straight layers around her bare shoulders as she took a deep breath. "It's not, is it?" She nodded a little, closing her eyes, and then looked right at me. "There are people who would refer to me as one vicious bitch. And they wouldn't be wrong – it's required of any queen who wishes to rule her own king- dom, and I very much want that. But there is not one who could argue that I'm not fair, or I'm cruel without cause. No one goes hungry here, who is willing to work. A woman can walk the streets of the *Burrows* mostly without fear, and those who would jeopardize that face swift, severe consequences. That all sounds good, right?"

I nodded. "It does."

"It *should*. And it *is* what I strive for. But I do those things because it makes a good leader – not because I give a fuck. I *don't* give a fuck, about most people, not anymore. I think my presence in a room improves both the room and the people in it by at least four or five times over. I'm vengeful as a motherfucker, and I *never* forget when I'm owed a favor. I like violence. Not loud, impersonal guns – *blades*. Something where your hands get dirty. I like *pain*."

I kept my mouth closed because I didn't know what to say. I didn't know where she was going with this, but I didn't dare interrupt her.

"Do you know why I'm telling you these things, Alyson?" she asked, and I shook my head.

"Because you asked where I fell on the spectrum. Do you understand now why I said it was a difficult question to answer?"

"I do."

"Good." She smiled. "Back to that bone I had to pick with you then – you've turned yourself into an *outlaw*. I can't go back to Harriet after having your hands in my head, so what the hell is supposed to be my bright spot in the fucking *Apex* now?"

My eyes went wide. "I'm sorry. I'll be in the *Burrows* indefinitely, so maybe I can just... do your hair here?"

"Oh you were already going to do *that*, Alyson," she told me, pulling herself up to full height. "And it is a *small* price to pay for me risking my diplomatic status to get your grandmother out of the *Mids* before Adam Bishop tried to use her as leverage."

I nodded. "That's no problem at all, and I wouldn't dare complain. Thank you so much for doing this me for me."

"I didn't do it for *you*," Ruby snapped. "Paying for the medicine to make your grandmother more comfortable? *That* was for you. This is for Mari."

"*What?*" I asked, nearly choking on my tongue. "Did you know my mother?!"

She tipped her head, just slightly. "I didn't know her as your mother though. You had to have been just a little girl, at school during the day, but she used to do my hair, at the salon. I had to stop going once I was married – Baron didn't think it was prudent. By the time I had the autonomy to go back, she was gone. She was always kind.

The closest thing to a therapist I've ever had. I should have known, as soon as I saw you, but I'd blocked it out, like I try to do with most painful things. But when you cried about your grandmother, I looked you up. And now I know you inherited those magic hands."

I was too stunned to say anything. I knew my mother had worked at the salon – I'd spent afternoons there under her tutelage, before Lori was ever in the picture. It was my mother's legacy that had gotten me the coveted placement behind a chair to start off, instead of working my way up from the shampoo bowls. But it had never, *ever* occurred that Ruby might know her – that some of the same wisdom she'd given me, she'd been able to offer another young woman.

It made my eyes water.

"You should get to your grandmother, she's been asking about you," Ruby said, before I could formulate a response. "You should also know that moving her was ill-advised, but I understood why it needed to be done, and so did she. She insisted."

"She did?"

"Yes," she nodded. "The doctor at the facility, and the doctor attending to her now, they agree. She has very little time left. For that reason–along with a hefty payoff – they let me leave with her, taking no record, and with camera footage destroyed. The *Apex* doesn't know she's here. But I don't know how long that will be the case. Your saving grace is that the *APF* cannot operate in the *Burrows*. They want your sister though."

"Why?"

"I wish I knew," she said. "I live for exploitation of power, but I don't care to help the *Apex* do anything. It's a horrible fucking place – I grew up there, I should know. The last thing they need is another brilliant, stolen mind to help progress their agenda."

"So you won't turn us in? To make me owe you a favor?"

Ruby scoffed. "You already owe me enough favors, Alyson. But no. From *me*, you have nothing to worry about."

"Should I ignore the obvious implication that there's someone else to worry about?"

"Absolutely not," she shook her head. "You should keep *that* at the forefront of your mind."

With that said, she walked away, leaving me alone in the foyer with my brain working overtime and no idea where to go. Just like before, a maid came from out of nowhere, motioning for me to follow her.

Finally, it was time to see my grandmother.

The scene I walked into made me smile – Nadiah, seated right up against the side of the bed, her hand clutched around Gran's. Gran's eyes were open, which I thought was a good thing until Nadiah looked up, with tears in her own eyes. She mouthed something that made my chest hurt.

She's blind.

I'd seen that word on a list of issues associated with renal failure, so it wasn't surprising. Not that "unsurprising" made it better.

"Is that my Alyson? I'd know that energy anywhere. Come here lil' smart-mouthed girl." Gran held up her free hand, motioning for me to come to the other side of the bed, and I did. "Tell me," she said, "Is this some elaborate hoax to get me to tell your mama's business?"

I grinned, blinking back tears. "I wish it was."

"I know. I *know*."

"Then you know what the situation is. You *know* Nadiah is in direct danger, which means we all are," I said, ignoring the warning look Nadiah shot me. "If there's anything we need to know..."

Gran shook her head as she squeezed my hand. "Nothing you *need* to know. Nothing that will change the situation we're in now. But know that your parents were willing to give their lives to make this a better world for you. I can't give you any details, by design. I never wanted to be wrapped up in that – didn't want to give anybody a single lick of *nothing* against my child. But I knew *that*. That they weren't just sitting idly by, conceding to the oppression."

I pushed out a breath, closing my eyes as the meaning of her words sank in.

"They were part of an opposition group."

That possibility had played in my head many times since my conversation with Gran at the care facility, and I'd discussed it with Nadiah down in that tunnel. Now, it wasn't a possibility.

This was confirmation.

An answered question that launched a million more, ones that Gran had already admitted she couldn't answer.

This was enough though.

Suddenly, everything looked and felt so much different – all my memories taking on a brand-new context. I'd called up the memory of the last time I saw them hundreds, maybe thousands of times. I always felt the tiniest inkling they'd hugged us tighter, kissed us sweeter, lingered just a little longer than usual, like they may have suspected it might be the last time.

Might be.

So what happened?

The official line about the explosion at the gate between the *Mids* and *Apex* had always been "terror attack", by a resistance group from the *Burrows*. I remembered it – they forced it down our throats, playing it on the wall panel video screens like it was must-see TV. They'd executed the perpetrators. Reinforced the borders and made everything safe for us again, by implementing stricter rules than before, the ones we suffered under now.

I'd always thought they were just in the wrong place at the wrong time – civilian casualties of someone with a bone to pick against the *Apex*, or *APF*. Now though, I had to wonder... were my *parents* the "terrorists"?

Nadiah shifted the conversation to something else, and I followed her lead. There was nothing to gain but satisfaction of my personal curiosity, which could wait.

Spending time with Gran while I still could was a much more pressing matter.

I *look a mess.*

Maddox had dropped me off back at his place and then left to handle some sort of business, so I was free to examine myself now. Gran was safe, Nadiah was safe, I was safe, so it felt – marginally, at least – like an appropriate time to find myself in the bathroom mirror, taking inventory.

Of my bumps, nicks, and bruises, yes, but also of the bags under my eyes, past-expiration date braids, and some unidentified odor I was sure had embedded itself in my hair from our time in that damned tunnel.

I had to do something about it.

I found a pair of scissors and snipped, cutting my long braids to the length where my hair ended, around my shoulders. What I would do with it once the braids were out, I didn't know, but I *knew* it was well past time to do something about it.

And maybe changing my hair would help shake the *Mids* off of me.

I sat down in front of a bookshelf and picked something that sounded promising – *History Untold.* With the large book settled in my lap, I started the process of unraveling my braids, sometimes with one hand while I used the other to turn pages.

I wasn't going as fast as I hoped.

My hair was dirty and tangled, still dotted with the occasional half-undone braid when Maddox came strolling in, head bobbing to whatever was playing in his ears, and a large paper sack of something that smelled *amazing* in his hands.

Any other time I'd thought I was embarrassed in front of him was *nothing* compared to right now.

At least it would've been, if he'd done anything except give me a sympathetic smile as he dropped the bag in his hands onto the counter, then came towards me.

"You need help?" he asked.

Yes.

"You don't have to," I told him. "It's a slow process, and I—"

"Only because you're using your hands – there're combs and shit in the bathroom." His eyebrows went up, like he'd realized something. "But you didn't want to snoop around."

I nodded, and he grinned.

"Okay," he said. "Let's get this finished."

A few minutes later, I was seated between his legs, working through the much-easier process of taking down my braids with a proper tool. Between the two of us, it took less than thirty minutes to get the rest out, then dispose of the smelly, matted pile of synthetic hair left behind.

"You need me to wash it for you?"

My eyes were wide as I looked up at him, wondering if I'd heard what I thought I did. "Did... did you just offer to wash my hair for me?"

"... yes? I mean, I'm not a professional like you, but I do a decent job with my own, and I've got products and shit here. Unless you—"

"That would be amazing," I interrupted, before he could offer whatever other options he thought there were. Him helping me take my hair down, helping me wash it, were things I hadn't considered, but I wasn't about to turn it down, though I felt nervous as hell about it.

Especially once I realized he intended to do it in the shower.

"You don't have to get naked," he told me, chuckling over what had to be a ridiculous look on my face. I'd followed him into the bathroom, thinking he was just showing me his products – high-end stuff I'd only ever seen in the salon, and couldn't afford to use on my own hair – but then he'd taken his clothes off.

It wasn't that washing my hair in the shower wasn't sensible – it was pretty much how I always did it, to use as little water as possible.

I'd just never been in a shower with Maddox – or hell, *any* man – before.

But, as the course of my life over the last few months had

proven... there was a first time for everything.

I stripped down to my bra and panties and got in the shower.

It had been a long, *long* time since I'd had someone else's hands in my hair, and I'd forgotten just how good it felt. The clarifying shampoo had the best kind of slight tingle, amplified by the fact that Maddox knew what he was doing – his fingers were firm and nimble along my scalp, massaging and cleaning so good I couldn't help closing my eyes.

"Feels good to you?" he asked, laughter in his tone as he pulled the shower head down from the wall, using it to rinse the cleanser from my hair.

I tipped my head back, keeping the water from running down my face. "Yeah. It does. Thank you."

"You're welcome," he told me, as he replaced the shower sprayer, and picked up the shampoo again for a second round. "You were reading when I came in – you found something interesting?"

"Yeah, actually. I was looking at the *Burrows* history, kinda hoping to run into something about this bombing that happened in the *Mids*."

"The one you mentioned, where your parents died?"

My eyes narrowed. "I mentioned that to you?"

"Yeah," he chuckled. "Damn near bit my head off about it, the day I took you to see Blue. You *kinda* blamed the *Burrows* for their death, since I guess a resistance group from here did it?"

I sighed. "Yeah. I remember, but the thing is, I'm not sure I had the real facts about that now."

"If your facts came from the *Apex*, I can guarantee it. But, if it was a group from the *Burrows*, you'll find it in one of these books around here. Or you can ask Mos – he's been working on a database, with some others. Trying to build us an internet."

"That explains why Nadiah was so intent on getting back to him today," I laughed.

And why Ches was so eager and nice to Nadiah when we were here before. She knew Nadiah could help...

Maddox laughed too. "Nah, I doubt that's what those two are up to."

"Oh my *God*, don't say that!"

He laughed harder. "Fine, I won't say it, but you know I'm right."

"Definitely not the point."

He was still laughing as he pulled the shower head down again, stepping in front of me this time. When I tipped my head back, I was looking right in his face while he worked – shower spray in one hand to rinse away the shampoo, the other hand slipping through my hair to make sure it was all out.

He had me surrounded.

And he was staring.

"What?" I asked, when he lowered the sprayer, but didn't move to do anything else.

"Nothing. You're just really fucking beautiful, that's all."

I raised my head, sending rivulets of clean water streaming down my face from my freshly washed hair, but that was better than being exposed like I was with my head tipped back. "Thank you."

"You're welcome."

Without turning, he reached backward, hooking the sprayer back in place. A moment later, his hand was under my chin, tipping my face up to his. With his free hand, he wiped the water from my face.

And kept staring.

"What is this?" I asked, without intending to. The question was on my mind, sure, but I hadn't meant to speak it out loud.

"What is what?"

"*This*," I repeated, like that one word explained anything. "You bringing me coffee, and sending help, and me staying here, and you washing my hair. And staring at me. What is this?"

"I don't know what you want me to say."

"I want you to tell me the truth."

"The truth is that I don't know," he shrugged, then wiped fresh streams of water from my eyes. "But if you want it to stop—"

"I don't."

"Then why the hell are we talking about it?"

Because it feels too good to be true. Because this has to be some vivid dream.

I didn't say that though.

I said, "I don't know," which wasn't untrue.

But then his lips were on mine, and I didn't care to think about it anymore.

All I cared about was his tongue in my mouth and his arm around my waist, and kissing him back with just as much heat as he was giving me. I pressed myself against him, digging my fingers into the firm ridges of his body, tracing and caressing his slopes and lines.

A little surge of satisfaction rushed through me when I felt him growing hard against my stomach. That satisfaction spurred me to slip a hand between us, cupping him through the wet fabric of his boxers.

"*Shit,* Aly," he groaned against my mouth. "I promised myself I would stay out of you for at least a few days."

I nipped his bottom lip with my teeth, a trick I'd learned from him that night at my house. "Why would you do that, Maddox? Inside me is *exactly* where I'd like you to be."

For a moment, he went still, giving me a look that sent a ripple of fear over my soaked skin.

And then, he turned me around, pressing me against the smooth wall of the shower. Bra off, panties off, boxers off, and then he was inside me from behind, with none of the resistance of that first time, at my house. My body adjusted, happily contracting around him, adding to our natural, delectable friction.

"Feel good to you?"

Shit.

There was that question again, with a different object of my enjoyment this time.

"*Yesss,*" I whimpered, as his teeth sank into my shoulder.

Good wasn't the word though.

Incredible was a much more accurate depiction of what I was feeling as he stroked me from behind, hooking an arm under my thigh to lift it, giving him better access. I slipped a little on the wet floor, but Maddox had ahold of me, keeping me in place as he moved. Without my own leverage, I was powerless to do anything except take what he was giving – a position I wouldn't have given up for the world, at least not at that moment.

He turned me, urging my upper body down, with my hands pressed against the back of the shower. He moved behind me again, one arm around my waist, the other hand pressed to my clit as he slammed into me over, and over, and over until my thighs were trembling and I'd lost the strength to keep myself up. That was when he turned me around, hiking my legs around his waist to press me into the corner of the shower. We knocked into the shower sprayer, turning it right on us, but that was okay too.

Neither of us cared enough to move it.

He was buried in me so deep, pressed so close, our mouths fused so tightly together, he felt like a part of me I'd been missing without knowing it was gone. He stroked harder, faster, deeper, chasing whatever my body craved without me ever opening my mouth to say it. He just *knew*.

That freed my mouth for other things – kissing and moaning and yelling myself hoarse as he drove me right over my peak and kept going until he hit his. Even once we were done, we didn't pull apart – we stayed like that, exchanges slow kisses until the water went cold, and we had to get out.

"Hey, hold up," he called after me, when I tried to exit the bathroom in search of dry underwear. "I'm not done with you." He put his arms around me again, pulling me close in front of the mirror.

"What do you mean?" I asked, meeting his gaze in the mirror's reflection.

I must've sounded a little too eager, because he smirked as he pressed his lips to my neck, offering a few kisses before he looked up again.

"Time for conditioner. Then dinner."

SIXTEEN

After a week, Aly's grandmother passed.

It happened the day Mos and I were supposed to meet her – Nadiah had referred to it as a double date. We all rode out there together, intending to spend time visiting, and then have dinner out somewhere, as a group. It sounded nice, and seemed like it would make Aly happy, so it was fine by me.

But when we got there, and Ruby was the one to meet us at the door, I knew something was wrong.

So did Aly.

In the days after that, she cried about it, but mostly she was resolute. I didn't get the feeling she was just being strong for Nadiah – there was some of that, for sure, but this was something else.

Like she'd already conditioned herself into expecting it, so it wouldn't hurt so bad.

That was the part that kinda fucked with me, but I'd realized long ago that it was what this world did to you – it was damn near a defense mechanism. If you already expected the worst to happen, maybe it would lessen the effects on you.

Maybe.

In the meantime, it was a fucked-up way to live.

I was worried about her.

But then, she broke down in the ruins.

That was where they spread their grandmother's ashes, out into the water. It was a long hike – one Ches had an attitude about. To her, all she saw was me being off the grid yet again for a whole day. But after she pressed the issue, I made it clear I didn't give a fuck.

When the day came, I woke up knowing where I would be.

By Aly's side, while she and her sister paid their last respects.

The whole way there she was fine – it was the journey back that brought the breakdown.

And there wasn't shit I could do to make it better.

By the time we made it back to the *Burrows*, it was late, and all she wanted to do was sleep. Since the sisters – understandably – didn't want to be apart, I set them up in a bigger room than the one Nadiah had taken for herself, in the residential area of Ches' compound. And then, I left them to their grieving.

Since Ches was blowing me the fuck up anyway.

Even though I wasn't in the mood for whatever the hell might go on, I went anyway. I didn't want to have ignored something that created a worse mess that I'd be the one cleaning up later. When Mos wanted to tag along with me, I didn't object – something about Mos seemed to bring out her better behavior.

"It's about goddamn time," was the first thing out of her mouth when I walked through the door of her office. I was tempted to just turn around and walk right back out, but Mos clapped me on my shoulder, urging patience.

"What is it, Ches?" I asked, swallowing my agitation.

For Mosley's sake.

Her nose wrinkled. "Really? That's how you greet me now, no deference at all anymore?"

"Since when did deference become a requirement?" I countered, eyes narrowed. "What, you want me to bow to you or something?"

She stood, her bob swinging as she paced across the floor to where I was standing. "I *want* some goddamn respect. Ruby's knights bow to her."

Your ass ain't Ruby.

I wanted to say that shit, bad, and another day maybe I would've. But I was tired, and emotionally drained already, and I just didn't goddamn feel like doing this with her – since it seemed like *all* she wanted to do. So instead of saying the thing that would have taken a conversation I already didn't want to have into a conversation I *damn* sure didn't want to have, I said something else.

"That's never been the dynamic here."

Which was true.

In the entirety of her "reign", Ches had never treated me like I was one of her "subjects". I was the *prince*, the honored son and next in line to the throne, followed by Mos. Not that I was concerned about any perceived perks of that – outside of the obvious, of not being put in the position of an attack dog.

Or rather, *a lap* dog.

"What the hell do you mean, that's never been the dynamic?" she asked, turning to walk away, back to her desk. "What do you think we've been doing here?"

I crossed my arms. "I think I've had your back – from the moment Baron set you up with all this, even though the way you did Ruby was foul."

"You only think that because she made your dick hard. Your little crush had you under her spell."

I chuckled. "Ches, a *spell* isn't what made it dirty that you fucked your best friend's husband to use him for power."

"You call it dirty, *I* call it calculated. Shrewd. Getting what was mine, and you didn't use to have an issue with doing what was necessary to keep it. Or do you wanna act like *your* hands aren't dirty too?"

"I've never been on any snake shit Ches, and you know it. I've whooped ass, spilled blood, stolen, all that. Not proud of every moment, nah, but I got no problem admitting it. But fuck over somebody that trusted me? Nah – we're not the same when it comes to *that* shit."

Her nostrils flared as she shook her head. "No, we aren't. *You've changed.*"

My face pulled into a scowl. "*I've* changed? You hear this shit, Mos?"

Across the room, Mos shrugged, making it clear he wasn't trying to get pulled into it. I didn't blame him. Hell, I wanted *out*.

"Are you denying it?" she asked. "Cause it's plain as day – as soon as that little *bitch* showed up looking for her sister, you've been acting real different."

"*Watch your fuckin' mouth*," I growled, sparking a half second of fear behind her eyes before she smirked.

"See? *See*?" she said, directing her words at Mos. "*Watch my fuckin' mouth*?" she repeated. "Over a girl you've known... two months? Is the pussy *that* good, goddamn!"

"Ches, *chill*," Mos urged, sitting forward in his chair. "Come on, this is us, you don't have to get like this."

"Oh shut the fuck up," she snapped at him with a snarl. "You've been so busy face deep in that other girl's pussy you've barely come up for air. I knew better than to let you have her."

Mos drew his head back. "*Let?*"

"Yes, *let*," she said. "You have a fucking job here, remember? I thought maybe she could help, but it looks like she's just another distraction."

"I'm here because I *want* to be, Ches," Mos said, quietly–not to be confused with meek, or timid. He was mild, and no lie, I felt a certain responsibility to protect him. But I'd also raised him to let nobody – not me, not Ches – walk over him. "The minute that changes, I will walk outta here and not look back – or what... you gonna *force* me to do something for you? Huh? Have you climbed so high *you're* the slaver now?"

That seemed to bring her back to earth. Ches swallowed hard, shaking her head. "Mos, I—"

"I will slit whoever's throat I have to – mine or yours – but I will *never* be controlled – mentally or physically – again. We have to be clear on that."

"Of course, Mos," she said, with a measured, sympathetic smile that didn't reach her eyes. "I'm sorry. I was upset, and I spoke out of turn – you're free to do as you wish – I can only hope that those wishes still fall in line with our family's best interests."

So we're family again now?

I fought the gaping urge to roll my eyes at that shit while Mos nodded.

"They always have. For me, and for Maddox."

Ches didn't bother with the fake smile when her gaze came back to me. "Is *that* right?"

I scoffed. "Yeah, believe it or not. Even though I thought your shit was foul, I rocked with you out of loyalty, and lately? Hell, *I* have been acting more in your 'best interests' than you have. I'm trying to keep a bullet out of your back."

"Oh *God*," she groaned. "Here you go again with this – how many times will I have to tell you – you don't understand. *Nobody* likes a leader when they're in the process of gaining power. But they either fall in line, or they get crushed underfoot."

"How do you plan to make them?" I asked. "Fall in line, that is?"

She smiled. "I'm glad you asked." With a huff, she rounded her desk, opening a drawer to pull a folder out. "From *Division Four*," she said, pulling a glossy printed picture out, and laying it on top of the desk.

Weapons.

A *lot* of weapons.

"From *four*?" I asked, incredulous. "Sula Archer is gonna sell weapons to you, that's what you're telling me?"

She shook her head. "No. Sula Archer's soldiers are."

I looked at Mos to make sure I wasn't losing it, but he was wearing the same skeptical expression I was. "That sounds like a setup."

Something she *should* be familiar with, since over the last year she'd gotten good at it.

"It's *not*," she insisted. "I've done due diligence and made sure – they don't care about loyalty – they care about *money*."

"Which is gonna come from *where*, when all our shit is drying up because nobody wants to fuck with you anymore?" I asked. "This is what I'm talking about, Ches!"

"*I* will worry about that part," she said, nodding. I couldn't pinpoint why, but something about her sudden shift concerned me to the point of discomfort. "You just be ready to make this happen when I need you. I trust nobody else to do this for me. Give me a few weeks to get the money – you get the weapons. And get ready to turn my babies into an *army*."

"Soldiers die." I met her gaze, trying to figure out what was going on in her head. "Is that what you're looking for? That's what you want?"

"Of course not," she snapped. "But they know what they signed up for – sometimes casualties are necessary for war, and their sacrifice will not be in vain. Will you help me or not? I can get someone else to do it..."

"Nah," I told her. "I got it."

I'd studied, and practiced, and bled – I knew the ins and outs better than anyone she might convince to step up.

I would do it if for no other reasons than to save the lives of the people who'd stayed loyal to Ches.

"You sure you don't need to run it by Aly first?"

I didn't respond to that because it would only prolong a conversation I was already well past over. Instead, I turned, pushing my way through the doors of her office.

I needed to punch something.

I could smell blood as I walked into the warehouse.

From the outside, it *looked* abandoned, but you could hear the crowd, buzzing with commentary and excitement about the last fight. They were rowdy, and drunk, packed tight between the unfinished walls, crowding the bar for more of the free-flowing liquor they'd already paid for with the cover charge.

Another one of Ches' enterprises.

But I wasn't trying to think about that – I was focused on the smell of violence.

That shit was more than a little intoxicating, and I breathed it in, deep – blood, sweat, liquor, half-rusted metal from the cage. I pressed through the crowd, seeing nothing but my destination – the man standing off to side, with a mangled clipboard in his hand.

"Bash. What's up?" I asked, shaking hands with him as I approached.

"Nigga, everything now that you came through – I should ask what's up with *you*. You only show up when you're working out aggression, and you've been here a lot," he remarked, in his musical division four accent.

I shrugged. "Just trying to get what I can before you pack it up and move on," I told him, which was half true. "What you got for me? Can you get me in?"

Bash scoffed. "You know better, Mad. We can *always* make room for your wild ass. Hell, I got a big motherfucker fresh outta the camps in *ten*, just itching for a fight. If you're ready, you can go now."

With no hesitation, I pulled off my sweatshirt. My hair was already out of the way.

"Always ready," I told Bash, handing my stuff to Mosley, who'd followed me here from *Underground*. He took it without a word, knowing it was useless to talk me out of it. "Let's go."

"*Yooooo!*" Sebastian screamed into the mic he'd had tucked into his pocket. "We got Maddox Hatcher in the building one more fucking time. Place your bets *now*."

He said some shit about my impending opponent – shit I didn't care about, so I tuned him out. It didn't matter who it was – what mattered was that in just a few minutes, I'd get to work all my frustration with Ches out on someone trying to do the same thing, which made it equitable.

The crowd wanted entertainment, Bash wanted to make a cut off of it, I wanted to kick somebody's ass, and whoever was coming in this ring with me wanted their ass kicked.

It was a perfect setup.

Everybody left a winner.

Once upon a time, I'd gone into the cage for fun – for the thrill of broken bones and splattered blood, for the pussy thrown at me because I'd won, for that status of being the man on top. Now though, it was different. Win or lose – once you stepped out, you were too tired to be pissed anymore.

The shit was therapy now.

They closed me in with some big motherfucker that looked like *two* big motherfuckers put together. That was fine though – he may have been bigger than me, but being big made him slow, and he didn't seem to be that bright either.

His big ass could hit though.

I discovered that when I stumbled backward a little, dodging a different blow. He landed the second, which I hadn't seen coming, catching me under the chin with a jab that made my teeth rattle.

Wouldn't make *that* mistake again.

Not in my damn face. I took a few body shots, enjoying the numbing quality of the pain that came after, but I knew better than to do that too often. Only when I needed the opening, knowing he pulled back from his blows so slowly it gave me time to land three or four of my own. In between those, I kept him moving around the ring, tiring his big ass out while I jabbed and crossed, rearranging his face to a satisfying pulp.

Bare hands.

Bare feet.

No protective gear, none of that shit.

Just bruised, bloody knuckles, sore ribs, and a swollen jaw, by the time Bash stepped into the ring, holding my arm up to declare me the winner while my big lump of an opponent lay motionless at my feet.

I felt a *lot* better.

Much of that good feeling – that endorphin high – dissipated as soon as I stepped out of the ring. I was searching the crowd for Mos, ready to have a drink or two and then get the fuck out of there.

My gaze fell on Aly instead.

I could have handled it *much* better if the look on her face was horror. That was a common reaction to watching people draw blood from each other on purpose. And that reaction wasn't wrong – the shit was barbaric, honestly.

That wasn't it though.

Maybe it was still the grief of spreading her grandmother's ashes earlier, or maybe she was tired, or confused, or maybe I was trying to find any explanation other than the obvious.

She looked *disappointed.*

That fucked with me.

A lot.

Or maybe I was projecting.

Whatever it was, she didn't crack the slightest smile as I climbed down, to move toward where she, Mos, and Nadiah were standing. Wordlessly, she handed me the stuff I'd originally given Mos, and I put it all on, swallowing the burning question in my mind, since I would've had to shout it to ask it.

What the hell are they doing here?

A familiar face – two familiar faces – caught my attention at the bar, answering the question for me anyway.

Goddamn twins.

"Do you wanna go?" was the question I *did* ask, when Aly's face still hadn't changed by the time I was dressed again. She reached up, swiping a hand along my jaw, and when she pulled back, her fingers were streaked with blood.

"Yeah," she nodded. "I wanna go."

So we left.

We walked back to my place in overwhelming silence I didn't know how to counteract because I wasn't sure what was going on in her head. As I walked, my knuckles raw and stinging in the cold air, going to the cages seemed like less and less of a good idea.

I felt like shit.

Mentally, and physically now.

At my place, Aly still had nothing to say. She took me to the bathroom and tugged me outta my clothes and hers, and we showered. She cleaned my bleeding hands, and bandaged them, and bandaged the cut on my jaw too. And then, on my couch, she sat and looked me right in the face, finally asking a question.

"Does it make you feel better?"

My eyebrow went up. "What, the fighting?"

"Yeah."

I shrugged. "Depends. Most of the time, yeah."

"Do the women ever fight? Do they allow that?"

Frowning, I looked into her eyes, trying to figure out where the hell she was going with this, because she *couldn't* be going where I thought she was going. "Yeah, women fight all the time. More vicious than the guys, actually."

She nodded. "Okay. How do I sign up?"

"Aly, *what*?" I laughed, shaking my head. "Nah, that's not... *nah.*"

"Why not?" she asked. "Mos said you fight to escape. Because you're angry. Well, I'm a little fucking angry too."

"You're gonna go get beat up because you're mad at me for beating somebody up?"

Her face pulled into a scowl. "No, *asshole.* First – I can probably fight. *Probably.* Second – nobody's mad at you."

"You know what... you could probably hold your own, with the right motivation. Otherwise nah babe. But what are you mad about?"

She pushed out a sigh, dropping her gaze to her hands. "I'm mad at Gran. For leaving us. I'm mad at her body, for betraying her. For getting sick. I'm mad at the Apex for making everything so fucking *horrible*, and making the medicine and care so expensive. I'm mad at her for not telling me everything she could've. Things she *should've*. I'm mad at myself for being mad about it. I'm mad about a *lot*. Where's my escape?"

"Somewhere *healthy*," I countered. "Not somewhere that will leave you bloody, with a fucked-up face."

"So it's fine for you, but not for me. Got it," she snapped, pushing herself up. I was quick though, grabbing her and pulling her right back down to my lap.

"It's not fine for me either," I admitted. "But it's how I cope when I need to, without getting lost in liquor, or pills, or pu..." I let that trail off, knowing that wasn't a good line of conversation to open – not when Aly was on edge like this.

I hadn't caught myself in time though.

"Pussy, huh?" she asked. "Why didn't you go for some of that? There were women all over the place, salivating over you outside that cage. Pussy galore."

"The only pussy I *want* was supposed to be in the bed, resting, after a hard day," I told her – I had no problem being up front.

"So you beat somebody with your bare hands instead? That sounds logical to you?"

I shook my head. "Who the fuck said anything about logic, Aly? It's *not* logical, and neither is this conversation – I feel like you're talking around whatever the hell your problem is, instead of just laying it out!"

"That's what you want? You want me to just lay it out?"

Based on her tone and volume... shit, *did* I want her to lay it out?

Before I could offer an answer, she was up, off my lap. I intended to reach for her again, but I couldn't do anything but sit back, surprised.

She was taking her clothes off.

Maybe clothes was an overstatement, since she was just in panties and one of my shirts, but she had both off in a flash, and was back in my lap, tugging my boxers down. I was confused as hell, but it took nothing for my body to respond to her, allowing her to sink onto me with a deep sigh as I anchored my hands at her hips, stopping her before she moved.

"Aly, what the fuck is going on?"

She shook her head, then looked up to meet my eyes. "I don't know. But I don't drink, or do drugs, and you don't want me to fight. I *need* the escape though. So, pussy it is, I guess."

"You mean... nevermind."

I lessened my grip and let her move.

There was no competition – the warm, slick tightness between her thighs was a helluva lot better than being in a sweaty cage with another guy. She settled into me, barely moving, but with the pain in my side, that was fine.

I let her go like she wanted.

And even though it hurt like a bitch because of my jaw, when she kissed me, I kissed her back, with everything I had to give.

I wrapped my arms around her, holding her tight when she buried her face in my neck, crying, but still moving, still looking for the escape. I took over, stroking up, and up, and up, until her nails dug into my shoulders, thighs tightening on either side of mine. This differed from before – no sweat, no cursing, no words at all. Just a quiet, necessary release.

She didn't move, and I didn't either – after a few minutes had passed, I realized her exhaustion, mental and physical, had gotten the better of her.

She was asleep.

Instead of trying to move, I reached for the blanket at the end of the couch, pulling it over both of us, so I could join her.

SEVENTEEN

I could listen to her talk about him all day.

Between us, I'd call Nadiah the "fun" one – the one who knew people, the social one. But I'd never heard anyone make her gush the way she was, as we walked side by side down a *Burrows* sidewalk, headed to breakfast. Sure, she'd talked about Mos a lot after that initial trip here, when they first met. But now that they could be *together*?

She had stars in her eyes, and I loved it.

"We should find a place, you know?" I asked her as we turned a corner. "Here, in the *Burrows*. It's been like two weeks now, and if we're making this permanent, we should have something of our own. I have to figure out how much a place costs..."

Nadiah raised her eyebrows at me. "Why? What's wrong with the setup we have now? I'm helping with the internet set up with Ches' people, so I can stay there as long as I want, and be close to Mos. Are you not happy staying with Maddox anymore? Are you two having problems?"

"No, not at all," I smirked. *Problem* was not the word for what Maddox and I were having, probably much too often. So often it was probably clouding our judgment. "I know we're post-apocalypse and all, but it's too soon for us to be living together. I don't want us to get tired of each other."

"You're feeling like that?"

"No, but I want to get ahead of it, I think. I've never had an adult relationship, and I move in with the first one? It's not sensible."

Nadiah shrugged. "Who the hell *cares*, Aly? Look at what's going on around us – yes, we had to lay Gran to rest last week, which still hurts, but the *other* things? We're free. We're walking to breakfast, at a restaurant. There are kids playing together over there," she pointed. "And look at *that* – according to the sign, that is a whole café, just for *coffee*. Six months ago, would any of this have sounded possible to you?"

"No. No, you're right, but it feels too good to be true. Like this has come way too easily. It hasn't been expensive enough."

Nadiah sucked her teeth. "Uh, have you forgotten the tunnels already? Forgotten Adam Bishop at our door?"

"Of course not," I told her. "That's not what I'm saying."

"Then what *are* you saying?"

"*Ugh.*" I adjusted the straps of my backpack as we headed up another street. After breakfast, we were supposed to go shopping, to replace our toiletries and other little things we needed. I was looking forward to filling my bag and still having money left, but honestly the sheer possibility of that only contributed to my current feeling. "I'm just waiting on the other shoe to drop. Because there's no way it isn't coming."

"What if they already have?" Nadiah pressed. "And you're doing all this worrying for nothing?"

"I don't think so."

Nadiah stopped walking, to laugh. "Wow. What did Maddox do?"

"Huh?" I asked, turning to face her. "What does that mean?"

"It *means* he must have made you feel some kind of amazing if you're looking for the trap, wondering if it's a setup. So what did he do?"

What *hadn't* he done?

I sighed. "It's stupid."

"I bet it's not."

"It is though."

She shrugged. "Fine. But tell me anyway."

Okay.

I'd woken up in bed alone.

Which, wasn't abnormal at all – I knew where Maddox was, because I could hear him on the other side of the wall partition, working out. So I got up to watch, just like I had several mornings since I arrived, because watching his display of incredible strength, his muscles flexing, sweat dripping off his beautiful skin...

It was a nice way to wake up.

When Maddox worked out at home, he played music on a little speaker – he explained that it was so the cords of the earbuds didn't get in his way. He played it low – for my sake, since it was early, and it was always hip hop, with heavy up-tempo beats that created a certain vibe.

I bumped the speaker.

Well, I knocked over the whole setup, actually, and it cut to a different song. Luckily, it was the end of his workout anyway so I hadn't interrupted anything – he laughed. Teased me about being clumsy. And let the song play while he cleant up the space, and I went to make us coffee.

It was a beautiful song – a *love* song. I couldn't help smiling over it when the woman sang a line about her lover being the coffee she needed in the morning, and sunshine in the rain. I stopped what I was doing to listen, my face growing warm as the lyrics sank into me, about someone being the best part of your life.

And then I realized Maddox had stopped too, to listen.

And stare at me.

Water in the desert.

Pain relief.

I'll follow you anywhere.

That was the gist, and Maddox was looking at *me*.

And then he was *on* me, and *in* me, sweaty and salty, but I didn't care about that at all. What I cared about was his sudden, driving need to be inside me while *that* song was playing, while these lovers gave a back-and-forth plea to hear their love declared out loud.

"You see now why I said it was stupid?" I asked Nadiah, once I'd finished telling the story. I expected her to nod along, agreeing because she got me, but no.

"If *that* is stupid, sign me up," she said. "Because *oh my God*, I know which song you're talking about, and... *oh my God*. You two are getting married."

"Please don't do that," I groaned. "We've been here two weeks. I've only known this man existed for *two months*."

"That means *nothing*," Nadiah countered. "I *cannot* believe that happened this morning and your reaction is that me and you should find a place together. Have you *lost* it?"

"That question presumes I had *it* in the first place, little sister."

"You know, you're right."

I sucked my teeth. "That's *not* what you were supposed to say. You're supposed to be reassuring me!"

"I'm not reassuring *shit* for you," Nadiah laughed. "That strong, sexy, *sweet* man thinks you're the best part of his life and you want to move in with your little sister."

"In my defense, what I *want* is my little sister out of Franchesca Catlan's house, because I don't trust that lady – I just led with the other stuff, okay?" I told her, motioning for us to walk again.

"Ches isn't that bad – she has a hard exterior."

I grunted. "Sure."

"I'm serious," Nadiah insisted. "Do you know how Maddox and Mosley ended up with her?"

I nodded. Maddox had told me a little of the story late one night. "Well, I know about Maddox, but not about Mos."

"Probably because it's awful. And not his story to tell I guess, and I won't go into detail either, but they rescued him from the *Apex*. He was in schooling there, early, being forced to code, and develop tech, and all that. But it wasn't *just* that. Tall, handsome black kid... you *know* what they made him do, right?"

I sighed. "I can imagine, unfortunately."

"Yeah. He was only fifteen when Maddox and Ches got him and few other kids out. He hasn't been back to the *Apex* since. Won't even go into the *Mids*. Too close."

"Wow."

"Right. I know Ches is a little hard, but she rescued him, and a lot of the others, from horrible situations. She can't be all bad, right?"

"I don't know her well enough to answer that question," I admitted. "I just know I've never gotten a great vibe, like there's an ulterior motive with her. And let's not forget that *she* was the one who drove Maddox into a goddamn *cage fight*."

Nadiah sucked her teeth. "From the way the bets went, it seemed like Mad is a regular around there. And besides that, you *know* watching him beat that guy up made you hot. Grief or not."

"*Even so...*"

"Uh-huh," Nadiah laughed. "Seriously though – maybe if you came around, you could catch her vibe better, you know? Maybe have dinner or something?"

"We'll see," I conceded with a sigh, as we turned another corner, onto a smaller street. We were almost at *Café Azul*, the restaurant where Maddox had taken me to meet Blue when we were here the first time. I remembered the food smelling amazing, and had wanted to come back since then – I was happy for the chance to bring Nadiah.

But something was wrong.

"I think we're being followed," I told her. I slapped a grin on my face as I turned to look behind us, hoping it wouldn't raise any suspicion.

At first, Nadiah laughed, but when I didn't join her, her eyes went wide. "Oh, you're... you're *serious?*"

"Yes," I hissed. "There are two guys. They've turned every time we turned, stopped every time we stopped. I think they're trailing us."

"Why though? Do you think maybe the guys did this? For protection."

I shook my head. "I told Mad where we were going – if he thought I needed protection to get there, I feel like he would have said something. Or escorted us here himself. No, this is something else."

"Something like what?"

"I don't know."

The hairs on the back of my neck stood up, and I glanced back at the same time a dark van turned onto the narrow street, approaching us from behind. So far, my instincts had been too on point to not trust them now.

"Nadiah, listen – get to the end of the block – that stop sign right there. Make a left and keep going. Do *not* stop until you get to *Café Azul* and ask for Blue. If he's there, mention me, mention Maddox."

The van was on a slow creep, but still coming, as if it were waiting for a certain moment. I didn't have to glance back to know the guys I'd noticed were getting closer.

"*Aly...*" Nadiah said, but I shook my head as I pulled my backpack from my shoulders.

"Just do what I said, please. I'm about to stop walking – you keep going. Once you get past that trash can – *run.* As fast as you can go, okay?"

"I... okay."

I nodded, and stopped, unzipping my bag. "Go."

She did.

I let my gaze drop into my backpack, rifling around in it until my hand closed around what I was looking for.

"Can I help you guys?" I asked the two men following us as I let the bag drop to the ground. Behind me, I heard the change happen as Nadiah's footsteps turned into a sprint. "Uh-uh-uh," I said, brandishing that rusted chair leg I'd kept all this time, just in case it came in handy again. They intended to follow her, but were surprised enough by me turning on them with a weapon that neither tried to pass. "I *asked* if I could help you."

They wore masks now. They hadn't before, when they were keeping enough distance that their features were hard to make out. The van was still a little further back, idling. Waiting.

To take me and Nadiah.

It was two – maybe three, or more – against one. I'd faced those odds before, and knew my chances weren't great, but they weren't just going to stand here long.

I had to act now.

Instead of trying to get close, I used the bit of distance in my favor, cranking the chair leg over my shoulder and then throwing it, beaning one man right between the eyes. Whoever was driving the truck must've seen that, because it sped toward us now, as the guy who wasn't writhing on the ground, holding his head, reached to grab me.

Without thinking twice about it, I aimed my knee for his groin, as hard as I could – he went down as soon as the blow connected. I didn't stop for my bag, I took off, following the same directions I'd given Nadiah – get down the street, turn at the stop sign, don't stop until you get to the café, not for anything.

The guys hadn't stayed down long.

They were right on my tail, declaring me all kinds of vulgar names as I sprinted down the street, lungs burning. As I approached it, I wasn't sure why I thought *Café Azul* would be some sanctuary, but it was the only thing I had to hold on to at the moment. I had to *try*.

For all I knew I was walking right into a net – nothing was stopping them from coming in after me, and I was leading them right to Nadiah. Still, something akin to relief twisted in my gut as

I snatched the front door open, tripping over the mat as I ran inside.

When I hit the ground, I knew it was over – the door hadn't closed behind me. But when I turned to look out of the front glass, I saw the guys who'd been chasing me climbing into the van before it sped off.

My relief was short-lived though.

I was snatched up from the ground by beefy-looking men in sweat suits and dragged through the back halls of the restaurant while I struggled. It wasn't until they pulled me into a familiar, smoke-filled room that I settled some, my heart still racing as they deposited me in front of Blue, who took a long drag from his hookah.

"Alyson Little. I see you found yourself."

"What?"

I glanced where he pointed, to where Nadiah was sitting a few feet away, eyes wide.

"Last time I saw you, you thought you were looking for her, right? There she is, right there – you welcome for that."

I swallowed my annoyance, remembering it wouldn't get me anywhere with him. "You didn't find her – I sent her to you," I said. "For *help*. Unless you're part of this too."

"I heard her story." He blew out several rings of smoke. "But remember not to play too close with fire, Alyson Little, don't get burned. I don't take part in criminal activities of that nature, and I don't fuck with that implication, you feel me?"

"I do. I'm sorry. But I just almost got snatched and shoved in a van – you'll have to forgive my impropriety," I told him, nostrils flared.

"Already forgiven, any friend of young Maddox is a friend of mine – every friend of the kid can't say that though. I don't like that."

"Meaning what? One of his friends did this?"

"Don't put words in my mouth Alyson Little, I don't like that."

I sighed. "Do you know who did this? Or *why*?"

"I *don't* know who did this Alyson, and I don't like that. I got a vital tenet for you though – you got a price on your head. Heard it this morning from my scouts – you shouldn't be exposed like this without protection. If I know, Ches knows. And if Ches knows, she didn't tell young Maddox. He wouldn't have let you out the house."

"Do you think Ches is behind this?"

"I can't speak on that – all I can tell you is that a snake in the grass will eat however many birds it finds in the bush, and take the bird out of your hand too, you feel me?"

My eyes narrowed as my brain twisted and turned around his words, finding the underlying meaning in Blue's blended idioms. After a moment, I nodded.

"Yeah. I feel you. And I need a favor."

"Lay it out there, Alyson Little, what is it you need?"

"I need to call someone."

"Which one do you think I should reach out to first?"

Ches posed that question from across her desk, where a map of *The Americas* was spread out. This was a specialized one – the *Divisions*, one through ten, were clearly marked, but this one had the added details of listing the people who ran them, the way their territories were laid out, and the valuable resources each division produced.

I was proud of her.

This was more like the shit she used to do – actual strategy.

"I've been thinking about what you said, about needing to mend fences, and I think you're right," she admitted, after a deep sigh.

"Once we're armed, I want to rebuild alliances. I sent Tremaine's husband back to her, and I won't tell Sula that her people sold me the weapons," she said, dead serious. "So those are possibilities, right? And what about Mal? Division five."

I nodded. "Mal is a possibility."

The only possibility.

There was little chance either of the other women would spit on Ches if she was on fire, let alone align themselves with her. But I wasn't going to blow her vibe when it was obvious she was trying.

"And maybe Lowe, from seven. Or Hunter, up in two. The men don't get bogged down in the pettiness, you know? They want to make money and maybe get a little sniff, huh?" she joked, which... *wow*.

"What has you in such a good mood?" I asked, and she grinned.

"Just looking forward to the next few weeks – this will be an exciting time, Mad – we're *building*, without stopping to ask permission. I'm going to need you focused."

"As long as there's a plan, and we're keeping shit legitimate, you don't have to worry about me."

Whatever she planned to say was interrupted by her pager going off. A few seconds later, Mos burst through the door of the office, out of breath and panting, holding up a tablet in his hand. "The *Apex* put a bounty out, on Nadiah and Aly," he announced, turning the screen in our direction. There were pictures, in the braids they'd both abandoned since then, but still.

"How the hell did we not already know this?" I asked, turning to Ches, who looked up from her pager, eyes wide.

"This is the kind of things my scouts in the *Apex* should have warned me about. What is that you're looking at?" she asked Mos, pointing to the tablet. "How did you get that?"

"Nadiah and I were putting in some work, after hours. Not just to get our own internet going for the *Burrows*, but to see if we could tap into the *Apex*. I didn't want to get any hopes up, but we got it this morning. Well, we almost got it, but then Nadiah was meeting up with Aly, and I wanted to keep going – to keep working on it. I pulled up their news, and *this* is the first thing I saw. They've turned them into some public enemy, and even if the *APF* can't operate here..."

"It doesn't mean someone won't try to deliver them, to get the money," Ches finished, saying what I was thinking. I looked down at my pager, buzzing at my waist. "Many people around here wouldn't blink an eye about it, if this gets around."

"It's already around," I barked, standing up as my eyes scanned the message on my screen again. "This is from Blue – Aly and Nadiah are there. Somebody tried to grab them on their way to break-fast, in a black van." I turned to Ches. "How the *fuck* did we not know about this?!"

"I'm trying to find out now," she said, pointing at her own pager. "In the meantime, you need to go get them – bring them here, they'll be safe. No one will try anything *here*."

She was right – they'd have to be crazy, and even crazy mother-fuckers could end up dead.

I grabbed a set of keys from the wall, knowing I'd want the protection of a vehicle instead of my bike, and I'd need the room too.

"You coming with me?" I asked Mos, who agreed.

"He'll be right back," Ches said, stepping forward. "If you've got internet access inside the *Apex*, we need to talk."

"That shit can wait." I motioned for him to come on. "Like you said – we'll be right back."

I knew Blue was good people, no matter how much he got on my nerves. He wouldn't let anybody touch Aly or Nadiah, and I was beyond relieved that they'd got to him. But the more I thought about it, the more I grew concerned about Aly's mental state.

In just a short time, she'd been through a *lot*.

It had to be taking a toll on her.

Mos and I were headed downstairs when the front doors to the compound opened. I took the last steps two at a time, already pulling my gun from my holster – nobody came through the front like that unannounced.

Except, apparently, Aly and Nadiah.

"Go get your stuff," Aly told Nadiah, wearing a stony expression that didn't change when she looked in my direction. It took a second to realize she wasn't looking at me – Ches had come out of the office and was a few steps behind me.

"Well, we're glad to see you're safe, but what is *this* about?" Ches asked, stepping forward. "You burst through my front door, demanding people around my house... it could be considered rude."

Aly's face broke into the slightest smile. "Yes, I suppose it could. We'll be leaving shortly. Nadiah?"

Nadiah had stopped moving when Ches spoke, and now appeared torn. It was obvious she wanted to follow Aly's directions, but didn't want to offend Ches, since this *was* her house.

Ches saw it too.

"Nadiah," she spoke, her tone coated in honey. "I thought I'd been a gracious host. You've had the run of the house, we've kept you fed, and warm. I've never once questioned your relationship or access to Mos – you've been treated well. What on earth would make you want to leave like *this*?"

Nadiah straightened, giving Ches a curious look. "Leave *how*, Ches? We came through the front door. I'm getting my things. I'm going with my sister. Is there something offensive about that?"

I looked to Ches, wondering the same thing, and she shifted under the weight of everyone's gaze.

"No, I guess not. It just seems rather abrupt. Especially after you supposedly got chased down for an attempted abduction."

Aly scoffed. "Supposedly? There's no question about it. There's a *bounty* on our heads. Blue knew about it. He was surprised *you* didn't."

"Maybe his scouts are better than mine," Ches shrugged. "But a bounty on your head only makes it more ridiculous for Nadiah to pack up and leave – it's safer here than out there. For both of you as a matter of fact. You should stay too, Aly. Here with your sister."

"We'll pass."

Ches smiled. "Oh, but I insist. See, you're affiliated with me, and it's not good for business if people think I can't protect my own. You'll stay. Both of you."

"We *won't*," Aly countered, stepping forward. "Nadiah – get your shit and *let's go*. Thank you for your hospitality, Ches, but you can consider any 'affiliation' my sister and I have with you, dissolved. Your kindness has been appreciated."

You could hear a pin drop.

I defied Ches all the time, because I had the leeway to do so, built up over years of loyalty. Nobody else – besides Mos – went against her like this, because they were all scared.

But Aly wasn't scared of *shit* when it came to protecting her sister.

Nadiah scurried off to the room she'd been using, with Mos right on her heels, to help, and to talk. I moved toward Aly, wanting to know what had her ready to force the issue of Nadiah not staying with Ches anymore. And if the plan was that they'd both be staying with me.

"So where will you be staying now?" Ches called out before I could ask myself. "Since my home is not good enough for you and your precious sister anymore."

Aly turned to her, stone-faced. "Ruby's."

If looks could kill, Ches would have dropped Aly with the glare she gave upon hearing Ruby's name. "Ruby Hartford? The woman who had your sister working as a whore until you came to her rescue?"

Ches knew that shit wasn't true, but she threw the jab anyway, thinking it would land – that first day in the *Burrows*, it would've.

This wasn't the same Aly though.

This Aly grinned at that shit. "Yeah. Ruby Hartford. Says a lot, doesn't it?"

"Oh, you've started wearing big girl panties now, have you?" Ches asked, stalking down the rest of the steps. "This is cute and all, but take heed, *little girl* – I'm not an enemy you want."

"You're right, Ches. You're not. Which is why there hasn't been a single *shred* of unprovoked hostility on my part. So if the venom is getting to be too much for you – I would suggest you put away your own fangs."

With her face pulled into a snarl, Ches opened her mouth to counter Aly's response. Whatever she was about to say, it was interrupted by the buzzing of her pager. She whipped it in front her face, eyes narrowed at whatever she saw on the screen.

"I have something to handle. Make sure your sister takes *all* her shit when she leaves."

"Won't be a problem," Aly countered.

One last eye roll and Ches was gone, leaving me to turn to Aly with my eyes wide.

"Damn – did you have to come at her like *that*?" I asked, and she nodded.

"Yes, actually. Ches is the type of woman you can't show any fear. I had to make it clear to her I wasn't scared, and wasn't backing down, even though..." She sighed, and shook her head.

"What?" I asked. "Why are you so hell-bent on going to stay with *Ruby*, of all people?"

"Because *Ruby* isn't trying to kidnap me!"

My eyes went wide. "Aly, you *can't* think Ches..."

"I don't know *what* to think, Mad. All I wanted to do was have breakfast this morning, and instead I'm throwing chair legs!"

"*What*?!"

She shook her head. "Nevermind. Just know whoever tried us this morning? One of them will have an ugly knot tomorrow, and the other will have a sore dick."

"You *fought them*?"

"*I had to*," she insisted. "Not that I'd call it fighting so much as quick instincts. But whatever you want to call it, I am sick to death of having to do it. I thought I would be safe here, Mad, and it doesn't look like that's the case."

I grabbed her hands, squeezing them between mine. "I get your reservations, I swear I do. But you don't have to pack up and leave, go all the way out to *Ruby's*. She lives on the other end of the *Burrows*! I know you don't like Ches, but you *will* be safe here."

"Maddox, what if I told you I saw one of those kiss print neck tattoos, on one of the attackers? Would that change your mind?"

"*Did you* see one?" I countered.

"Maybe." She sighed. "They had on masks, covering half of their faces. But I struggled with one, before I tried to put my knee through his pelvis. The mask got pulled up, and it could've been something else. *Could've* been. But I need something more concrete than that. I *know* Ruby wouldn't do something like this. I can't say the same for Ches."

I didn't want to let the shit go.

At all.

But I knew it wouldn't go the way I *wanted* it to go if I pressed.

She and Nadiah would both be safe with Ruby – I didn't doubt that for a second. My only other reasons for pushing the issue would be trying to force her to trust Ches, or forcing her to do what *I* wanted her to do, and I wasn't trying to drive down either of those lanes.

I knew better.

"Okay. Let me take you."

She smiled and shook her head. "Our ride is waiting outside. I contacted Ruby from Blue's place, and she sent someone to meet us here."

"Damn. So you were pretty decided, huh?"

"I was," she nodded. "And I hope that's not something you're going to take personally."

"Not at all." I grabbed her chin, tipping it so her head was held high. "I like it. Good girl from the *Mids* fucked around and got a little *bad girl* in her now."

She smiled.

Beautiful ass smile.

"Actually, I fucked around and got a little bad *boy* from the *Burrows* in me, and I mean... you see how that turned out."

I laughed, leaning in to press a kiss to her lips. There was more I wanted to do – and say – but I heard Mos and Nadiah approaching, so I tucked it in for another time.

"I'll see you tomorrow," I said, kissing her temple.

Her smile melted into a smirk, and one of her eyebrows hiked up. "Are you telling me, or asking me?"

"*Telling.*"

She bit down on her lip as she looked at me, then pulled in a sigh.

"Then I guess I'll see you tomorrow."

EIGHTEEN

I was in front of Ruby Hartford's house at the crack of dawn.

I paged Aly, and she came through those regal front doors smiling, ready to go.

Like she'd been waiting for me.

She was wearing the same jacket and boots as the first time I met her, but the braids were gone now, replaced by her crown of natural hair, styled into a fro.

Her eyes were different too now – that wide-eyed wonder was gone, replaced with the practicality and cynicism that would keep her alive in a world like this. But there was something else too when she met my gaze.

Deep affection.

Mutual affection.

"You came to get me on your bike," she said as she approached. "I'm surprised."

"I came to *see* you," I corrected. "I didn't think you'd want to leave."

She shrugged. "Nadiah was wrapped up all night back and forth with Mos on some tablet he gave her, and while I trust Ruby not to hand me over to the *Apex*, she's not the warm and fuzziest company."

"Ah. So you were bored?"

Aly shook her head. "Not exactly. For the first time in a while though, I felt a little lonely."

"Why didn't you say something?"

"How, on the pager? Isn't it for emergencies?"

I reached for her hand, pulling her close enough to tuck under my arm. "Do you think I don't consider your feelings an emergency?"

"Mad..."

"I'm *serious*," I insisted. "If we're apart, and you need – or want – to talk, I consider it a priority, because I consider *you* a priority."

"We've known each other for like two seconds."

I scoffed. "Okay, so tell me the appropriate length of time for me to feel how I feel about you. Can you write a timeline for me?"

"You *know* I can't."

"Okay, then stop playing and accept my untimely feelings for what they are. I don't care if we're not level with it right now, you'll catch up."

She tipped her head back, a smile on her lips as she met my gaze. "I didn't say that."

"Didn't say what?"

"Didn't call your feelings premature or unreciprocated."

I frowned. "Okay then, '*we met two seconds ago*' was...?"

"An observation."

"Okay," I nodded. "I have an observation too."

She tipped her head to the side. "What is it?"

"You are *really fucking beautiful.*"

"*Stop*," she laughed, wriggling in my arms as I planted a kiss against her neck. "You play too much."

"I'm not playing. *You* play too much," I countered. "Ms. Pointless Observations."

"*Pointless?*" Her eyes went wide. "There was a point, excuse you!"

"Okay then, tell me your point."

"It was *going* to be that it was sweet, and flattering, that you felt that way about me after such a short time, but *nevermind* – it's pointless," she said, ducking under my arm to escape my hold.

"Nah hold up, I take that word back, let's rewind."

She laughed as I stepped away from the bike to catch her again, this time wrapping both arms around her waist. "Nuh-uh, Mad, you said what you said."

"Did I really though? You have a witness to back that up?"

"*See,*" she giggled. "Like I said – you play too much."

"Stop trying to put that on me. I have something for you." I released my hold on her to go back to my bike.

"Like a present?" she asked, and I laughed as I went into my trunk on the back.

"Damn, do I already have you spoiled like that?" I pulled out her backpack, holding it up. "I'll make sure it's a present next time, but for now, this will have to do."

Her eyes went wide. "You found this?!" she gushed, taking it from my hands to open and rifle through it.

"Yeah, I went to talk to Blue after you and Nadiah left. Scoped things out, checked if anybody saw anything."

"Did they?"

I shook my head. "Nah. It was a side street, in the morning. Nothing useful yet. I've got eyes and ears on it though."

"Using people you know through Ches?" Aly asked, not bothering to hide the skepticism in her tone.

"Damn, you really don't trust her, do you?"

"Not even a little."

"Do you trust *me?*"

She pulled in a breath. "Maddox, don't—"

"Just hear me out?" I asked, holding my hands up. "I've known Ches a long ass time, but I'm not blind, okay? No lie, in your shoes, I don't know that I'd trust her either. *But* – she knows how I feel about you. Knows how Mos feels about Nadiah. If for no other reason than for *our* sake, she wouldn't let anybody harm you. Mos and I are family to her, and despite her bullshit, that still means something to her. It makes the two of you family too."

Aly let out the breath she'd pulled in and tilted her head. "Are you trying to convince *me*, or yourself?"

"*You*," I told her, confidently.

Ches wasn't *that* far gone, not yet.

I looked down as my pager buzzed, checking the screen before I held it up.

"Look," I said. "This is her seeing if I'm with you. She wants you to come by – she feels bad about yesterday, wants to apologize."

Aly laughed. "Does she *really* think I'd believe a single word of apology from her mouth?"

"You'd be crazy if you did," I admitted. "It won't be sincere. She's not sorry. But she *wants* peace, which is what this is about, I guarantee you. It's an olive branch – that you *don't* have to accept, I won't be mad or anything if you don't. Ches was rude as fuck yesterday, honestly."

"You're right."

I nodded. "But, if you want to accept, I can bring you back with me. You'll be safe. And she might have new information about the kidnapping attempt, her scouts usually deliver first thing in the morning."

"Do I have to go, to hear the update?"

"No," I shook my head. "I'll hit you with anything important. You do *not* have to do this. At all."

"I need to think about it, so I'll catch another ride. But thank you."

"You're welcome. I lied about there not being a present."

Her eyebrow hiked up. "What?"

"You didn't notice the gift I left? In your sketchbook? I hope you don't mind."

"You went through my sketchbook?!" she screeched, snatching it out of the bag she was still holding.

"Everything was spilled out on the ground," I explained. "I took the notebook off some kid and had to flip through to make sure it was yours. You're good. Like *really fucking good.*"

"I'm *really fucking embarrassed*," she countered, clutching the sketchbook over her face.

"Nah, don't be," I told her, pulling the book down. "Let me show you this." I took it from her hands, flipping to a certain page. "Look – you drew me, and I drew you. I mean, mine isn't all detailed and shit like yours, but you get the picture."

For a long moment, Aly just stared at the piece of paper I'd slipped into the book, instead of using one of her pages. After a while, she looked up, meeting my gaze. "You are such a damn *fool*," she got out, before she burst out laughing at my stick-figure drawing with tits and an afro that was twice the size of the rest of the drawing.

"You don't like my art?" I asked, making her laugh harder as she reached up to cup my face in her hands.

"I think you need practice." She pushed up on her toes, pressing her lips to mine. "I can teach you."

I used my free hand to catch her around the waist, keeping her close. "I'd like that."

"I would too."

We kissed again, slow and sweet, until I really needed to head back to *Underground* for a briefing. I watched her until she was tucked back into Ruby's house before I pulled off to get to the other end of the *Burrows.*

*Somebody better have **something** for me.*

Τhe vibe was off.

I felt it as soon as I walked into *Underground*, but I'd felt that so often in the last few months of dealing with Ches' antics that I brushed it off and went on about my business, only stopping when my pager went off again.

"Need to talk to you. NOW. – Mos"

I frowned.

What the hell is this about?

Instead of continuing on to Ches' office, I detoured to the computer room where I could usually find Mos. When I got there, I found the door locked and the lights off, neither of which was a typical state. I moved on to his room, which was locked too.

"*Mos*," I called through the door as I knocked. "You in there? Open up!"

After a few seconds, I heard the bolt disengage, and the door opened just enough for me to slip in before Mos locked it behind me, looking jittery and stressed as fuck.

"You want to tell me what the hell is going on? Why is your door locked? Why is the computer room locked?"

"To keep *me* out," Mos answered, scrubbing a hand over his head. "Ches, man. I *knew* something was off, but I didn't want to believe..."

I grabbed him by the shoulders. "Believe *what*? You're not telling me anything right now."

"I don't know where to fucking *start*."

"Just pick a place and talk," I demanded. "You've got me on edge and shit already doesn't feel right."

"Because it *isn't*. You know I got into the *Apex* internet yesterday, right? All the shit happens with Nadiah and Aly, they pack up, leave, all that. You go out investigating, I stay here trying to dig into as much as I can, until Ches pulls me off – claims she doesn't want me to trigger any security measures and get caught – as if *I* would get caught. But whatever, she seems scared, so fine – I'll go back to working on things for the *Burrows*."

I nodded. "Okay... that doesn't sound off."

"It didn't seem like it to me either, until she pulls me from the computer room too this morning. Worried about power surges and detection, brushing off my assurances that none of that is a concern. She locks me out of there and then has her goons check my room for other devices – takes all that too."

My eyes narrowed. "But you had shit that didn't get taken, right?"

"You know me Mad," Mos laughed. "Of course I had shit that didn't get taken. But I knew there was something she must not have wanted me to find, so I didn't put up a fuss – I went with it. As soon as they left me alone, I locked the door, and hit Nadiah up."

"You paged her?"

He smirked and shook his head. "Nah." He pulled a cell phone – not one of the *really* old school ones that could only pull a cellular signal, like the ones he was trying to get working on a network for Ches. A sleek, glossy smartphone, like the ones they used in the *Apex* – phones we had in abundance, but couldn't do shit with here. Unless...

"You figured out how to make it work?"

"*Been* figured out how to make it work – just had to make sure it was consistent, and had some reach on the signal. Nadiah was the one to help me pull the last of it together, and the first one to test it from a distance with me. We rigged it to use the cellular signal."

My eyes went wide. "So both of you are damn geniuses?"

"Nah – Nadiah is the genius. Ruby has *Apex* internet access, and computers too. Perks of being the queen I guess. Nadiah hacked the *APF* warrant database, found out exactly what crimes they were accused of. Treason, dereliction of duty, *kidnapping* for their grandmother."

"That's fucked up..."

Mos shook his head. "It's not the most fucked up part though."

I frowned. "Okay, then what is?"

"The APF has like a database, I'll call it, where all their tips and information, case files, all that, is digitally logged – backups. This includes transcripts of phone calls related to the cases too."

"Mos... where are you going with this?"

He sighed. "Aly was right, Mad."

"Right about what?"

"About not trusting Ches. *She* did this. Nadiah found it all – the intake report from one of the scouts, the phone calls between officers about it. She told them Aly and Nadiah were 'her sons' girlfriends', and that she had access. She negotiated a reward amount, which is what gave them the idea of doing a bounty. And she got them to suppress the news coming into the *Burrows,* which is why it was so delayed for it to get back to us. They were supposed to be delivered to the gate tomorrow."

Stunned wasn't quite the right word for what went through me. I slipped my fingers under my hat, digging my nails into my scalp as if scratching would make this shit make sense.

"She called us her sons, but she did this shit. *When?*"

"The correspondence started about a week ago. The day after she told us about those weapons she was trying to get."

My head dropped back, and I closed my eyes, digging my teeth into my lip to keep from letting out a roar. "Money. That's why she was being skittish about telling me how she planned to pay for that shit, cause she knew... *fuck!*" I put a thumb to my temple, trying to ease the tension building in my head. "She stood and lied right in my goddamn face. Called me her motherfucking family, and then... how the hell did she pull this off? How was she communicating with them?"

"Her pager, and scouts. If Aly and Nadiah hadn't been able to dodge this shit, she would've gotten away with it. There was a place where they flat out asked her, won't your 'sons' be mad at you?" Mos stopped speaking, shook his head. "She was going to pin it on your cage fighting. Try to say it was somebody you fucked up, getting back at you."

I opened my mouth, but I couldn't get shit to come out.

What the fuck *could* I say, faced with all this?

Even with everything going on, I'd wanted to believe she did still share the same deep-seated loyalty we'd developed early on. Our history should have *demanded* that shit. And now she was willing to betray Mos, betray *me,* for... I didn't understand what she was looking for.

"She wants to be on the same level as Ruby," Mos spoke up, as if he'd read my mind. "That's something I've always seen – something we've talked about, but she tried to make a play for some power here with the *APF*. They laughed behind her back – called her primitive and shit, since she had to communicate with the pager, since we don't have a landline phone established here at the compound. She got a promise that if she delivered Aly and Nadiah, something could be arranged."

I blew out a sigh.

There it was – not just money, but *power*, that thing made Ches ruthless and blind in her pursuit. I wanted to blame it on the abuse we'd suffered in the *Apex*, all those years ago, but she'd come out of that with some kindness left. She met Ruby, we got Mos. Ruby had been the one who got us out of the *Apex* and into the *Burrows* in the first place, where Ches had flourished, even *before* she betrayed her friend.

She'd clawed her way to a position that should've been everything she wanted, and somehow... it still wasn't enough. Didn't seem like it would *ever* be enough, until she was alone.

She and I needed to have a fucking conversation.

"How long ago did you find all this out?" I asked, my brain working overtime to make sense of it all.

"I hit your pager while I was talking to Nadiah, she *just* found all this, within the last thirty minutes. All the stuff about Ches is just one file, and she hasn't gone through everything yet."

I nodded. "Okay. I need you to get in touch with Nadiah, tell her and Aly to stay put. Ches used me this morning, to get Aly back in here."

Fuck.

I was glad Aly had enough sense not to come with me, to want to take a moment to think about it. She'd seen this situation much more clearly than I had.

"Actually..."

I looked up at Mos, alarmed by his tone. "What is it?"

"Aly had already left for that meeting with Ches, before Nadiah found everything. She said Aly left maybe twenty minutes after you did, and she's not responding to any of Nadiah's messages."

"*Shit...* twenty minutes after I left? And we've been talking for... goddamnit, she's probably already here." I flexed my fingers, pacing the room for a moment as I tried to think. "Okay, you've gotta get out of here. Take the phone, and anything else you can throw into a little bag – act normal. Get down to the garage, get a bike, go straight to Ruby's."

He frowned. "What about me helping you here though?"

"The best thing you can do to help me is getting out of here before hell breaks loose – so I only have one person to worry about, instead of two. Tell me you've got me on that, Mos."

I knew he wasn't happy about it, but he nodded. "Yeah bro. I got you."

"Good." I slapped hands with him, pulling him into a quick, tight hug before I bounded out of the room, heading for my original destination – Ches' office. Mos wasn't a fighter, but I'd taught him enough that he could hold his own if he needed to. Not to mention, he carried a blade just like the one I kept tucked at my belt, even inside the compound where weapons weren't technically allowed.

I hated that I felt like I might need it. Any beef with Ches aside, I cared about the people she referred to as her soldiers – I'd fought beside these folks, protected their lives like they'd protected mine. I chilled with them, drank with them – liked them, when they weren't tapdancing on my nerves. I hoped I could let my knife stay where it was.

That hope was short lived.

As I ascended the first of the two levels of stairs to Ches' office, three figures came into view, like they were there to guard the landing, which wasn't that unusual.

Juju, Bandz, Jab.

I was all set to give my usual greeting, since I hadn't seen them in a few days, when I noticed something.

Juju didn't look any different from usual, except for the fact that her eyes wouldn't stop moving, a nervous flittering from me, to her crew, to the door of Ches' office.

Bandz was standing a little funny.

Jab had a big ass knot, right in the middle of his forehead.

"... you motherfuckers...," I growled, more to myself than them, because they knew what the fuck they'd done. I didn't question or second-guess it – I pulled my knife and aimed, sinking the wide, jagged blade into one of Jab's thighs and then the other before I turned to Bandz, armed with just my fists.

Jab didn't have enough heart to pull that blade out of his leg.

Juju's defensive fists didn't mean shit as I hammered my fists into Bandz, thinking about him daring to go after Aly, *knowing* who she was. I had no plans of stopping until I'd rearranged his face to my satisfaction, and then it would be Jab's turn. Juju could try all she wanted to pull me off her partner, but they were paying for *this* shit. Didn't take much to deduce that she'd been the driver, and was as guilty as the other two as far as I was concerned. I didn't hit women, but once I was done with the others, chances were low I'd feel any guilt about tossing her over the stair rail or something.

Or maybe I'd let Aly do it.

Suddenly, I realized Juju wasn't hitting me anymore. Before I could process where she might have gone, hot electricity surged through me, overloading my nerves and leaving behind the distinct sensation that my skin was on fire.

I slumped backward as the connection between my limbs and my brain broke, leaving me unable to move. Bandz was out, but the animalistic scream that burst from Jab let me know I should've been paying a little more attention to Juju.

He may not have been willing to pull that blade out of his leg, but *she* was.

She stood over me with it now, her face pulled into a snarl. "Well, well, *well*. Look at Prince Maddox *now*," she said, her usual bubbliness twisted into a mocking tone. "You were *always* in the way. She didn't need us because of *you*." I noticed the taser in her other hand just before she pressed it again, sending another wave of hot, paralyzing electricity through my body. "But then you got distracted. By some *irrelevant bitch* from the *Mids*! You wouldn't look my way, but you fall all over *her*?!" Juju's lips curled into a snarl. "Oh Mad, I'm going to enjoy *this*."

She held the knife high, like she was getting ready to plunge it into my chest. Before she could, her head rocked to the side, the knife and taser clattering to the floor just before she hit it herself, crumpling into a heap at my feet.

"Wow, sis. You like totally rocked that bitch."

"*Completely* rocked that bitch. Like, wow. I feel powerful right now."

"Like *super* powerful, it's totally how you should feel."

A relieved sigh blew from my lips as the feeling came back to my limbs. I'd *never* been so glad to be subjected to the twins and their back and forth – never been happier to see them than when they stood over me, peering down.

"Are you okay, Mad?"

"Yeah Mad, are you okay?"

They were both wearing rose-gold brass knuckles, dotted with lethal-looking studs. Dee was the one rubbing her hand though, so I assumed she was the one who'd thrown the punch.

"Yeah," I groaned, dragging myself into a seated position, though my head was still swimming. "Are you?"

"I feel *great*," Dee said. "Like, totally amazing."

"You should feel amazing, totally," Dem encouraged. "You got that bitch out of here."

"All the way out of here – *I got her*."

"Where did y'all come from?" I asked, interrupting their loop as I looked around. Juju was still knocked out, Bandz was a mess, groaning through something that still kinda resembled his mouth, and Jab had dragged himself, bleeding, halfway down the stairs.

"We ran into Mos, on the way up from the garage," Dee said, her eyes on her sister as Dem sashayed down to where Jab was, put her foot against his back and shoved, sending him rolling down the rest of the stairs.

"Yeah," Dem called. "We were coming in from the garage and ran into Mos. He's so cute."

"Totally cute. Super adorable."

"*Totally* adorable."

"Okay, I gotta get into this office," I said, hauling myself to my feet. I reached to grab my knife, then glanced between Dee and Dem. "I have to have a hard conversation with Ches, and I need to know... you with them, or you with me?"

Dee laughed. "Maddox, *please*. We don't even like Ches, Sula sent us here to keep an eye on her."

My eyes went wide. "*Seriously?*"

"Seriously, *please*, Mad," Dem chimed. "We're only here because Sula sent us. We don't even like Ches, we're *just* keeping an eye on her."

I shook my head. I'd had no delusions they were besties with Ches, but *damn*.

Made sense though.

"Well come on then," I said, climbing up the first of the stairs that would put us right at her office. "Let's go."

I 'd never been with the mean girl shit.

Even back in high school, where some girls seemed to thrive on the negative energy, talking behind each other's backs, the fake sincerity.

Which was why, when Ches presented me with her too-wide smile, saying "I'm *so* glad you took me up on this offer. It's important that you and I come to an understanding." as she showed me into her office, it didn't mean a damn thing.

I'd *never* trusted her, not really.

Damn sure wasn't about to start now.

"I agree," I told her. "You and I *should* come to an understanding, since it seems we have the shared connection, you know. Nadiah and Mosley, me and Maddox. There's no need for tension there, when we could have peace instead."

"Oh I agree – there *will* be peace. Because you and your sister will be in jail cells, or whatever the hell the *Apex* does with you. Me, Maddox, and Mosley will run the *Burrows*, as it was always meant to be. Or... I don't know, maybe we'll move into the *Mids*, once the *Apex* is done with their... restructuring."

My eyebrows went up. "Restructuring?"

"You should know this," Ches jeered. "The *Mids* have been a fucking dump for years – the *Apex* will break it open, sell it for parts, basically. This end of the *Burrows*... we're only separated by the ruins. I have every intention of claiming some of that newly available space for myself."

"Good luck."

Her eyes narrowed. "Good luck? *That's* what you have to say?" She leaned forward over the desk. "You have a lot of fucking nerve, sitting in my office with your head held high, like you weren't laid out on my floor, scared as hell, just a couple months ago."

"People change. Necessity of this world, isn't it?" I asked, keeping my gaze level with hers. "According to Maddox, you used to be a good person too."

"Oh *really*," she snarled, nostrils flared. "You know what, he's right. Franchesca Catlan, warrior for the weak *is* gone. It's just Ches now – *ruler* of the weak. I've been there before – helpless, battered, looked at like I was *nothing*. Well, nothing but a warm body to be poked and prodded, spit in and spat on. Holes to be used – that's all."

"But you got away from that – you *survived*. You had people who depended on you, people who *loved* you."

Her snarl shifted back to that wide, ugly grin. "You're right. I *did*. But then I saw my chance to make sure I was *never* the weak one again. And I took it. Just like I'll take *every* shred of power that comes my way, until I have what I need to turn the people who used and abused me and everyone else into the ones begging for the pain to be taken away. *Nothing* will get in my way. But... this isn't your concern, is it? I'm not surprised that you've focused on my story – you're not the bright sister of the two. You didn't notice I told you up front – you won't be here, Alyson Little. I'm delivering you to the *Apex* today, and once your sister knows, she'll come running, and I'll hand her over too. It was stupid of you to walk in here. Not even Maddox will save you."

I smiled. "Oh, no, I heard you when you said Nadiah and I were going to jail, I was just curious about your motivation. You're a fascinating woman, Ches." I stopped, looking up as a distant, pained scream cut through the air, then shook it off. "All of this, the betrayal, the attempted power grab... it's all about vengeance, huh?"

"Well, I won't lie, the power feels pretty damned good too."

"Good enough to help you sleep at night, knowing you've betrayed *everybody* that ever trusted you?"

She shrugged. "Necessary sacrifice. Relationships are overrated anyway."

"Why am I *not* surprised to hear you say that?" Ruby stepped from the shadows near the back of the room, blade in hand.

Ches sprang to her feet. "How the *hell* did you get in here?!"

"How the *hell* do you think?" Ruby purred. "Even *your* soldiers know who the real queen is around here. They were more than willing to look the other way."

"You lying bitch."

"Ohhhh..." Ruby's eyes narrowed as she lifted that blade, pointing it at Ches. "That is rich, coming from *your* mouth."

"What the hell do you want, Ruby? Why are you here?"

"I'm here to hold court, Franchesca, but just like the second-rate villain you are, you've already admitted everything. So I find you *guilty.*"

"Of?"

"Conspiring against my honored guest. Collusion with the *Apex. Acts of aggression,* bitch. Ohhh," Ruby moaned. "I have been *waiting* for this, and here we are."

Ches snarled. "Try me if you want to. You might think you're hot shit because you have that blade, but you take one step toward me, and I'm ending you, like I already should've."

"Oh you mean *this?*" Ruby asked, gesturing her head toward that sword. In a smooth motion, she lowered the blade, holding the hilt in my direction for me to take it. When I did, she smiled, then ran a hand over the sleek ponytail she'd had me do for her before we left her compound. Then, she turned back to Ches. "Now come and end me, bitch."

I shrieked, jumping out of the way as Ches dove over the desk, fingernails bared like claws. Ruby easily dodged that, pivoting to aim a kick across the top of Ches' back that sent her to the ground.

That was where any appearance of a clear winner ended though.

Ches was up off the ground in a flash, going at Ruby hard, in a matchup that would have been right at home in the cages. Behind us, the locked double-doors to the office rattled, like someone trying to get in, prompting me to push the heavy armchair I'd been using up against them, holding Ches' people back as long as I could, until the rest of Ruby's reinforcements made it.

She hadn't wanted to wait.

It never occurred to me that the invitation Ches extended was anything but a trap, and Ruby had agreed. She was the one who'd cooked up this plan, for me to come to the meeting anyway, distracting Ches at the door while Ruby used her powers of persuasion – and the brute force of the knights she'd brought with her – to get into the office from the back entrance before Ches and I made it up the stairs.

We were here when I got the pager message from Nadiah that confirmed what I already knew.

Ches was a snake.

And true to her name, it seemed like she was about to wiggle her way out of a bad situation when she caught Ruby under the chin with a blow that made the other woman crumple. Ches turned to me, her face bloody and sinister, like I was next on her list, which was fine by me. I'd walked in here prepared to do whatever I needed to do.

But that didn't happen.

From the ground, Ruby snatched Ches by the ankles, dragging her down hard. In seconds, she was over her, grabbing her by the arms and yanking with such force I heard *something* snap from the stress, whatever it was making Ches scream in pain.

Ruby drew herself to her feet, wiping blood from her eyes before she held out her hand for her blade.

I didn't hesitate.

"I have been *waiting* for this day," Ruby said, kicking Ches over onto her back. "To avenge the woman I loved – the friend I cherished – the person you killed to become... *this*."

"*Ruby*," Ches sputtered, crying. "*Please*."

"You don't have to beg, Franchesca. I consider this an honor."

Ruby smiled, then drove the blade through her lost friend so hard that when she stepped back, it remained, blood pooling around it until Ches stopped moving.

"Rest well, my friend."

NINETEEN

Nothing was keeping me from getting through that door.

When I realized something was blocking it, keeping me from being able to slam my way through it, I wracked my brain trying to think of another option. As soon as it hit me, I turned to head downstairs to the garage, to take the elevator that led to her office.

I was right at the head of the stairs when the door opened.

Ruby Hartford walked out first, her face swollen and blood-streaked, but her head was held high. Fresh blood dripped from the blade in her hand as she approached me – she slid the flat part over the black leggings she wore, wiping it clean before she stopped in front of me.

Aly stepped out of the room behind her.

Downstairs, there was a commotion – heavy footsteps and shouting – but my attention remained on the two women in front of me.

Where the fuck is Ches?

"Maddox Hatcher," Ruby spoke, lifting the blade and placing it flat on my shoulder. She'd always been good for theatrics, and that hadn't changed. "As her closest thing to kin, you should know – Franchesca Catlan has been relieved of her position of power over the upper *Burrows*." She raised her voice for that last part, for the benefit of the audience who'd gathered on the first landing, blocked by a line of Ruby's knights from coming any further.

"She broke the code – engaged in acts of undue aggression, allied herself with the *Apex*, among other crimes, committed, attempted, and planned. None of which can be allowed to go unpunished. She has been executed. *I* executed her," she made clear, quieting the sudden murmur of the crowd. "She will be buried as an honored friend, not a criminal, because I fucking say so. Those of you who cannot overcome your misplaced loyalty to her are free to submit yourselves to the *APF* at the gate between here and the *Mids*. Everyone else, you will now serve under Maddox Hatcher." She raised the blade, touching the sharp edge to my neck, where the kiss print tattoo was. "You should all get these removed or covered."

I was too stunned to respond.

Not by the position and power she'd just granted – neither of which I was sure I wanted – but by her revelation.

I executed her.

Meaning Ches was dead.

Ruby moved past me, tossing a "Let's go." at her knights as she went.

I didn't look back – my gaze was fixed forward as I forced my feet to move, past Aly, through the doorway, into the office.

There was Ches.

I wasn't sure how to feel about it.

I dropped to the floor beside her, head in my hands, conflicted. Logically, I understood that this was the natural end for her – the end that made sense. If it hadn't been Ruby, it would've been someone else, soon. Hell, it may have had to be me, considering what I'd been coming this way to say to her. There was little chance that conversation would've ended without blood.

And yet... *still.*

Somewhere way, *way* down deep, a ripple of pain bloomed in my chest. Flaws and all, the fact of the matter was that Ches had saved my life – *changed* my life. And it had absolutely been for the better.

She'd become family.

Not just to me, but to Mos too, and I wasn't surprised to hear grief in the sharp intake of breath that came when he made it to the door of the office.

She'd been *somebody* when neither of us had anyone left. Looking at her lifeless body, I wondered, as I did often lately, who she could've been if that "group home" hadn't pulled her into its' grips, destroying most of her light. Past the point of repair.

But then Aly put a hand on my shoulder – intended as comfort, but it was a reminder of who Ches had become. She knew what could've happened to Aly and Nadiah – the kinda shit they did when you had no one, when you were just another number in the system. And still, Ches had worked out a plan – had *used me,* planned to blame the shit on me if it worked – that would put Nadiah and Aly in that position, all for *nothing,* as far as I was concerned.

The conflicting emotions made my head hurt.

"Mad, what should we do?"

That didn't come from Mos, or Aly, or either of the twins – it came from one of the people who was supposed to see me as their leader now. For many of them, that wasn't a shift – they communicated more with me than Ches, reported to me among a few other people she'd declared as generals.

It was a shift for *me* though.

I had no idea what to fucking say.

"Let's get this cleaned up." This time, it was Aly who spoke, threading her fingers through mine as I lugged myself back to my feet. "Her body should be moved and stored respectfully until the cremation and everything. I'll find out from Ruby what the plans are for the memorial service. Once the order has been restored here at the house, go home. It's been an emotional day."

She delivered those words with confidence, so they moved. No attempt at intimidation, just certainty and kindness, tucking her rightful disdain away.

And they listened to her.

Didn't question it.

She pulled me away from commotion to cover her hands with mine, and squeeze.

"Hey. I know she meant a lot to you. I am *so* sorry," she said, staring up into my face.

I shook my head though. "Nah, *I'm* sorry. I told you you would be safe here because I trusted her, and that was a mistake. You were put in danger because of me."

"I knew what I was walking into," she told me, with a little smile. "Not gonna lie – I was scared as hell. But I knew I couldn't keep running, so here I am."

With a deep, exhausted sigh, I wrapped my arm around her. "My brave girl from the *Mids*."

She laughed. "You know what? I accept that."

"It's the truth."

"You want to know what else is the truth?" she asked, and I nodded.

"What?"

She grabbed my hands again and pulled. "You should let me get you home. You look like you could use some rest."

———

I dragged myself to the meeting with Ruby.

I wasn't looking forward to it, but I knew it was coming. A few days after the memorial service for Ches, the summons arrived, and I went.

"You've grown into an incredible young man." was *far* from the first thing I expected out of Ruby's mouth when I sat down in her office, but it was what she had for me. I'd known her a long time, but this was the first time I'd met with her alone since she'd stepped into the leadership role after the death of her husband.

So really, I didn't know what to expect at all.

"Uh, thanks," I said, not knowing what else to say to something like that. Ruby must've known, because she grinned.

"You're welcome, Maddox. And I hope you view this promotion as the honor I intended for it to be. I had my own sources, inside Franchesca's operation – I know that you've been a trusted advisor and voice of reason, even when she decided not to listen. I know that your peers respect you. They already saw you as a leader – they know you value their lives, in a way Franchesca did not. You're young, yes. But it's a good fit for you."

I ran my tongue over my dry lips and nodded. "I understand why you'd think so Ruby, but I have to be honest – I have no desire to deal with the drugs and guns and shit. I don't want to look over my shoulder, or harass people about paying what they owe, none of that."

"Then don't," she shrugged. "That was what *Ches* dealt in – no one says you have to. If you choose not to, that is fine by me, and I am almost certain that Blue would be more than happy to pick that end of the business up. You'd still have the club and the restaurant, still have the legitimate import business with the spices and such, and that barbaric fight club, or whatever the hell you call it."

My eyebrows went up. "You're serious?"

"Absolutely. Maddox – I don't give a shit if you and your people start a dance crew and charge for shows – just make sure my cut of whatever you do is on time, keep the crime down in your area, and represent the people of the upper *Burrows* when it's time to make decisions. Ches got greedy, but that's all that was *ever* required of her. It's all that will ever be required of you."

"Ches showed up to represent us?"

Ruby snorted. "Hell no, she couldn't show her face near me in public. I cast her votes myself," she admitted with a shrug. "But with you in that position, we can return to the way it should be. Mosley and Nadiah have been working with my techs, and almost have a *Burrows*-wide network in place, so we'll have electronic communication soon, like the *Apex* and the other divisions. Work out a plan for me and submit it for approval."

"I can do that," I agreed. "But I wanted to ask you something."

"About Ches," Ruby stated, rather than asked.

I nodded. "Yes, about Ches."

"Okay. Go ahead."

"Aly told me about the conversation that happened in the office. Told me what Ches gave as her reasoning, behind this mess."

Ruby smiled. "Ah, yes. Righteous vengeance."

I nodded, and took a moment. "Yeah. Do you buy that?"

Like me, Ruby considered her words before she answered. "I do, Maddox. I didn't know Ches before the horrors she endured – horrors you *both* endured. I met her after, and I fell in love with her spirit. That undeniable strength she had – a quality I didn't have, and wanted for myself. A survivor, *'you'll never take me back there again'*, mentality. A blessing and a curse."

Ruby straightened in her seat, propping her elbows on the arms of her chair. "Franchesca taught me how to be strong. I was already a bad bitch, but one with no backbone. Our friendship infused my spine with steel, and I am forever grateful to her for that. In exchange, she helped herself to my husband. At first, I thought it was about sex – I mean, for him, it was. But for her it was about *never going back there again*. It was about access, and power. So from there, they got what they got, and I got necessary cynicism. I only cared that she had him because it was a betrayal of our friendship, but when he was with *her,* it meant I wasn't getting my ass kicked, or being used like a whore. Which gave me time to develop the darkness I wrap myself in now. That whole situation, it made us. It brought us *here*. Baron dead. Ches with the upper *Burrows*. Me with my crown. I was content – widowed, with access to big strong men, with big strong dicks. Power. Beauty. Money. I had –

have —no true complaints. Is that *ever* a vibe you picked up from Ches?"

I sighed and shook my head. "No."

"Of course not. Because once they broke Franchesca in that place, she never got fixed. She never stopped seeing their faces. She came to the *Apex* with me once – saw a group at lunch. Four guys, at a table – maybe they did everything together, including her, in that horrible place. She's dying inside, but there they are... having lunch."

My eyes went wide. "*Wow.* She said nothing about that."

"She wouldn't have. It was a hard day. But then she started fucking my husband shortly after that, so you'll understand if my sympathy waned."

"I do."

"Good. To cut a long story short, yes. I believe Franchesca may have been driven by, blinded by revenge. I don't believe you were subjected to quite the same horrors she was, so your demons may look different. Or more likely, you've beat them all away already in the cage, back when you were self-medicating."

I chuckled a little. "Something like that. Talking about it helped, but Ches never wanted to do that."

"No," Ruby shook her head. "She didn't. But, with that said, I pulled her history from the doctor you all use over there. She didn't have the equipment to confirm before her death, but I gave her permission to look, afterward. Franchesca had a tumor in her brain," Ruby revealed, with a little sigh. "That would explain the recent change in behavior, her demeanor."

I sat back, scrubbing a hand over my face. "She didn't say anything about being sick. And there I was, being an asshole because—"

"No," Ruby interrupted with a little smile. "Nothing makes this your fault. Nothing makes *you* responsible. She should've stepped back. She should've asked for help."

"*I* should've known something else was going on."

"You didn't because she didn't tell you. Or anyone. That was *her* mistake. Taking on undue guilt about it is just going to make you sick too."

I frowned. "So, you don't feel any remorse about killing her, knowing this?"

"Not a shred," Ruby answered. "She had that coming – she *earned* that, well before this tumor came. But because she was my friend – because I still loved the person who taught me *so much* about myself, I don't think of what I did as *killing her*. She was already dying, Maddox. I gave her mercy."

I considered it for a moment, then nodded. "Yeah. I guess that makes sense."

"I know this is futile, but I'm going to say it anyway – don't make this more than it is. I'm not suggesting that you shouldn't mourn Ches. More than anyone else, you have a right to. What I *am* suggesting is that, just like me, the person you're mourning was already gone. And that is not your fault. Don't let misplaced guilt tell you it is."

"I hear you, Ruby."

"Do you though?" She smiled, and stood, extending a hand across the desk, which prompted me to mirror her actions. I was being dismissed. "I'm giving you two weeks to get back with whatever plans you have for the upper *Burrows*. Please use any resources you have available – if you need property lines, demographic information, anything. We have it."

"Thank you."

"You're welcome. I think you will make an excellent leader, especially with Aly by your side. I know you see the potential in her – please don't underestimate it."

I lifted an eyebrow. "Absolutely not. I don't need to be concerned about all the favors she owes you, do I?"

Ruby's grin turned into something else – something... proud – as she nodded. "See? Smart man," she chuckled. "But no, you don't. Both of you had legitimate grievances against Ches – you both wanted her blood, but so did I. Aly negotiated her debt by conceding to my presence in the room."

"Are you telling me you wouldn't have pulled rank and done it anyway?"

She scoffed. "Of course I would've, nothing would have kept me out of that room. But I liked that she had the guts to make that deal, so I accepted it."

I laughed. "You like Aly, don't you?"

"Something you and I have in common," she admitted. "Albeit, a very different fondness than what you feel for her. Every queen needs a protégé.

Those words made my next few blinks a little harder, but I didn't hate the thought of that. A penchant for violence aside, Ruby was a good leader, and possessed strength and general bad-assness I knew Aly admired. It wasn't up to me either way, but I didn't mind Ruby's influence at all. Not if it helped Aly fully blossom.

"Good luck to you, Maddox," Ruby said, really dismissing me this time. We shook hands again, and I climbed on my bike with no intention of going straight home first. I needed to make my way to the empty stretches that separated us from the division borders, so I could just *think*.

So I could process not just today's information, but *everything* over the last week. I couldn't help wondering if this was what Aly had felt, when her life had shifted so fast, in such a short time. The confusion, the guilt, the anger, the *fear*.

I didn't know how any of this shit would go.

So I'd stay on the bike until I figured it out.

I found them.

It was the tiniest mention, with minimal details, but as soon as I ran across the words, I knew they were about my parents.

"... working with a consultant from the Burrows, a team of activists attempted to arm an APF truck with explosives. This act of protest was never meant to have casualties – not even APF officers. The goal was for the truck to make it back to base where it would be parked among hundreds of other APF vehicles not in use. The explosive would be detonated overnight, handicapping and distracting the APF long enough to secure other parts of the resistance. Instead, the team was discovered, and an officer opened fire, detonating the explosives at a transit gate, resulting in hundreds of deaths. The failed exercise sparked increased police presence, stricter laws, and much harsher punishments for perceived crimes. This reaction from the Apex suppressed any attempt at resistance in the Mids since then."

Damn.

I closed the book I'd been looking through, unsure of how to feel.

The strongest reaction was guilt.

All those people who died, and all the ones who didn't – all affected by my parents' failed mission. How much different would my life look if they'd succeeded – if they'd gotten away with it. Would it have been the start of a revolution in the *Mids*? If so, would we have survived it?

Or what if they hadn't done it at all?

Not even an attempt?

Would they still be alive now? Would Gran?

Would I ever have known there was a possibility of life outside the Mids?

Would someone else have done it?

But all of that was irrelevant.

The *fact* was that they'd tried, and failed, and everyone left behind had been forced to face the consequences. They'd sacrificed themselves, and not a single one of us had been better off for it.

That made me angry.

But somewhere in there, tucked way down, there was a bit of pride. No, it hadn't worked – it had gone horribly wrong. But it took courage to try something like that – to try to save the world as you know it. Courage that most people didn't have, but they did. They'd *tried*.

It was okay to let that, privately at least, count for *something* right?

"Isn't this the coolest library?" Nadiah called from the doorway as she stepped into where I was. I'd been surprised to find this huge room full of books at Ches' compound, but I was glad it was here – I needed to learn as much as I could.

"Yeah," I nodded, looking up to find her with her usual smile on her face. "It's all cataloged and everything."

"You gonna read them all?"

I grinned. "Maybe. Surprised to see you by yourself," I teased, and she wrinkled her nose at me.

"I could say the same for you – where's Maddox?"

"Still not back from his meeting with Ruby," I sighed. "That's why I'm in here keeping myself busy. Picking up a few things along the way I guess."

"Anything interesting?"

I thought about it for a second, then opened the book back to the page I'd been on before. I slid it across the table toward her, and she stepped forward. Her eyes moved fast over the words, identifying and absorbing. Then, she looked up, meeting my eyes.

"You think this is about mom and dad?"

"I do."

"This is messed up."

"It is."

Nadiah sighed, then dropped into the seat across from me. "Can I tell you a secret?"

"Of course. You can tell me anything."

"Even if you might wanna bludgeon me after you hear it?"

My eyebrow went up. "Yes. Even then."

She wet her lips with her tongue, then met my gaze. "I don't think Adam Bishop showed up at our house *just* because I hadn't responded to the scholarship."

"Oh?"

"Yeah. After we went to the *Burrows*, after I met Mosley, and had access to the computers, all that... my classes just weren't doing anything for me anymore. I had a project I was working on – the project that earned the scholarship, actually. Drones. The *Apex* hasn't re-mastered them yet, but I did. Well, almost. I talked to Mos about it, and he helped me figure out this last piece, but when I made it back to class I couldn't make myself finish it. I knew they'd just confiscate it, and someone else would get credit. The instructors pressed me about it, and I stopped going."

My mouth dropped open, and I leaned forward. "Did I hear you right? You *stopped going* to school?"

"They were all over my back, Aly! I didn't know how to tell you, and it didn't seem like anybody cared anyway. Instead of going to classes, I spent my days at the library, trying to figure out if I could get a job, studying and researching, looking up stuff about that bombing."

I shook my head. "Nadiah, how long did you think you'd be able to keep that up?"

"I don't know," she shrugged. "I didn't know *what* to do. And then Adam Bishop shows up at the door. The *same* Adam Bishop whose name was in all those lying ass press releases about the bombing that killed our parents."

"I didn't realize. Didn't recognize the name."

She nodded. "Yeah. He's a scary dude."

"Now *that* I could tell."

Nadiah chuckled, then pushed out a breath. "Are you mad at me?"

"Mad? No. Do I wish you wouldn't scare the hell out of me? *Yes.*"

"I'm *sorry*," she whined, sounding so pitiful that I wasn't sure I *could* be mad, if I wanted to.

"It's over now, so nothing to be sorry about. Ruby assured me she would put an end to the whole bounty thing, and I have no reason not to believe her," I said, offering a reassuring smile. "We're safe. At least for now."

"Speaking of Ruby... Mad has been gone a *long* time. You don't think she's torturing him or anything do you? She is *terrifying.*"

I laughed. "Yes, she is, but to answer your question, no, I don't think she's torturing him. I think it's a big undertaking for Mad, to be promoted like this. I'm sure he's just processing."

That made a huge smile spread across Nadiah's face.

"*What?*" I asked, and she shook her head.

"Oh nothing. I just love how you know him *so* well already."

"I wouldn't say that at all," I denied. "But I'm enjoying getting there."

Nadiah's lips twisted. "Mmmhmm girl. Anyway, I'm going to go find Mosley."

"Of course you are," I teased. "I think I'm going to call it a night too though."

"We should have breakfast or something tomorrow," Nadiah suggested. "The four of us."

I nodded. "Okay. I'll let Maddox know. I love you."

"I love you too," she told me, blowing a kiss in my direction before she headed out. I wrote the book down in the log to show I was checking it out, to take with me to Maddox's house.

Home.

I t was late when he came in, but I was awake. In his bed, reading, with the help of a book light Mosley had gifted me.

I could tell he thought I was asleep, based on his deliberate movements. He was trying to be as quiet as possible in the removal of his heavy boots, getting something to drink, and then climbing into the shower to wash the day off.

I stayed where I was.

Listened.

Waited.

And then, after what felt like forever, he joined me in the over-sized bed.

"Rough day?" I asked, propping up on my elbow. I'd turned on the lamp light so he'd know I was awake, instead of letting him poke around in the dark. Even in just that soft illumination, I could see the exhaustion that laid on him. Could *feel* it almost.

He nodded, hooking an arm around my waist to drag me on top of him. I put my head down on his chest, settling into his body.

"Ruby told me about the deal you made."

My head popped back up, and I met his gaze. "Are you mad at me?"

"No. She tried to have you abducted. As good as signed a death warrant on you and your sister, basically. If Ruby hadn't gotten her, I probably would've had to do it myself, once I confronted her. It was inevitable."

The pain and fatigue in his eyes were so, *so* clear. "But that doesn't make it hurt any less?"

"No," he shook his head. "It doesn't. I'll be good though."

"I know you will," I assured him. "Except for the times you aren't, and that's okay too."

His hand came to the middle of my back, for a lazy back-and-forth stroke. "I appreciate that. Appreciate *you*."

"Yeah, well the feeling is mutual."

I pushed myself up, bringing my lips to his. What was intended to be sweet and reassuring shifted to something else, something deeper, as he took over my mouth.

"I'm gonna need you," he said, when we pulled away from each other.

The corners of my mouth turned up. "You have me."

"I mean in this new role, that Ruby put me in. I mean, the other way too, but you already know that. I'm saying, I *can* do this by myself. But I don't want to. So I need you."

"Then you'll have me," I told him, settling back into a comfortable place in his arms. "Tell me what you need first."

"A plan," he answered, immediately. "I have some of it – a lot of it – in my head already, just have to refine it. But I don't want to be in this position symbolically. Or worse, *selfishly*. I want things to be different. Better. And I feel like you probably have ideas about that."

I sat up, staring at him, sprawled wide across the bed. "How much different? How much better? And for who?"

"The most we can. On all counts."

My gaze landed on the nightstand, on the book I'd been reading – *The Anatomy of a Revolution*. I looked back to Mad and nodded.

"Yeah. I have a few ideas."

ACKNOWLEDGMENTS

If it weren't Alexandra, Jeanette, and Love, there wouldn't be a "Wonder".

Periodt.

Ladies, I cannot say enough about what your encouragement has done for me, but I hope you know how deeply I appreciate you.

Thank you.

To my betas... y'all took one for the team with this one LOL. Thank you!

ALSO BY CHRISTINA C JONES

christina c jones
love, in warm hues

ABOUT THE AUTHOR

Christina C. Jones is a modern romance novelist who has penned many love stories. She has earned a reputation as a storyteller who seamlessly weaves the complexities of modern life into captivating tales of black romance.